remember me forever

Also by Sara Wolf

Love Me Never
Forget Me Always

remember me Forever

A LOVELY VICIOUS NOVEL

SARA WOLF

Entangled Publishing, LLC
2614 South Timberline Road
Suite 109
Fort Collins, CO 80525

Entangled Teen is an imprint of Entangled Publishing, LLC.

Visit our website at www.entangledpublishing.com.

Edited by Stacy Abrams and Lydia Sharp
Cover design by Louisa Maggio
Interior design by Toni Kerr

ISBN 978-1-633754997
Ebook ISBN 978-1-633754980

Manufactured in the United States of America

First Edition May 2017

10 9 8 7 6 5 4 3 2 1

For Nemesis.

I'm sorry. I wrote a bad book about us. (Not sorry.)

chapter one

3 YEARS, 43 WEEKS, 2 DAYS

IT SEEMS TO ME THAT OLD PEOPLE really like to tell you to enjoy your life while you're young. Said people are usually forty-nine hundred years old and drive Volvos. Not that there's anything wrong with Volvos. But there is definitely something wrong with being forty-nine hundred years old. This is primarily because having too much experience makes you boring and flat as week-old soda.

Exhibit A: Jack Adam Hunter.

Exhibit B: Immortal vampires, probably.

Exhibit C: Grandparents.

My grandma is the one and only exception to this rule in the entire world. My grandma is tremendous. When I was two months old she took me for a ride in the basket attached to her Harley-Davidson. I'm slightly positive this experience full of wind and exhaust and bawling crafted me into the dashing heroine I am today. Mom and Dad sent her to an old people's home, since I guess taking your infant granddaughter for a spin with your bike gang is the first sign of dementia or something. But now that I'm in Georgia, we are reunited at last. There were tears. And snotty tissues. That lasted for roughly five minutes. Now there's mostly a lot of insanity.

"I'm not one to question the validity of doing neat things," I say as I hand Gran another fistful of fireworks, "but if I were the sort of person to do that, you know, someone really boring and lame and definitely not me, my question would be along the lines of, 'what the hell are we doing on this roof at four in the morning, question mark.' At least four question marks go after that. And like, a very concerned emoji."

Gran makes a *tut-tut* noise and stuffs the rest of the fireworks into the chimney's mouth. There are so many that I can't see the dark brick inside anymore. We ran a fuse up through the chimney an hour ago, and now Gran ties it to the huge combined fuse of all the fireworks. She sits back on her heels and wipes wispy dyed-green hair from her eyes, flashing a wicked grin at me.

"As chairman of the Greeting and Farewell Committee of Silverlake Home for the Elderly, it's my duty to give the girls and guys here a proper sendoff. None of this funeral-procession, boring-priest nonsense. Viola was a good woman, with a lot of love for life. She'd never want a dull sendoff, but her kids are forcing that on her. Even after she's dead!"

"The horror!" I gasp in sync with her.

"Exactly." Gran points at me. Her eyes are the same as mine, reddish-brown. Dad's reddish-brown. "Horrible. The things people do these days to disrespect the dead are just awful. So we're going to respect my dead friend properly."

"By stuffing the chimney full of fireworks."

"By stuffing the chimney full of fireworks," she agrees. "When the nurse comes by in the morning and starts the fire, she'll light this whole damn place up! Viola would've gotten a good laugh out of that."

I smile and help Gran down the fire escape. She's tall and in shape for a seventy-year-old, but she's still thin, her fingers tiny. When we're back on solid ground and walking across the lawn to her building, Gran throws an arm around my neck.

"What about your funeral, eh?" she asks.

"You mean the one that is never going to happen ever because I am going to gather the seven Dragon Balls and wish for eternal life?"

She laughs. "Yeah, that one. What would you want for it?"

I muse it over for all of six and a half seconds. "Make-outs. Naked dancing. Maybe a cake."

Gran smirks at me as we walk up the whitewashed stairs.

"What? What is it? Why are you giving me That One Look?"

"Oh, nothing. You've grown so much, is all. You said 'make-out' without turning five shades of purple."

"Yes, well, now I am an extremely mature, responsible adult, and I can do things like discuss the trials and tribulations of adolescence calmly."

"Uh-huh," Gran says expectantly.

"Such as making out. I did actually make out with someone."

Gran waits.

"I mean, I punched him before I made out with him. But it was a *mature* punch."

Gran laughs, full and loud. I point at her as she opens the door to her room and sits on her bed.

"Don't you dare start naming stuff you want at your funeral. Because I know from movies that when old people say stuff it usually comes true, and if you die I will be exceptionally bummed out."

"It comes true because we're wise, dear."

"It comes true because you guys have freaky awesome brain powers that seem to do everything but grant you immortality. And teeth."

Gran laughs, easing out of her slippers and lying back on the bed. "Come here."

I lumber over to the bed and sit on it. She takes my hand and pets it, slowly, looking me right in the eyes.

"A lot of people in your life are going to tell you how they think you should live. Some might not say it outright at all. Some of them might just convince you without saying anything that you need to live a certain way."

She looks out the dark window dotted with stars, smiles, and then looks back to me.

"Listen to me carefully, sweet girl. Don't live any other way than the way that makes you happy. If you aren't happy, leave your lover. If you aren't happy, quit the job. If you aren't happy, do more to make yourself happy. Because you are the only one who can make yourself truly happy in this life."

I open my mouth to argue, but she hushes me.

"I know. I know other things and other people will make you *feel* happy. But they won't *make* you happy. That comes from you. That comes from your own heart. Letting happiness grow in you—that all comes from inside. Some people never learn that. Some people never let happiness in, or they let it in too late. Some people never let it in because they're afraid. But that's the worst thing you can do to yourself. That's punishing yourself. Lots of folks don't even know they do it. So. I want you to know. I want you to try to be happy, for yourself."

I feel my eyes watering. If I cry now, I might never stop.

"There was a girl," I say. "A-A friend. Sort of. She never—she never let it in. She was sick. Really sick."

"And where is she now?" Gran asks patiently.

"She…" I tighten my grip on Gran's hand. "She killed herself. And I was the last one—I w-was the last one to talk to her, Gran, and I—"

Gran's strong, thin arms engulf me, the smell of lilacs and musty linens wafting up from her.

"I could've—I should've seen it, I should've—"

"There was nothing you could've done." Gran's voice is iron.

"But I—I was with her, and I knew her, and I knew how sad she was—"

"She must have been very unhappy."

"We all knew that! B-But…but we thought—"

"And what about now? Do you think she's still unhappy?"

"She's…dead."

"Wherever she is now, she's happier than when she was here."

I pull away. "She's not! She's just *dead*. She can't feel anything. If she…if she'd kept living, she could have had the chance to be happy again, here, with everyone—"

Gran's eyes are somber, but they glint. "That sounds an awful lot like someone else telling a girl how to live her life."

My mouth gapes with a retort, but I close it. She's right. Who am I to tell people Sophia would've been happier if she'd kept holding on to life? It's not my place. Gran moves her arms and hugs me closer, drawing my head to her chest, and I let her. It's like coming home.

"Cry for her, sweet girl, not for what you did or didn't do. And then get up. Find what makes you happy," she murmurs. "Life is too long to be so sad. I'm sure she'd want you to be happy."

All of Sophia's twisted, angry faces compound in my mind.

"I don't think so," I say.

"But you said she was your friend."

"Yeah, but—I hurt her. I did things to hurt her."

"On purpose?"

My breath catches before I can say yes. I mull over my

kiss with Jack. Our war. The laughter and the righteous anger and the tender, soft moments. The memories sting, like lemon juice in a paper cut.

"N-No. I was trying…to help?"

Gran raises a thin eyebrow. I shake my head.

"That's how it was at first. I was trying to help another friend, Kayla. But then…but then I started to really like him. I was hurting Sophia by liking him. Every second I liked him was more hurt to her. S-So. I take it back. I wasn't trying to help. I was being selfish."

"It sounds like you were trying to be happy with this boy."

I scoff. "But that hurt her. Us, we hurt her a lot. I got between them. I— She probably felt like she had nothing left, with him moving on. So she…she…"

The white dress on the green lawn flashes in my mind. Sophia's blue eyes, empty, her hair like a banner of corn silk and moonlight, caked with blood where her head met the ground. The tiny silver bracelet that said TALLIE glinting back at me.

She'd lost everything. And I took the last person in her life from her. I did it without even thinking, without even considering how it might hurt her. I just barreled ahead and did what I wanted to because I was selfish. Because I wanted to be happy.

Because I wanted love when I knew I didn't deserve it.

And now, I'll never deserve it.

I am the evil thing.

I am the darkest dragon who ate the saddest princess.

My thoughts are rudely interrupted by Gran's finger flicking my forehead.

"I can hear the cogs in your brain turning. Don't go down that road. That's arrogant. You think too much of yourself and your effect on people. If she went and killed herself, she did it because her life was miserable and she'd thought about it for ages, not because you did one little thing."

"But I contributed. I—"

Gran leans back in her bed and huffs, pulling the cover over her. "I'm not gonna argue with you when you're all wrapped up in self-pity, you hear? Come back when you're thinking clearly. I wanna talk to my granddaughter, not a silly martyr who's trying to take all the blame."

I go quiet. Gran must realize how rare an occasion this is, because she sighs.

"I'm sorry, kiddo. I know it's hard. But you're making it harder on yourself." She leans up and kisses me on the cheek. "Come back at nine. The nurse lights the fire then."

A small, grim smile tugs at my lips.

The drive home is all dark roads and a pale, gold-white gibbous moon lurking on the horizon. The same color as Sophia's hair. I hear her voice clearly in my head.

You tried to help. You tried to help, and for that I can never thank you enough.

I drive back to the nursing home at eight in the morning, and Gran and I park our butts in lawn chairs, with sunglasses and lemonade, and wait for nine o'clock.

Then nine comes, and the chimney spews fireworks—oranges and blues and greens incinerating the clouds. Gran laughs and toasts the sky, toasts her dead friend. I lean back in the chair and do the same with a soft, quiet nod.

chapter two

3 YEARS, 44 WEEKS, 2 DAYS

WHEN I WAS NINE, Dad packed up and left. It was clear and sunny. I was wearing overalls, and the air smelled like blackberries, and I watched him until he got in the cab and it sped away. I tried to run after him, but my legs were too short.

He taught me something really important that day.

When things get hard, people leave. Not that I blame them. Hard things are real tough to deal with, and they sap your energy and time and attention. So people leave because it's easier, and they can use that time and energy elsewhere, on something that isn't so difficult. Dad left because Mom was nagging too much—because she was stressed about raising me, and they were constantly short on money because they were raising me. It was stressful for him, and her. But that was because of me. Mostly it was my fault. They would have been happy if they didn't have me. I've never worked up the guts to say sorry to either of them.

But now I'm going off to college. I'm older. I don't need them quite as much anymore. I'm different from the little girl who tried to run after the cab.

The sun tries to choke my eyeballs. Waking up at two in

the afternoon every day means I'm a rock star. Or a zombie. Possibly both. Rock stars do cocaine, and cocaine is basically zombie dust, right? Right. I know *so* much about drugs. I'm going to college and I know *so* much about drugs. I'll be fine.

"Isis?" There's a knock on my door, and Dad's voice filters in. "Why are you mumbling about drugs?"

I'm talking aloud again, aren't I? I jump out of bed, throw on a pair of jean shorts, and smooth out my sleep-crumpled T-shirt, then fling open the door. Dad's disapproving face stares down at me, hair dark and streaked with silver, his eyes the same warm brown as mine.

"That's a great question, Dad, and here's the answer: I've been practicing saying no," I announce. "To drugs. In my sleep."

Dad's face remains unamused. I hug him and prance downstairs, past dozens of family portraits. The walls are clean and white and the carpets plush. The banisters are shiny cherrywood, and the flight of stairs leading down is massive, like something out of a fairy tale.

"There you are, Isis! Good morning."

"And there's the wicked stepmother," I mumble. She is not actually wicked. On a scale of Angelic to Wicked, she is definitely a four, which is, like, Absently Selfish or something. The same level as substitute teachers and guys who blast their car bass way too loud when you're trying to sleep. I just call her wicked because it makes me feel good. Wicked good.

Kelly looks up from the entrance hall, blond and blue-eyed, with wrists thinner than a stork's legs and enough makeup to choke a magazine model. I've never seen her undone and messy, not even at night and not even on Sundays. She's nearly ten months pregnant, but even so she looks like she walked straight out of a Sears ad —wholesome pastel sweaters and all. She has twins and yet doesn't even look slightly ruffled. I have a sneaking suspicion she's an android, but I haven't found her battery charger yet.

"There're croissants for breakfast, and I made your favorite—whipped-cream pancakes!" Kelly smiles. "That's your favorite, right? Your father said it was."

"Yup. I loved those. When I was, uh, four." I grin until it becomes awkward. Dad doesn't know anything about who I am now, and that's painfully clear. "Look, thanks a bunch for going through all that Martha Stewartian effort! But I've got other breakfast plans."

"No you don't," she says lightly.

"Uh, yes, I do. With friends."

"Which friends? You don't have friends here in Georgia."

"I'll have you know I have friends all over the space-time continuum. And some of them have telepathy. And, like, fireball-making powers. Do you like fireballs? I hope so. Because they don't especially like people calling me friendless."

Kelly's perfect porcelain face hardens. It's familiar, since I've been here two weeks and she makes that face every single freaking time something comes out of my mouth. She hates what I say and who I am. I can tell. I don't fit into her perfect mold of what a teenage girl should be. She wants to tell me I'm ridiculous, or over the top, but she wants me to like her, first and foremost. I brush past her and grab my purse and keys from the table in the hall.

"How about some shopping?" Kelly offers when I'm halfway out the door. "You and I could go wherever you'd like! There's a great place downtown—"

"How about some no?" I say. "With a side of no thanks?"

"That's too bad." Kelly forces a smile. "We should spend some one-on-one time together. I'd really like to get to know you."

"You really wanna know me? You wanna know, what, that

I peed my pants in third grade? That I like bad pop music and merry-go-rounds and the color orange?"

"That's a great place to start!" she says.

"You want me to like you. You don't care about who I am; you just want me to like you. But it doesn't work like that. It doesn't happen overnight."

"What's going on down here?" Dad asks, coming into view over the stairs. "And why are you using that tone of voice with Kelly, Isis?"

"What tone?" I half laugh, half scoff.

"There it is again. Don't use that tone with me, I'm your father."

A hot knot works its way into my throat.

"Sorry," I mumble. "It's kind of hard to remember that when you haven't been around for eight years."

I slam the door behind me. Gravel crunches under my furious steps. Kelly unwisely gave me free use of her "old" black BMW that's practically pristine. She has three of them, all in different colors and with different drop-tops and pimped-out tires. I get in and slam the door, starting it and pulling away from the landscaped lawn and palm trees in stately rows. Even the kids' playhouse out back is made of marble, with its own tiny working fountain. The twins wave at me as I pull out, and I wave back. They're fine. They're young and naive, and I can't fault them for either of those. They're just kids.

Like I was, once.

This is the lap of luxury, and I'm sitting in it like a whiny kid on a mall Santa.

It takes the entire drive to the beach to calm my raging nerves. I agreed to come for the summer because Dad sounded like he genuinely missed me and wanted to see me off before college, and only because Mom seemed to be doing so much better. Somewhere in the vast and fabulous labyrinth that is my head, a game-show buzzer goes off. *Bzzzt!* Wrong. Dad just wanted me here because he feels guilty, and he's trying to make up for a huge amount of lost time. But he can't. Unlike Mom, he never came back for me.

Kelly hasn't changed—I have. I can't stand her anymore. I'm a different person now. Two years ago, when I last visited, I was quiet. I was sad. I didn't fight or argue. I was in the middle of dealing with Nameless. The last time I came here, it was right before—

I shake my head.

The last time I came here, I was pure. And simple. And clean.

Dad still thinks I'm that little girl of two summers ago, and so he treats me like her. Like I should respect him. Like I should care about what he says.

But I don't.

Because he left me. Twice.

Can't ever say that to his face, though. That'd mess up what little family dynamics I have left. Dropping the news I wasn't going to Stanford didn't help improve his view of me, either. He'd already gotten a stupid *my kid goes to Stanford* T-shirt and everything. Who gets those, anyway? Tourists and people with no fashion sense. Dad wouldn't know fashion if it bit him in his history professor ass, and he was definitely a tourist—staying in my life for only a few weeks at a time.

I heave a sigh and park. Goldfield Beach is tiny, dune grasses swaying between gentle swells of gray sand. The water is choppy and dark today, like a really pissed-off witch is making a brew that doth kill many dudes. It's the Atlantic—the Atlantic I grew up on in Florida. The smell of salt and sunbaked stones fills my nose. Seagulls politely scream at each other over pieces of crab. The ocean is big and doesn't really care what tone of voice I use, or whether I go shopping or choose Ohio State over Stanford.

I kick my shoes off and run. Running and I got a divorce after I lost enough weight. But right now, running is the best. Even the BMW's got Kelly's stench all over it. Running is the only way I can truly leave the bullshit behind.

Running on the beach is a fun and unique experience. There's a lot of sand. I trip on a rock and stub my toe so hard I possibly now have weird, deformed hobbit feet. I'm so out of breath I feel like vomiting. A seagull almost poops on my arm.

"It's okay, buddy!" I shade my eyes and look up at the sky. "Luckily for you, I am both stunningly good-looking and benevolent. I forgive you!"

He drops a fat deuce on my shoulder in gratitude.

I sigh. It could be worse. I could be surrounded by people. On the moon. And one of those people could be Jack Hunter.

My stomach twists like a yoga prodigy. Icicle eyes fill my mind, frost over my heart, and I summon what's left of my fire to melt them away. Not now.

Never again.

I'm far away from the car. Its fancy German headlights can't watch me contemplate life in the incredibly-wistful-yet-also-somehow-sexy manner I am famous for. Infamous for. Am I even gonna be infamous anymore? At East Summit High I left my mark, but at Ohio State I'll be nothing. I'll be the gum on a busy New York lady's shoe. Less than that! I'll be that one piece of bread no one eats because it only has one open face and is sort of always stale no matter when you buy it!

With everything that happened after Sophia's death, I hadn't given myself time to worry about a new school. But now that it's less than a week away, I'm starting to freak. I'm almost a goddamn college freshman! I'll have a dorm and a roommate and actual classes where grades actually matter!

They'll define the rest of my career-slash-life-slash future prospects with Tom Hiddleston. I have to start taking things mildly seriously now! Ugh! Just thinking about that word sends shivers down my spine. Serious. Seeeerious. Cereal-ous. Trix are for kids. College is not for kids. College is for grown-ups.

I don't feel like a grown-up.

I'm more worried about Mom than anything, but she and I planned every-other-weekend visits. Even her therapist says my mom's doing better, especially since her horrible ex-boyfriend's imprisonment. I'm glad Leo's in jail—not just because he threw me against a wall and cracked my head open and nearly killed me–slash–made me temporarily forget Jack, but because bad dudes should be in jail, period.

In the Columbus airport when Mom saw me off, the color in her cheeks was back, and she'd smiled more in a week than I'd seen in my whole life.

Or maybe she was just trying extra hard for me.

I pick up a flat, smooth rock and try to skip it across the water. It drowns instead.

East Summit High School sort of wilted after Sophia died.

Nobody would come out and say that, of course, except me. Queen Bee Avery, the most popular girl in school and my begrudging half friend, came to school less and less, and finally stopped altogether. We learned a few weeks before graduation she was in a psych ward, undergoing intensive therapy. For her, prom was out of the question. The social order of East Summit was thrown in the blender and turned on high—girls scrabbled to fill the void and take the prom queen crown.

Avery showed up to graduation, though, and she walked to the podium when her name was called and got her diploma. She looked pale and haggard, and her parents were in the crowd, giving thin-lipped smiles of dry encouragement. I got the feeling they'd thrown her in the loony bin for show, to get her "better" quickly and without caring about whether or not it was really helping her get better. And then, before any of us could blink, she was whisked away to a private college in Connecticut, instead of UCLA like she'd planned. Even if she was a bitch, I keep hoping she'll end up all right. Or at least happier. But Sophia was her redemption, her idol, her friend. If I lost all three of those at once, I'd be broken, too.

Wren stared at Sophia's casket like it was a TV show, something not real. Kayla—my best friend and Wren's girlfriend—helped him through the worst of it, visiting his house every day and staying with him in the nurses' office during school when he crumbled. It broke her heart and mine to see Wren so horribly, twistedly sad. Sophia had been his friend when they were younger for so long. I reminded him to eat—brought him burritos and potpies—and when he couldn't eat, I texted to remind him to sleep. I probably didn't help much. I probably could have done more. Prom came and went, but none of us attended. We spent it at Sophia's grave instead, saying good-bye in our own ways.

By graduation, Wren learned to smile again. MIT was still a very real thing for him, and he'd left early in the summer to earn a few extra credits, or to escape Sophia's death. Both, probably. Kayla was torn up by it, but since she's going to school in Boston in September anyway, she's hurting a little less. They'd been growing closer after Sophia's death. Dunno if they'd done anything serious—Kayla mostly just hugged him. No kissing that I could see, and Kayla refused to dish on what they do in private, more out of respect than embarrassment. She's grown so much by helping him. She only talks about *Vogue* once a week now!

I skip another rock. It flies over the waves and jumps twice before sinking.

I'll miss Kayla. I already do.

The summer was mostly me and her, having last sleepovers and last quiet bottles of wine in cow pastures while looking at stars. We didn't go to parties. I didn't feel like it. She hadn't been friends with Sophia, but it was still a death that affected her closest friends and her boyfriend. We'd promised to text every day. And Instagram. And Snapchat. And Facebook. Basically, we'd made a promise to talk. A lot. We might not see each other so much, but a warm blanket of comfort settles over my heart when I think about her. She has my back. I have her flawless backside.

I've never liked funerals. And now I like them even less.

I cried. Of course I did.

Jack Hunter, though, didn't cry at all.

He should have, but he didn't. He stood in the corner by his mother, who cried enough for the both of them, her black dress and his black suit mingling as she leaned on him to keep standing. His hair had been gelled into perfect place, his face an opaque mask of the darkest ice I'd seen yet, just like his nickname in high school—the Ice Prince. The skin below his eyes was bruised with exhaustion, and his cheekbones seemed somehow sharper. I shivered looking at him. He wasn't putting on the lifeless, emotionless act anymore. He just *was* lifeless. He was empty. The spark had been sucked out of his eyes, leaving pale shells behind. His entire body, his entire physical presence, seemed like a shell—an illusion made of mirrors and brittle frost that would shatter at the slightest touch. He was chilling to look at, like something that shouldn't be still living or still moving. A mannequin. A zombie puppet.

I tried once. To bring him back. At the wake, in the musty-smelling funeral home laden with sorrow-cookies and sad-cakes, I said something about Sophia, how the priest who called her a selfless and beautiful girl didn't really know her at all. Jack had been holding a cup of water, staring into it as he stood in a corner away from the noise and crying people. He looked up at me, took in my face—red from my own crying—and closed his eyes.

"It's over," he said, too calmly.

"What is?" I asked, my stomach roiling. He pushed off the wall and walked away with one last word.

"Everything."

He stopped coming to school after that. I talked to Principal Evans about it, and he said Jack had dropped out. Harvard hadn't revoked its early acceptance offer, and Jack could still theoretically go even with straight Fs for his last two quarters. But both of us knew he wasn't going. He didn't care anymore.

When April came, at the almost-two-month mark of his absence, I went looking for him. I wanted to look for him before that. Hell, I *really* wanted to. I fought not to. I thought he needed space; I thought it would help if I stayed away. The last thing that'd help him would be seeing me. Having the crazy girl who was once your nemesis track you down would be stressful for even the most practiced ice prince. Besides, I wouldn't know how to help. I would just mess things up more. Say the wrong thing. Do the wrong thing. Like I had with Sophia.

But when Mrs. Hunter came to my door one late afternoon, crying and begging for me to find him, I knew I had to start looking. Even though she only knew Jack and I were maybe-friends, maybe-enemies, she was desperate enough to ask every one of his acquaintances for help. None of them could—Wren and Avery were too wrapped up in their own grief.

I was the only one.

I waited until spring break. And then I started chasing a ghost.

Mrs. Hunter gave me the note Jack left—it was simple and written on plain white paper. He said he was leaving, not to call the cops, and that he loved her. Mrs. Hunter had, in her desperation, gotten the bank to hand over his account information. She told me the money for Sophia's now-pointless surgery had been refunded to him, and he'd then gifted most of it to someone, taking a mere four thousand for himself. Four thousand was enough to live on for a bit, sure. But almost three months was pushing it.

He'd left all his stuff in his room, too. The only thing he took was his father's cigar box with Sophia's letters inside. I looked for any sign of him at Tallie's grave—Tallie, his and Sophia's daughter who died before she was ever born. Nothing. He wasn't there. A rose was left on Sophia's grave, wilted. It had to be weeks old. If he'd come back after that, he would've put down a fresh flower.

Then I checked the hospital. The kids I used to hang out with there, Mira and James, said Jack came to see them the day after Sophia's funeral. He told them he was going away for a long time, and he gave them each a massive brand-new teddy bear as a farewell gift. They'd been Sophia's friends, but it was more than that. Sophia, before the tumors started transforming her personality, loved them. They were like Tallie to her—the child-Tallie she would never have, and Jack knew that. Jack treated them like that.

I called the Rose Club in a last-ditch attempt to find him. The operator insisted he quit months ago.

And that was it. All my leads, suddenly dead. Jack was slipping from my hands like midnight sand.

And then someone named Lily called. She'd overheard the Rose Club operator's conversation with me. She was a friend of "Jaden," Jack's escort persona there, which I insanely doubted because the only friend Jack allows himself to have is his reflection and/or his own massive dumb brain. I let her chat my ear off and agreed to meet her at a café in Columbus.

Lily was blond and beautiful and almost six feet tall. From her expensive purse and perfume, I called her out instantly as an escort. She didn't deny it, which made me like her more. She wasn't wasting my precious time as I tried to save Jack.

Save?

I shake my head and watch the salt spray of the ocean douse a rock. "Save" is the wrong word. I can't think like that. I can't save myself, let alone another person. But for a while, I wanted to. I really wanted to. Jack, of all people, deserved help. I thought I could help a little. I thought I could do at least that much for him, after everything we'd been through. After what I felt for him.

I laugh and chuck a rock, not bothering to try to skip it.

I was an idiot.

The old Isis wouldn't have given up when Lily told me Jack came to visit her before he left town. He wouldn't say where he was going, but he gave her a manila folder and told her if a girl named Isis ever started snooping around at the club, to give it to her. So she did.

"He must really like you," Lily said, inspecting her nails as I put the folder in my purse.

"Yes, well. Cobras also like mongooses. From afar. On separate sides of electric fences."

"No, listen"—Lily leans in, one cool hand over mine—"I've seen a lot of men, okay? I've seen all types of people, too. Jack—Jack is something special. He'll deny it, but he either cares with his whole heart about someone or not at all. He doesn't half-ass things. The people he bothered to leave good-bye stuff for—those are the people he cares about in his life. You're one of them."

My heart felt like a sumo wrestler had flattened it. I tried to inhale to say something, but every breath stung. I didn't want to believe her. How could I believe her after he just ran off like that?

Lily took off soon after, leaving me to sneak glances at the envelope.

The old Isis wouldn't have given up after seeing what was inside.

He didn't leave me a note or a giant teddy bear. He left me a ticket to Paris, with the words "I'm sorry" scribbled on it in his large, neat handwriting.

My eyes burn now like they did then. He was trying to get rid of me.

No, c'mon Isis, don't be dramatic. Nothing good happens when people get dramatic. Examples: the Titanic, those rabbits that die when their hearts beat too fast, every episode of *Pretty Little Liars* ever. Jack may have been heartless, but he was also…? Also what? Also definitely not caring about me. He didn't even say good-bye in person, and then he sent me a ticket out of the country. He obviously wasn't in Paris himself, asking me to join him. That idea is almost stupidly romantic. Jack's a lot of things, but "stupid" and "romantic" are on the rock bottom of his attribute list, along with "nice" and "generally tolerable."

I told Kayla multiple times that I wanted to backpack through Europe, mostly jokingly. He was nearby to hear it, though. He must've seen through the joke and realized I really wanted to. Figures.

I pull the ticket out of my pocket. It's worn and crumpled, and the plane left six days ago, but I couldn't throw it away or use it. He must have used Sophia's surgery money to buy it for me, after all. No way in hell could I ever accept (or reject) something like that. So I just kept it. A braver Isis would've used it. A not-guilty Isis would've used it.

If I close my eyes now, I can remember when I went into Jack's room to look for clues as to where he went. The beach fades, and I'm lying on his bed, looking at the ceiling and wondering where he is on this hellacious butthole we call Earth. And if he's safe. Happy is too much to ask for. But as long as he's safe, and keeps being safe, one day he can be happy again. Or so I think. I don't actually know for sure. I'm real arrogant, saying these things like I'm sure of them. I never had anyone I love die. Jack's had three.

He might never be happy again.

He might be broken forever.

His room fades, and the ocean comes back. The knot in my throat returns with a vengeance.

"I hope you're safe, you idiot," I whisper to the waves.

All I can do is hope and move on. I can't wait around. I have my own life to live. I just wish things had turned out differently, is all. Not like, us dating. Because that would be horribly, stupidly selfish-slash-impossible in the face of Sophia's death. I just care about him. As a nemesis. As a rival. As the only person in the world who can challenge me, I want him to be acceptably healthy and functioning so we can meet up and fight again one day. Because the fighting was fun, and I learned a lot and grew a lot from it. Just the fighting. That's all I miss. That's all.

My heart gives a little shuddering squeeze. I start crying. To remedy this, I take my shirt off and wipe the seagull poop on the hood of Kelly's BMW. I start laughing.

And it's great, except for the part where I start crying harder.

chapter three

IT WAS THE BOY'S CROOKED GRIN that gave it away.

He grinned in that special way young boys do when they're about to conduct mischief. Possibly violent, and painful. Also possibly illegal, and definitely probably fun for them. Not so fun for the people it was conducted on.

That's why I follow him. Because I know that grin. I know it like I know parts of my own soul. I'd made that grin once or twice in my life, when I was a stupider, angrier boy who'd lost his father and had to take it out on the world. I made that grin before I raised the bat on Leo. I made that grin once while escorting a woman because she found assault scenarios terribly, horribly sexy.

I vomited for an hour after that session and tried to scrub her off, tried to scrub the evil out of me, out of humanity.

It never worked. It never will work. Humanity will always be dark. They will always try to inflict pain on one another, no matter how much they say they don't want to.

I learned that three months ago, after Sophia's funeral.

I learned it in my car, escaping Ohio. Escaping the pain I'd left behind.

I follow the boy down the quiet city streets, and he leads me to two more boys. Freshmen in high school, probably. Skinny, with tight jeans and earbuds hanging out of their pockets. No muscle. No experience. No courage. That's why they corner the homeless man between a Dumpster and a wall scrawled with candy-colored graffiti gone brown on the edges. Rotten. They laugh and push him. The homeless man wears a flannel shirt and filthy pants, shaking hands clutching a half-eaten banana he likely fished out of the trash. His gray beard is down to his chest and knotted, his face sunburned. The man babbles under his breath so low and fast it sounds like a chant or a curse. He doesn't want to die. He spends every day trying not to die.

"What's that, you crazy fucker?" A boy leans in, holding his hand to his ear in an exaggerated motion. "Speak up, we can't hear shit if you don't say shit."

The second boy brings out his phone and holds it up. "I got this. I'm recording, so do it."

The third boy frowns. "No way, man, someone's gonna see."

"No one's gonna see," the second boy snaps. "We got his back." He turns to the first boy. "We got your back. C'mon!"

The first boy hesitates, and that's when I know. The first boy is not the real threat. Neither is the third boy, who looks uncomfortable, like he's about to run away at any moment. It's the second boy, the one with the camera, who is the true coward. Hiding behind a lens, just like Wren did that night in middle school. But unlike Wren, he's smiling. Wren never smiled. Wren looked comatose, brain-dead. Wren looked like he was putting his soul somewhere far, far away to escape from the violence. Camera Boy, on the other hand, is instigating it, egging it on, goading it with all the small sickly power he has in his gangly teenage body.

Before I punch the camera out of his hands, I briefly thank

whatever god is listening that I've lived long enough to learn the difference between just bad people and truly terrible people. Some people never learn that, and they get hurt.

Like Isis.

Like Sophia.

My heart contracts painfully, and I punch again, this time at his face. The camera boy staggers, nose bleeding through his fingers. His friends jump, backing up quickly. The homeless man squawks and huddles in the corner, covering his head with his scrawny arms.

"Who the fuck are you?" the second boy shouts.

"Nobody hits Reggie!" The first boy ducks into a fighting position.

"Get out of here," I say. "Or you two are next."

"Fuck you!" The first one lunges, and I duck to the side and pull his arms behind his back in one fluid motion. He struggles, trying to kick and head-butt me away, but my grip is steel.

"You there," I say to the third one. "Help your friend up and leave. When you're around the corner, I'll let your friend go."

The third one is sweating profusely, eyes darting between his bloodied friend and his immobilized one. He finally makes the right decision and pulls the camera boy to his feet. Camera Boy scrabbles for his phone and limps around the corner with his friend, vibrantly swearing. I wait a dozen seconds, then shove the first boy forward. He backs up, pointing at me with a furious, twisted expression.

"I'll get you for this, you piece of shit!"

"No," I say coolly. "You won't."

This makes something in him snap—his pride, maybe. He rushes me again, and this time I'm forced to show no mercy. I knock my elbow into his diaphragm, and he collapses on the ground, gasping for air. I extend my hand to the homeless man.

"We should go. His friends will be back."

The homeless man uncurls, watery blue eyes connecting with mine. He nods, slowly, and uses my hand to help himself up. I make him walk in front of me, guarding the rear, all the way out of the alley and to the front of the strip mall, where there are cars and too many witnesses for the boys to try anything else. The homeless man's gait is strong and true, but a limp hampers him. A veteran, probably, who's fallen on hard times.

"Thank you," the man croaks.

I scoff. "I did it to stop them. Not to help you."

"Whatever reason, bless you. God bless you."

He did. God blessed me, I think as I watch him go. *And then he took it all away.*

I shrug away that thought. I'm far better off than most people. But it's that same privilege that sickens me. I'm eighteen. I'm, by all nationality counts, Caucasian. There's some Italian in me, on Mom's side, and Russian on Dad's. But I'm decidedly white. And male. I am not hideous to look at, nor is my brain crippled by general idiocy. Mom and I never wanted for money. I am lucky. I am *privileged*.

The homeless man hobbling down the boulevard needs God's blessings more than I do.

Sophia needed God's blessings more than anyone.

The traffic becomes white noise in my ears, washing against me and around me. People pass, their faces blurring indistinctly. Nothing feels real—it's a world trapped in a snow globe. The colors of the strip mall are washed-out instead of bright. The smells are Styrofoam and wood, tasteless where there should be taste. Nothing is right. I'm not right.

But I'd known that for a long time. I'm not right. I stand out too much. I'm too cold. I am not like the rest of the faces in the crowd. I don't feel as deeply as them. I don't vibrate with as much emotion as they do. I don't have as many friends, and I don't want them. I want to be alone.

If I were more like a normal person, warmer, would I have been able to tell what Sophia was about to do? Would I have been able to understand her better? Would I have been able to see her despair and stop it?

If I were more like Isis, would I have been able to save her?

That's what you do, her voice echoes. *You protect people.*

My fingers twitch, the knuckles bloodied. She's wrong. I hurt them.

I turn and head back to my car.

I came to meet my employer, Gregory Callan of VORTEX Enterprises. This little side trip to the strip mall was for an ATM I could get cash from. I got sidetracked by the homeless man and my own anger.

Unlike Isis, who was convinced Gregory was shady, I gave him a chance. I had to, after what he did for me. He found me, somehow, when no one else could. After Sophia's funeral, I left Ohio and drove and drove, without caring where I ended up. I stopped at run-down bars and pubs, picking fights and passing out behind their trash cans with swollen lips and twisted knees. I drove myself into hell with an iron hammer—relentless, barely stopping to sleep or eat. Sophia's face haunted me in every moonbeam, every shadow in the desert sand. I tried desperately to escape her—no, to escape the guilt. I was thin, delirious, and covered in old wounds when Gregory found me in a seedy Las Vegas motel.

How he found me, I'll never know. I tried to fight him against the grimy walls of that place, but I was too weak to even land a punch. He locked my arms behind my back and smiled affably. I still remember his words.

You call that a punch? It's a disgrace. If you want to die, that's fine with me. But do it after I've taught you how to fight properly.

I passed out in his arms and woke to the gentle sun of morning and the dry air of the desert. Gregory had taken me to a ranch in the middle of nowhere, where a massive, silent man in a bandanna and oil-spattered jeans served me thin broth and changed my bandages. I tried to fight him, too, but I was too exhausted and weak to even form a fist. The man's name was Littlehawk, and he and Gregory had been friends for their whole lives. They'd formed Vortex Enterprises together, recruiting the most promising police academy trainees and martial arts tournament winners, training them to become bodyguards for hire, as they had been so long ago.

Trainees came to Littlehawk's ranch soft, and they left hardened by weeks of hauling firewood, fetching water, and wrangling the wild herd of horses that lived there. On top of it all was shooting practice, awareness training, brutal obstacle courses, and mixed martial arts training in all sorts of styles: wing chun, karate, muay thai, judo. The Nevada sun baked the clay of inexperience into hard ceramic, and I watched the recruits from my window as I recovered, and I envied them. They gave their all to the training, pouring their best effort into it. I was like that once—devoted, hardworking. Lying in that bed, powerless, I wanted nothing more than to be out there with them, filling my head with sweat and soreness instead of guilt and darkness.

When I was well enough, Gregory and Littlehawk gave me that chance. And it saved me.

I haven't looked back since.

Vortex Enterprises has my loyalty, if only because I owe a great debt to the men who run it. They pulled me from the edge when even I couldn't.

The September air swelters around me, crickets crying

out lonely songs in the tall golden grasses on the side of the highway. The heat wave is the last dying gasp of the brutal, once-in-a-century summer that hits Ohio. The city of Columbus has never looked drier or bigger. The sky is a pale white-blue and goes on forever. My white dress shirt sticks to every sweat-stained crevice of my body, and the dark suit over it is uncomfortably hot.

I shouldn't be here.

I should be in Cambridge, Massachusetts. At Harvard.

I should be settling in to my dorm room and learning to tolerate the idiot who will be my roommate for a year. I should be taking classes now, typing notes on the laptop Mom bought me. But I returned the laptop, and I returned my dorm room. I returned it all. I rescinded my tuition and closed my bank accounts and packed a single backpack and left a note on the kitchen counter that told Mom not to worry.

And then I left.

That world, the innocent little fishbowl of young-adult angst people like to call college, isn't meant for me. I am mentally older than they are. I always have been. I am smarter than they are. I always have been.

I'm amazed you manage to get your head off your pillow in the mornings.

Isis's voice rings clear and bright in my ears. But I'm better at ignoring it now. It's gotten fainter. I haven't seen her for half a year, and yet her voice clings in my brain. It's incredible. Incredibly annoying. It's either a testament to her infuriatingly persistent personality, or a testament to my unwillingness to let go of the last few moments in my life I recall being truly happy. Happy? I'm unsure if I was ever happy, even with her. It's a mishmash of fuzzy memories and stolen moments of tenderness, all laced with the searing edge of guilt that is Sophia's face.

Maybe I was happy. But it's pointless. There's no real value in being happy.

There's no real value in something that doesn't last.

I take a right onto the shipping roads of Columbus, where eighteen-wheelers gather five deep and Matson containers choke the dusty, fenced-in lots. Two massive cranes noisily rearrange blocks of containers, loading and unloading with creaking, dutiful slowness. Men in orange vests and hard hats weave among containers, checking the contents, marking things on clipboards, and shouting obscenities at one another over the ordered chaos. Gregory—a tall, broad-shouldered man with an impressive salt-and-pepper mustache and tweed suit—stands in a near-empty lot. A shorter, yet somehow even beefier, young man stands next to him, wearing a dark suit like mine. His posture is tense yet relaxed, his hair spiked and his eyes dark. A dragon tattoo twines up his neck. It's Charlie Moriyama, Gregory's right-hand man and most trusted bodyguard. I saw him once or twice at the ranch, where he came to talk to Gregory and even taught some of the judo classes. He kicked my ass the first time I sparred with him—the only person at the Ranch besides Gregory to do so. I hold a grudging respect for Charlie; he's brash and immature at times, but extremely talented.

Across from both of them is a woman with black hair tied up in a neat bun. She shuns a business skirt for a woman's suit, looking every part a professional. But a professional of what, I can't quite tell. Gregory's training kicks in; there's no obvious weapon lump on her, and any jewelry that would mark her as a drug dealer or tattoos that would out her as a gang member are well hidden, if they exist at all. She doesn't even wear makeup. Odd, considering most of the people who contract Gregory's services are usually extremely wealthy and appearance-conscious.

Gregory sees me coming and waves me over. He plays the jolly old man bit almost too well, but it serves to hide the vicious businessman, wizened soldier, and master black belt beneath.

"Jack! Vanessa and I were just talking about you."

I sidle up beside Charlie, who crosses his arms and grunts. "You took too long," he says.

"Had to make a detour. Road construction."

"Yeah? Is this the same 'road construction' that got you on the news last week?"

"C'mon." Gregory smiles. "Let's at least try to pretend to be friends when in front of— " He turns and cocks an eyebrow at the woman, as if asking her what she is.

"Let's call me a potential client for now," Vanessa says. Her blue eyes are sharp and riveted to my knuckles. I wipe the blood off on a cloth I always keep in my pocket for this exact purpose.

"—in front of a potential client," Gregory finishes. "Besides, Jack's entitled to his five minutes. If I didn't know any better, I'd say you were jealous."

Charlie scoffs. "Jealous? Yeah, boss, I'm real jealous of wannabe Batman over here."

I'd risen in the ranks faster than anyone at Vortex. Of course Charlie's jealous. He's been in the business for years, even though he can't be more than twenty-two. He had to claw his way up by his hangnails. He thinks I'm pampered and spoiled. And I am. To a degree.

"I wasn't aware what I did in my free time was up for criticism by you," I say.

Charlie throws a glare at me. "It's up for criticism when you decide to use your training to beat the shit out of guys who steal Popsicles from 7-Eleven."

"They mugged a woman," I counter smoothly.

"They were small-time idiots pulling off small crime!" Charlie snarls. "But your little savior complex had you wasting time on their stupid asses."

"My time. Not yours. It's hardly any of your concern."

"You got us on the news! We're Vortex, not goddamn Walmart!"

"They never got his name or a picture of him," Gregory steps in. "Really, Charlie, you can relax. We aren't here for a witch hunt; we're here for the client. Settle this later."

Charlie goes red down to his spiked roots. I glance at Gregory, and despite his smile he narrows his eyes slightly. He should've told Charlie to be quiet ages ago. Letting him blab in front of a client was Gregory's way of letting Charlie embarrass himself. It's the subtle kind of mind game Gregory loves to play. Most of the people he trains and hires are not clever enough to sidestep it.

"Vanessa," Gregory begins. "Would you do the honors?"

"I'm Vanessa Redgate," the woman says. "I can't disclose who I work for, but we're offering Mr. Callan a contract."

"Outside of your work's approval, I assume?" I ask, and motion around. "Considering the unorthodox meeting place."

Vanessa nods, "We are after a small, elite group of hackers who have been shuffling funds for the largest black market on the internet."

"The Spice Road," I say.

Vanessa nods again. "I'm impressed. I wasn't aware Vortex agents excelled anywhere beyond their muscles."

Gregory laughs and claps me on the shoulder. "Jack's a special case. Please, continue."

"Regardless, these hackers worked for the Spice Road. They call themselves the Gatekeepers. The people I work for have unanimously decided against using third-party—"

"Contractors," Gregory interrupts, flashing a smile. "We

prefer the term 'contractors.'"

Vanessa eyes him warily but continues. "Decided against using third-party contractors. But my supervisor and a great number of people within the project have worked for years to trace the Gatekeepers. We finally have a lead, but we don't want to risk deploying a team and spooking them into going underground. Training people for this particular mission is just not cost-effective, and by the time we do train them, the lead may have already gone dry. "

"So this is where we come in," I say. She nods.

"We have strong evidence that two people closely connected to the Gatekeepers recently transferred into Ohio State University as sophomores."

Ohio State. The name catches in my brain like a large fish in a too-small net. During my stay at the Ranch, and after I was well enough, I had a laptop. Gregory lent it to me, with one request: that I find a goal. It was a simple task to anyone but me; I'd lost everything with Sophia's death. Things like goals seemed stupid when I no longer wanted to live in this hell we call a world, but I couldn't deny Gregory. He'd saved me. So I focused on the only thing I felt I'd left unfinished, the only thing I felt I could do for the people I'd left behind.

Will Cavanaugh—Isis's abuser and ex-boyfriend, the guy she called "Nameless." I picked up where I left off before Sophia's death and found his trail, which consisted mostly of stalking his social media. He didn't post much, mostly complaints about basketball teams and games, but it was enough. I hungrily devoured everything he shared, looking through his old photos. One of them even had Isis in it, the old Isis smiling timidly. Seeing that picture only fueled my stalking higher. I tried to trace Will's IP address but never got very far; he stuck to his old methods of routing himself around the world to throw off tracers like mine.

One day, though, as I watched his family's Facebook feeds, his aunt gave me a vital piece of info. She tagged Will in a picture of her holding up an Ohio State University sweatshirt, beaming. The hashtag was #mynephewgotin. The picture disappeared shortly after—I assume Will got her to take it down, one way or another. But I already had the info in my hands.

Will Cavanaugh is going to OSU in the fall.

So Vanessa's words about OSU perk up my ears, and I listen closer. Could it be him she's after? He's a good hacker—Isis herself said he won hacking tournaments in middle school.

"The goal," Vanessa continues, "would be to maintain surveillance on these two without rousing suspicion. The ultimate goal would be to gather evidence, preferably hard copies and byte logs of their hacking activities, or their correspondence with the Gatekeepers themselves."

"How long?" Charlie grunts. Vanessa raises an eyebrow at him.

"Excuse me?"

"How long would the contract last?"

"For as long as you can feasibly maintain your cover at the university."

"So, it's open-ended," I say.

"Until you gather what we decide is solid enough evidence to incriminate both of them, yes."

I look to Gregory, who shrugs.

"It's not our type of gig, Vanessa," he says. "Surely you understand."

"It could be," I say quickly. "Charlie and I are the youngest in Vortex. We could feasibly fit in."

If I could get into OSU without rousing suspicion, I might be able to find Will there, too.

Gregory shoots me a quick look. "You could. But

why would you want to? This is information work, not bodyguarding. We don't do that."

"But we *could*," I press.

"You're asking us to sit on our asses and go to college with a bunch of privileged kids for a year?" Charlie scoffs.

"The tuition would be paid," Vanessa interrupts. "You would have to put up a show of attending class and maintaining decent enough grades to continue your enrollment. But your primary concern will be surveillance and secrecy. No one can know why you're there."

"Ms. Vanessa," Gregory says, "I'm sure you're aware Vortex Enterprises is a for-hire bodyguard company, not a stable of spies."

"I know that well enough," she says. "But you came very highly recommended from several politically connected friends of mine who've used your service. And no other company has such a"—she fixes me with a stare—"*diverse* range of ages among their employees. It's imperative we employ informants who look the part of college students."

"These two college students who are connected to the Gatekeepers," I muse. "Do you have names?"

"None that I can disclose prior to your acceptance of the work."

"You really think you can do this?" Gregory asks me.

I nod firmly. "It would be simple."

"For you." Charlie snorts. "But the rest of us are here to guard, not get ass-deep into some James Bond shit."

Gregory ponders this for a moment, then nods at Vanessa. "We'll do it."

"What?" Charlie looks incredulous.

"It's the beginning of the school year. You'll blend in fine," Gregory says, a steely edge in his voice. "I know you two can do this. You especially, Charlie. You've got the charisma for it. You always have."

Gregory pulls Charlie's arm and motions for me to lean in. "Listen, it might not be our usual gig, but it'll pay well. Whoever wants this, they're big-time. Maybe even government. It'll be good to have them in Vortex's debt. Do you understand?"

Charlie's eyes glint with slow realization.

"When would we leave, sir?" I ask.

Gregory shrugs. "As soon as possible, I'm guessing. I'll forward you the details when I get them. All you have to do is agree to it."

"I agree to it, sir," I say.

Charlie inhales, chest puffing. "I-I'm down for it, too, boss!" he says quickly, glaring at me. "I'm not gonna let Batman fuck it up."

"I have a name," I drawl.

"Jack, right. Jackman. Jackoffman," he corrects. The insults are so familiar they sting with a bitter sweetness, but I brush them off.

"All right, enough playground antics." Gregory straightens and smiles at Vanessa, extending his hand. "My boys here say they'll do it."

"Fabulous." She takes his hand and shakes it. "I'll be in touch with the details. Now, if you'll excuse me."

It takes only a second before she's gone behind a Matson container. She moved so quickly I could barely follow her stride. She must've had her exit planned minutes in advance. Charlie shivers a little.

"Damn spooks."

"She doesn't seem so bad," I say.

"Of course she doesn't seem bad to you. You're practically one of them already, all robotic and cutthroat. I'd bet you'd kill your girlfriend if the boss asked you to."

My hand shoots out to his suit lapels before I can stop myself. The world becomes horrible white static again, blurring Charlie's face, dulling Gregory's assertive voice that tries to convince me to let him go. I shove him higher against the Matson container, the smell of dust and sweat and steel turning to ash in my nose. He's awful. An awful puppet. I could crush him so easily, snuff his life out like I did to Joseph that night by the lake, like I almost did to Leo, like I did with Sophia.

Because, after all, I let her die.

I killed her.

There is fear in Charlie's dark eyes, and it's the only thing that keeps the roar from consuming my brain. I shove him away and stride back to the car. Gregory keeps up with me, motioning for me to roll down the driver window. I do, reluctantly.

"Look at me," Gregory says, voice suddenly dark and commanding. I meet his gaze. "Are you going to be able to do this? Or do we need to revisit our training?"

My body flinches out of instinct, out of the physical memory from the training sessions with Gregory. The memory of blood oozing from my ears and my fingernails black and falling off. No. I don't need to learn the hard way again.

"I have myself under control, sir," I say slowly.

Gregory stares at me, through me, and then nods and pats the hood of my car.

"Get packing, then. You've got college to attend."

We return to the motel Gregory is paying for us to stay in—two serviceable twin beds and nothing much else, but it's better than sleeping in our cars. Better than the gravel he made us sleep on during training. Charlie grumbles obscenities and jumps in the shower immediately. I order Chinese takeout and open my laptop. Gregory, ever punctual and eager to get started, forwarded us the dossiers. The two student faces stare out at me from their files. One of them is tan, jockish, with a fair face and dark eyes like a cat's. Kyle Morris from Lakeside City, Michigan. The other—handsome-looking, brown hair, and a symmetrical face with eyes like frozen steel.

Will Cavanaugh from Good Falls, Florida.

I was right.

I was right, and now the game has truly begun.

chapter four

3 YEARS, 44 WEEKS, 6 DAYS

SOMETIMES WHEN LIFE KICKS you in the ass, you have to kick it back.

In the nuts.

With steel-toed boots.

Essentially, if someone, *anyone*, kicks you, it is very mature to take the high road and not kick them back. But it's not fun. And I'm all about fun. One hundred percent fun. One fundred percent.

I smirk at my own pun. One pundred percent. My father groaning across the breakfast table is the only indication that I've been thinking out loud for the past five minutes.

"Isis, eat your food," he pleads.

"No, Dad, I gotta go." I stand up quickly from my chair. The twins pelt each other with oatmeal.

"You'll sit down and eat your breakfast with the rest of us, Isis, or so help me—"

"Where are you going?" Kelly interrupts him and smiles sweetly at me.

"Home."

Kelly's eyes light up at the prospect. Dad's darken.

"Isis, your ticket doesn't have you going back until the thirtieth—"

"Dad," I whine. "My friend died and I gotta go kick life in the nuts."

"We're all going to die. *The Lion King* said so," one of the twins pauses in her oatmeal-throwing to say, her bright blond braids contrasting with her blue eyes as she blinks.

"Exactly!" I motion at her. "See, Dad? She gets it!"

Dad's face turns red in his about-to-explode manner when Kelly grabs his arm and coos.

"Oh, darling, she must be so eager to get back to Ohio and start college. Remember when we were that age? I was so excited to leave the house and get on with my life! She's just feeling that good old independence bug. Delta loves me—I'm a gold flier. They'll let me change the date for nothing."

Dad lets out a frustrated sigh, his red face going with it. "Aren't you—aren't you happy here? This was supposed to be your summer vacation, with me. I haven't seen you in two years, Isis. Two *years*."

"I'm having loads of fun here," I lie vigorously. "And I'm gonna miss you." Another lie. *I don't even know you.* "I'm just, you know. Like Kelly said. I'm ready to go!"

Dad eyes me over his glasses, and after what feels like eternity, sighs. Kelly smiles. I've won. As I pack my bags, I realize there's really nothing for me here except borrowed BMWs and a family that was never really mine. And it took me nine years to figure that out.

You really are slow, aren't you?

The voice echoes so clear I'd swear Jack was standing nearby. But there's no one there. A lopsided picture of Kelly and Dad and their new family stares at me through the open doorway. There are no pictures of me anywhere in the house, not even as a kid. I guess Dad just didn't have any. Or maybe

Kelly didn't want them up.

I'm surrounded by people here, but I'm completely alone.

I snap my suitcase shut and sit on it.

I cry a little at the airport two days later. Dad doesn't cry at all. This tells me everything I need to know about everything I never wanted to know. The airplane takes off and I helpfully throw peanuts at the bald guy in front of me who won't stop farting. The stewardess thanks me with her eyes, but then he gets up and goes to the bathroom and leaves the door open afterward and we perish. For two slow hours.

Mom is waiting for me at baggage claim. I smell like man-farts, but she hugs me anyway, and that's how I know I'm really home.

Packing for college is like packing for war. You're not coming back. You don't know what's out there. There's a chance you may die (exams) and/or suffer life-changing injuries (hangovers, STDs). And if you do come back, you're lucky. But the enemy territory is just begging to be explored, and I've gotten all the training I need from basic (high school). I'll be okay.

I can't fit Ms. Muffin into my suitcase.

I'm absolutely not going to be okay.

Mom hears my wails of distress and comes like a tired hound to the slaughter.

"What's wrong?" she asks.

"Everything is over forever!" I throw myself onto my pillows. Mom waits patiently for a translation. I thrust my finger toward Ms. Muffin half hanging out of the bursting suitcase.

"Isis, she's a doll." Mom sighs. "You're going to college. Maybe it's time to get rid of her."

I bolt upright, my eyes as big as saucers and my mouth as big as a flying saucer.

Mom corrects herself. "Okay, okay. Ms. Muffin stays. But keep in mind, first impressions are everything, and the only people Ms. Muffin will impress are six-year-olds."

"Precisely, *Madre*. I don't want to be friends with people who aren't six. At heart. Only at heart. Because it's also fun to legally drive."

Mom shakes her head, laughing a little, and goes back downstairs to her pancakes.

I sneak into her bathroom with all the grace of an anime ninja and check her pill stock. She's full up—antidepressants, mostly. It worries me because they make some people kill themselves. But it also doesn't worry me, because they stop some people from killing themselves. It's the shittiest fifty-fifty gamble in the world, but it's all we have. It's all that'll keep Mom safe while I'm gone.

"What are you doing, Isis?"

I immediately slam the mirror shut. "Checking for rats! And mold. Both of which kill people. Did you know rats can leap more than ten feet horizontally? And they always aim for the jugular."

Mom tenses, her lips pursing like she's going to chastise me, but then she moves in, enveloping me in her arms. Arms that are a little thicker than they used to be.

"I'll be all right, sweetie," she murmurs into my fading purple-streaked hair. "It's okay. It's okay to stop worrying now."

"I can't," I say. "If I stop, something bad will happen. If I stop, I won't see it coming, I won't pay attention, and something will happen to you—"

Mom's grip tightens. "You've been so strong for me, for so long. Thank you."

I feel a familiar prickle in my eye and promptly deny it exit. Mom holds me at arm's length, looking me up and down as she strokes my cheek.

"And now, it's time for you to be strong for yourself. Not me. Not anyone. No one else but you."

I laugh, but it's watery. "I'm not—I'm not so good at that."

She smiles, eyes like gray mirrors full of love. "Then it's time to learn."

In the very back of my closet, I find a pink chiffon shirt Kelly sent me as a gift. But it's more than that now. It's the pink shirt Jack said I was— I was— I can't even bring myself to say it, and how lame is that, that I can't even say a *word*? Mouths are meant for saying words, and I have one, and I know words, but this one is hard. This one means something, so it's hard.

In this pink blouse, someone called me *beautiful* for the first time. Someone I respected. Respect. Someone I loved.

Love.

Love?

I shake my head and jam the shirt into the farthest reaches of my suitcase. You never know when you'll need a new curtain. Or a toilet rag.

Mom helps me load stuff into the car. I've got my trusty blue suitcase and my beat-up backpack from high school. High school. Hi, school. Bye, school. I shiver a little as I realize I'm not in it anymore. I'm officially out. Half of me wants to drink nineteen Red Bulls and dance the motherfucking hokey pokey nonstop for twenty-four hours, and the other part of me wants to crawl back into school, wrap it around me like a security blanket, and never come back out. I settle for rolling on the lawn and moaning with dread like a grubby caterpillar refusing to get out of its cocoon.

Kayla pulls into our driveway just as Mom loads the last

bag. I jump up from groaning on the lawn and rush over. She's right on time for our dinner date. Our last and final farewell dinner date. She gets out of the car in a blindingly beautiful white dress and sandals, her dark hair combed out to chocolate sheetlike perfection. She greets my mom with the graciousness of seven French queens and drags me into her car with the strength of seven Viking warriors. When we're on the road, she huffs.

"Is the stuff in the trunk really all you're taking? The Romanies travel with more stuff than you!"

"Ah"—I raise a sage finger—"but Romanies don't have an entire suitcase pocket devoted to Haribo gummy bears."

Kayla rolls her eyes. "You're so nuts."

"I prefer gummies to nuts."

"Oh do you?" Kayla arches her brow in that terribly cheesy double-entendre way, and I suppress the urge to pluck it off her face. Her face is a work of art, cheesy eyebrow or no. I don't ruin art. Except when I do. And then I get yelled at.

"Anyway," I say. "This is the last time we'll see each other until Christmas break, so we'd better crash a party or something equally entertaining yet memorable."

Kayla grins and merges onto the highway. "I know just the place."

I recognize the street before I do the restaurant. The Red Fern looms before us. The same place I arranged Jack and Kayla's first date. The one I stalked them at. But Kayla doesn't know that, of course. She picks a booth by the window and we settle in; she orders iced tea, and I order a root beer.

"If we were in Europe, we'd be able to order wine." Kayla sighs dreamily. "God, they have it so good there."

I frown, remembering the ticket Jack left me. It leaves a sour taste in my mouth.

"Oh yeah. Everybody loves the plague."

"That was centuries ago, Isis. No one has the plague anymore."

"The death metal fans of the world beg to differ."

Kayla rolls her eyes, and when the waitress returns with our drinks, she orders spring rolls for us to split. I look around nervously at the decor. The same colorful birds of paradise linger in the vases, and the crystal light fixtures look like seaweed suspended in ice.

"I've never been here," I say. "It's nice."

"Oh, don't lie."

A cold jolt runs down my spine and into my butt. It is mildly unpleasant. "What?"

Kayla sips her tea. "Jack told me you stalked us on our date."

"That was only because he was, objectively, a nasty-faced pus-butt bug-eater, and I had to—"

"I know you paid him to take me out," she interrupts. I gape like a particularly mute fish. "It's fine. I'm over it. That seems like so long ago."

"You—" I swallow. "You aren't super pissed?"

"Why would I be? It was one of the best nights of my life."

"When did he—"

"The night we broke up. The morning after Avery's party, when she—"

When she locked Wren and a drugged Kayla in a room. I don't say that, though, and it really doesn't need to be said. Kayla shakes her hair out.

"It was when you and Wren went to kick Avery's ass. Jack and I talked about a lot of things. That was one of them. He came clean."

"I never did. Shit, I never told you," I say instantly. "And I'm really sorry—"

"Don't be, idiot." She kicks me under the table. "It's over

and it was a long time ago, and anyway I'd forgive you for anything. Short of killing my baby brother. And maybe I'd even forgive you for that, depending on how much he'd spit up on me that week."

Our spring rolls arrive, and I drown my gratitude in sprouts and poser meat made out of innocent bean curds. Kayla talks about Massachusetts, and all the places she's going to visit with Wren. The East Coast will suit her—she's gorgeous and tan and tall, and a big city is all but required so the maximum amount of peons will be able to bask in her splendor as she blooms into the most beautiful woman in the world, and eventually, the queen of Westeros.

"I don't even like *Game of Thrones*," she offers, and I realize I was speaking my thoughts again. "Everyone is too white."

The books have fewer white people, and she would know this if she read more often.

"I've been reading *War and Peace*."

Correction: she'd know this if she read better, not-dumb books more often.

"Oh my God, you're a snob. I'm best friends with a book snob."

I flip my hair and order stir-fried rice. Kayla orders coconut curry. Somewhere outside, a man yells "FUCK" and another man yells "STOP" but we never see them and keep eating our appetizers gleefully. Life goes on outside the restaurant without us. It is all very dramatic. Kayla picks at her nails, a somber look replacing her faint exasperated joy.

"I'm going to miss you, snob."

I reach across the table and put my hand over hers.

"I'll always be with you," I say. She smiles, and I continue. "As a pair of disembodied eyes. Watching your buttocks with great admiration-slash-envy-slash-protective maternal instinct."

"Ew."

"Wren won't know what hit him when I materialize out of thin air on your first get-it-on night and punch him in the mouth."

Kayla glares.

"*Softly*. Sock him in the mouth *softly*," I correct. "With my pinkie."

Our dinner arrives and we eat like starved hyenas, which is an improvement, because on the ladder of voracious eaters teenage girls are just below great white sharks and above starved hyenas, which means we are actually behaving ourselves. The waitress doesn't seem to think so, and she wrinkles her nose when she takes away our dishes, the rings of food left behind like halos of glory. And indigestion. I duck into the bathroom for a second to wash my face free of peanut sauce. And it's then the memories come flooding back with a particularly heinous vengeance. Jack leaned against that counter. Jack touched that sink. Jack touched my face for the first time while he stood where the counter and the wall met. Jack's in every tile of this bathroom, and I can't escape it.

I don't want to.

He might be missing, gone from my life like a ghost, but here? He's still here. I can envision his tall frame here. I can close my eyes and be in the past again.

It's just a dumb bathroom in a Thai restaurant. But to me, it's so much more.

I wash my face and stare in the mirror.

This is the last dinner Kayla and I will have together for a long time. Four months, at least. I leave tomorrow. She leaves a week after. This is where it all stops, and begins again. Nobody knows what will happen, but I'm determined to keep her in my life. I won't lose her.

Not like I lost Jack.

"Everything okay?" Kayla asks when I come back to the table. "Diarrhea?"

"Oh, constantly. It's my superpower. Semiautomatic shitting."

Kayla's quiet, which either meant she didn't get my joke or she wasn't listening.

"You miss him, huh?" she asks quietly.

I know who she's talking about. It's hard not to guess when he's a giant pink elephant all but sitting on our faces. Spiritually. Spiritually sitting on our faces. But I play dumb because that's easier.

"Wren? Hell yeah, I miss him. I messaged that nerd on Facebook last night and he never—"

"I meant Jack, dummy."

I'm quiet. Kayla sighs and crosses her arms over her chest as she waits for the check.

"It's not fair. He just took off and left you."

I laugh, the sound bitter. "It's fine. There was nothing between us, anyway."

Kayla gives me another, sharper death stare. She'd learned from Avery well. "Don't bullshit me, okay? There's an entire school that can attest to your mutual attraction. Plus, I'm your best friend. And I dated him for a while. I know exactly how much you meant to each other."

"Obviously not a lot." I laugh again. "Since he left so quickly. Without saying good-bye."

Kayla's silent, waiting for more. I smile.

"Living is really weird," I say. "You never get used to it. But it happens anyway. And sometimes you find things that make it a little more comfortable, and you try to hold on to those things, and the tighter you hold, the faster they slip away."

I look out the window to the dusk-painted main street, gold streetlamps just starting to bloom. I'll miss this small town. It won't miss me.

"I think Sophia knew that the best out of all of us. Maybe she was the only one in the world who knew that. Maybe that's why she just…let go. Because the things she loved were leaving faster the tighter she held on."

"Isis—"

I turn back to Kayla. "I'm okay, I promise. I've just been thinking about her a lot. About what I could've done. Gran told me I couldn't have done anything. But I could've. I could've just…*let go*. I could have let Jack go, and maybe Sophia would still be here."

"That's not true!" Kayla protests.

"Maybe it is. Maybe it isn't. But the only thing I really know is in that alternate world where I let Jack go, Sophia is more likely to still be alive."

Kayla flinches. The waitress leaves the bill, but Kayla doesn't even notice. I motion at it.

"You gonna get that? We can splitzies."

We split the bill evenly. On the drive home, with the sky as dark and starless as cold ocean water, Kayla finally speaks.

"You didn't do anything wrong, Isis."

"No," I agree. "You're right. I didn't do anything wrong. I didn't do anything at all."

Kayla tries to break the dark ice that's layered over our conversation, and I try, too. The shadow of Sophia's death haunts us. Me. It haunts me, and it's ruining this good-bye, and I can't even stop it.

"Look, Kayla, I'm sorry. I'm just…just really sorry. I don't know when I got like this, and I promised myself I wouldn't—"

"But it's easier said than done," she interrupts. "I know. Wren's been like this, too. Don't worry. It's okay. I've had practice handling mopey."

Her smile is a little drained.

When we pull into my driveway, we sit in the dark car, watching the moths attack the porch light. They throw themselves at it, over and over again, like they want to catch fire and burn.

"I'm lucky I met you." I smile at Kayla. "And I'm triple lucky you have a thing for insane weirdos. Pretty much won the friend lottery."

"So did I." Kayla pouts. "Without you, I never would've realized Avery was using me."

"Jack helped."

She nods, grinning wryly. "I guess. A little."

"Do you remember the first time we met at Avery's party? And he made you cry?"

"Oh God, I was such a crybaby. I can't even believe how dumb I was. And that was just, like, ten months ago. I could've had a baby in that time."

"A crybaby," I insert.

"All babies are crybabies," she counters. I take on a wise old man squint and voice as I postulate.

"But are all crybabies…babies?"

Kayla courteously punches my arm, then sighs and leans back in her seat.

"Jack was the first one to bring it up. He made me start questioning everything—why I was hanging with Avery, did I really enjoy her company, how much of my feelings were hidden behind the shopping and the gossip. Without him, it would've taken me a lot longer."

"Wouldn't have killed him to put some damn sugar on it," I grunt. "Willy Wonka does it all the time, and he's fine! Possibly homicidal, but fine."

Kayla laughs and shakes her head. "You know Jack. He doesn't work like that."

I smile, the thing a little twisted but still whole. Kayla puts her hand on my shoulder.

"You two are…the same. I didn't notice it before, but Wren pointed it out to me. He's right. You two really are the same. So I think— I think even if he's gone now, he'll be back. People like you—you don't find very often. He'll be back."

"And when he comes back, I will behead him," I announce.

"You'll greet him," Kayla says sternly. "With a hug."

"I will greet him with a hug. To his torso. Which will be missing a head."

Kayla slaps her palm to her face, and I hug her, laughing. Laughing warm. Laughing true. Laughing for the first time in what feels like forever.

I'm not really losing my best friend.

We're just going our own ways. We're scattering ourselves to different winds, but we'll come together again. We are exploring a globe in different directions. Like Columbus and Magellan, boldly going where no stinky sixteenth-century European explorer and his crew of scurvy men have ever gone before! Except one of them died of fever, and, like, mutiny, I think, and the other was pretty much a racist bastard who enabled hundreds of years of genocide, so in a fit of good judgment I decide to nix that metaphor entirely.

"Thank God," Kayla breathes. "Can you get out now?"

chapter five

3 YEARS, 45 WEEKS, 0 DAYS

I'VE COME TO THE VERY ORIGINAL and unique conclusion that leaving home sucks ass. No one else has ever, in the history of humanity, come to this conclusion. No one except me. I am special.

"Isis, we're late!"

And late. I am very late.

Being late doesn't deter me from being proper about farewells, though. As Mom starts the car, I stand in the doorway and breathe in the musty air of eighteen years' worth of angst. I didn't spend all eighteen years here, but all the shit that happened in the last year and a half made it feel like that long.

Good-bye, little room.

Good-bye, girl I used to be.

I hug Ms. Muffin close and pet Hellspawn one last time and leave.

Mom drives slowly and carefully. I sip ginger ale and watch the highway flash by. Suddenly, a terrifying thought hits me upside the head with its sweaty palm.

What the hell did I do with my teenage years?

I didn't volunteer or play sports. I didn't become a radical warrior princess on my sixteenth birthday, complete with a talking cat and magically appearing clothes. Hogwarts didn't even send me a letter, and I haven't actually forgiven them for that. Wait until I go to London and find Platform Nine-and-Three-Quarters and slip through to the other side and unleash my rage. I'll make Voldemort look like a sock puppet. And I'll make out with Draco. And I'll train a bunch of house elves to fan me and bring me grapes—

I stop when I realize I'm writing mental Harry Potter fan fiction on my way to college. Focus! I need at least seven whole focuses if I'm going to make a fabulous impression. Or any impression at all. I'd rather make a bad impression than no impression.

As Mom pulls onto the exit, I sigh.

I didn't even kiss a boy. For realsies, anyway. Not-drunk.

I did other things. I held hands and hugged. Nameless pretended real hard to be nice using hugs and hand-holding. Once or twice he even hinted he thought I was pretty. But it was an act, just to build me up before he tore me down. And it was all before the big it. Little it. It's not even worthy of a prefix. It's just "it."

I have to leave that behind, too. There's no room for that. Not if I want to move on with my life. I've done my best to bury it, ignore it until it goes away, and it's sort of worked. I got far enough to sleep in a bed with Jack without freaking out. So I'm getting better, and that's real good to know.

It gives me a little bit of hope where there used to be none.

Jack helped me realize that I'm not unlovable. I'm not hopeless.

I'm not all ugly.

Or maybe I realized it on my own.

Either way, fighting with him helped me realize lots of

stuff. I grew up all kinds of ways.

A sharp pain radiates in my chest, but I brush that dirt off my shoulder and watch Mom's smile.

"There's the sign, sweetie. Get the map out, will you?"

OHIO STATE UNIVERSITY looms in white lettering on a big sign on the side of the road. I pull out the brochure map and direct her onto the campus. Trees and rosebushes bloom like crazy, the emerald-green lawn dappled with buttery late-afternoon sun. The buildings are all old brickwork, ivy sprawling across windows, and Roman columns. The dorms are shabbier, but just as big. Hundreds of students are walking around, their parents walking with them, or standing outside the car and hugging them one last time, or helping them carry baggage into dorms.

Mom parks and gets out, and my stomach drops with excitement as I fumble with the door handle. This is it. This is how my childhood ends. Not with a bang, but with a silent scream.

I finger the cigarette burns on my wrist and make sure my sleeve is covering them. I take it back. My childhood ended a long time ago.

Mom can't really pick up my heavy suitcase or backpack, so I drag them up the stairs and she follows. The room is tiny and whitewashed and on the second floor, right next to the fire escape. There's no carpet, just cold tile, and the beds are so high up they seem made for, at the very least, Hagrid. Two beds are tucked into opposite ends of the room, a window glaring between them. Two desks are just beside the beds, with ass torture implements of the highest caliber—wood chairs. Two closets wait to be filled with shoes or condoms or failed exams or whatever else college kids fill empty spaces with. Broken dreams, maybe.

My roommate has already claimed the left side, so I plop

my stuff on the right. Mom fusses around with the bedsheets she packed and makes my bed. I watch her work, knowing I'll miss the sight of her doing little things like this. I inspect my roommate's closet—a guitar, lots of army surplus jackets and hiking boots. She's littered her desk with silver jewelry—studs, rings with skulls, necklaces with spiked orbs of death. Yep. We'll get along just fine.

Mom finishes the bed, and we walk downstairs and sit on the lawn, soaking in the sun. Mom holds my hand, stroking it with her thumb.

"I'm sorry, Isis," she tries.

"For what? Not birthing me a week or two earlier? I *so* wanted to be a Gemini. None of this Cancer nonsense."

Mom smiles wryly. "No, not that. For…I don't know. I feel like I didn't do a very good job. But I suppose every parent feels like that."

I squeeze her hand. "You did the best you knew how. We both did."

She nods and squeezes back. "I'm just glad I could be with you for your last year at home. Even if…even if it was difficult."

I know what regret looks like now. I saw it in every line of Jack's face at the funeral. I'll never forget what it looks like, even if the Zabadoobians abduct me and bleach my brain. Mom wears it like a shawl, lightly but drawing it taut. I throw my arms around her and bury my head in her shoulder.

"It's okay. I had fun. It was hard, but I had fun and I learned stuff, more stuff than I ever learned in my life, so I'm real happy I came to live with you. Thanks for being the best mom ever."

She puts one arm around me and into my hair and starts crying.

"I love you, Isis."

"I love you, too!" I laugh, the tears springing up. "I'll miss you."

I'll see her more than Kayla, but it still stings. I'm about as good at good-byes as Tarzan is at wearing clothes.

At least Leo's in jail. She'll be safe for a few years.

Mom insisted on giving me the old VW Beetle for college. She'd been wanting to get a different car for a while, and this gave her the perfect excuse. I see her to the Greyhound bus station and wave as it pulls out of the lot. I watch her with a sinking heart that sort of dovetails into a swoop, then lifts up as I drive back to the school again.

I'm alone.

Nobody knows me at Ohio State. I have to start all over. Hundreds of freshmen stream past me on the sidewalks, trampling the green lawn and my pure maiden heart as they look right through me. I'm more faceless than Emperor Palpatine before he took his hood off. A massive banner over the huge glass-walled library reads WELCOME BUCKEYES!

"More like welcome fuck-eyes," a voice to my left groans. A girl with seven earrings in one ear and a round, stocky face stands beside me. She's heavy and tall and powerful, her hair dyed bright pink and shaved on the sides. Her combat boots and flannel shirt tell me everything I need to know. Badass supreme. I simultaneously want to be her and fight her just to be able to say she punched me. She blinks hazel eyes thick with eyeliner at me.

"Uh, what?" she says.

"Was I thinking out loud? I do that sometimes. The doctors say it's probably mild Tourette's, but I say it's a higher evolutionary process of humanity. Someday the entire world will be like me and it will be rad."

The girl's pink eyebrows shoot up, and she laughs. It's a full, rich laugh, like stew instead of the giggly soup of most girls. She holds out her hand.

"Yvette. Yvette Monroe."

I shake it. "Isis Blake. But my friends call me Crazy. Or Idiot. Sometimes both at once."

Yvette smirks. "That makes two of us."

It's then I recognize one of the fabulous skull earrings she's wearing. There's another pair in my dorm.

"This is going to sound slightly stalkerish, but I can't help but notice you've decapitated Jack Skellington and put him on your ears."

"What can I say?" Yvette shrugs. "I like bones."

"So do I, actually, because our skeletons support a massive interconnected muscular structure, and without them we would be blobs of flesh. Also we wouldn't have middle fingers to flip people off with. Are you in room 14B?"

Yvette's eyes widen. "Yeah, so you're—"

"*My roommate!*" I screech. A passing guy winces and flips me off. I loudly inform him he has his skeleton to thank for that. Yvette seems pleased. She thumps her arm across my shoulders and I sink about two inches into the soft dirt.

"You first," she says, leading me back to our dorm.

"First for what? A three-legged footrace? Because I'll have you know I only have one really good leg, the other is kind of unshaved and unsexy—"

"First to spill your life story. Where are you from?"

"Uh, Ohio. Or I mean, no. Florida! Yeah, that's the one. I grew up there, then moved here senior year. What about you? Oooh, let me guess—hell. You're from hell."

"I am definitely from hell. Hell, Kansas."

"I like uncooked ramen noodles and driving like a maniac," I continue.

"I hate everything except bacon and pickles. And I don't drive."

"One time in third grade I stuck candy up my nose to impress a boy. Spoiler: he was not impressed."

Yvette looks impressed, then sighs.

"I started smoking because it's the first year of college and I already know I'm going to drop out."

And it's her honesty that kills me. It's the way she says it—all frank, undramatic, modest honesty. Something I never had. Something I should've had. Something that, if I had, would have saved someone's life, maybe.

"My friend killed herself," I say. Yvette looks over at me for a second, a minute that stretches into what feels like an hour and I never want it to end, because she's seeing me instead of looking through me like everyone else in this place. Yvette opens the door and we walk in, and she gestures to her bed.

"This is my half. That's your half."

I nod, and she smiles, pink hair lit from behind by the sunlight.

"Let's get some fucking food."

Fact: college is great.

I know this primarily because they serve clam chowder next to pizza, and gyoza next to burritos, and there is dessert every. Single. Night. If you so choose. And I hella so choose. Sometimes. Sometimes I eat a salad like a Grown-up™ because that's what I am now, I guess.

My Hagrid bed is pretty shitty, comfort-wise, but the terrifying thought of rolling off the five-foot drop at night keeps me securely in the middle and under the covers always. Yvette snores, and blasts Metallica when she does her homework, but otherwise we've been getting along fine. Better than fine. She's snarkier than me, sometimes, which is worthy of at least four Nobel Prizes, and she's smart. She isn't Jack smart or anything, but she's not Jack dumb, either. She's always hard and a little angry, but she laughs louder and gets angrier faster than anyone I've ever known, except maybe Kayla when I tell her she's pretty.

But Yvette's openness is a refreshing change from last year's secrets and passive-aggressiveness. She doesn't bring up Sophia's suicide, even though I told her about it the first day. She's not the type to pry, and I adore her for it. She smokes on the fire escape sometimes, and sometimes I go up there with her and try to smoke, but it usually ends with me puking, so we stop that right quick.

I'll tell her more about Sophia in my own time. Or maybe I won't. Maybe I'll just keep it inside, like I kept Nameless. But I won't let it fester this time. I won't let it hurt me. I won't hold on to the hurt like a ball of shattered glass ever again. Some shitbaby jerk taught me better than that.

My classes are great but sort of easy, in that weird, beginning-of-semester way. I mean, four teachers assigned ten-page essays due next week, but forty pages is a febreeze for me. I used to write twenty pages in my radical-yet-whiny pubescent diary on the daily. The only thing that's really hard is focusing, because the classrooms are huge auditoriums, sort of, which could easily be converted into gladiator rings if we moved the teacher's desk and got rid of the chairs, and really, the bland walls would look so much better with swaths of blood across them and also the lights are so bright, do they shine the lightbulbs? How do you shine a lightbulb so high up? Can their janitor fly?

Next to me in our seats in the very back, Yvette informs me janitors cannot fly. Vampires, however, can.

"Vampires are gross," I determine.

"Have you even read *Twilight*?"

"I've read so many things that are not that."

"It was the best. The vampires were the best. The make-outs were the best."

I shudder. Yvette, in her flaming skull T-shirt and ripped jeans, sighs like a fancy princess dreaming of boys.

"Imagine having sex with a vampire."

"Imagine going to church and praying to your lord and savior," I offer a counter-point.

She laughs and goes back to Tumblr on her laptop. The best part about college, I've decided, is the professors don't give a shit whether you pay attention or not. Short of dropping an F-bomb super loud out of nowhere, they ignore all the internet surfing and texting that goes on. We're paying to be here, not the other way around. It'll be different when labs come around, but right now it's Shangri-la, and please do not talk to me about labs, because the thought of me around combustible chemicals is so exhilarating I have to fight to not pee myself constantly in anticipation. Long live science. Long live explode-y things.

Mom calls every night, because that's what moms do. That, and like, sighing. But Mom's always sighed a lot, because she's sad mostly, but also because having a borderline nutso daughter like me would be trying on any mortal human's soul. Except, like, Beyoncé, but we all know she isn't mortal at all and also she has Blue Ivy who I *hate* because it's so unfair because Beyoncé was supposed to be *my* mom.

"Beyoncé's music is terrible," Yvette offers as we walk to dinner.

"Ah yes," I say. "Let me just mark that down on this neat little list I keep titled *The 25 Reasons Why You'll Be Joining Me in the Eternally Agonizing Lava Pit Portion of Beelzebub's Kingdom*."

"You talk to yourself so much. Is it like, a birth defect?"

"It's a side effect of the radioactive waste my mother bathed in while pregnant with me, yes."

Yvette opens her mouth to say something else, then closes it and turns the color of a ketchup sandwich—white on the edges, red in the middle. I follow her gaze to a group of girls, but before I can pinpoint which fly lady has her attention, Yvette snaps out of it, clearing her throat and grabbing a bowl for soup.

"Anyway," she says with much difficulty. "There's a music showcase down at Weigel Hall. It's mostly sweaty dudes dicking around with drums and Alice in Chains covers. You should come and educate yourself on the merits of true music."

"Wait, whoa, are we just gonna ignore the fact that you—"

Yvette suddenly repurposes a decent amount of soup as floor cleaner. "That I what?" she snaps.

"Uh, nothing. Never mind. Yeah, I'll come. Is there a cover fee, or?"

She relaxes visibly. "It's free. I'll see you at seven, then?"

I answer with a mean air-guitar riff, and she smirks and leaves. I take my pizza slice out onto the balcony, where the dying sun paints everything in pale golds and silvers. The tree shadows grow long, tangling in the shadows of passersby and untangling again.

And that's when I see him.

I try hard not to see him. I really do. My brain gives a sputter, and I forget how to swallow. My skin crawls, hot at first, then so terribly cold I might as well be in Alaska. I start sweating, and my eyes dart around, looking for all the exits off the terrace—the stairs, the back stairs, through the cafeteria and out the door. I don't even think about it, I just do it. I'm reacting instead of thinking as I pick up my plate and dump it in a whirling flash; two seconds is all it takes, two seconds and the terror has a complete and total hold over me as I dash inside the cafeteria and watch him approach through the window.

Curly, dark brown hair falls into his eyes. Steel-colored eyes, a blue so dark you can't see the light through them. The color of swords and the ocean, both terrifying, both sharp; both can kill you. He killed a little part of me. His eyebrows are thick and his mouth pleasant, and if you squint he could be in a British boy band, maybe, possibly. The freckles on his nose are still there, the freckles I'd written stupid poetry about. He's taller than I remember—taller than most of the boys here—and his biceps are huge; he's been lifting and it'd make any girl swoon, but it just makes me want to barf. All I want to do is puke, right here, all over the potted plant I'm hiding behind. But above the panic-static that's currently turning my brain to mush, another part of me screams silently.

What! The! Fuck! Is Nameless! Doing! Here!

Here, of all places, *here*, of all goddamn colleges. It has to be a joke. He has to be visiting a friend or something. He can't be enrolled here, learning here, sleeping within the same ten miles of me. He can't be. He just *can't*. I came here to avoid him. I moved to an entirely different state to leave him behind, and now he's found me again. No, shit, there's no way he's here just for me. It's a coincidence. His shitty, threatening emails earlier in the year were just last-gasp effort taunts, his way of—of—of what? Somewhere in the back of my mind, my sessions with Dr. Mernich—the psychologist I saw after Leo's assault—stick with me, burning dark and hard. Triggered. His way of triggering me. He wanted me to remember. And now he's going to get to see me remember. In person.

"H-Hey, are you okay?"

I look up. A girl with honey-colored hair and huge gray eyes behind glasses blinks at me. She smells faintly of musky roses. My stellar powers of observation alert me to the fact she has a chest even bigger than Kayla's and a thick, soft belly, but I barely register it through my haze of panic.

"I'm decidedly not okay," I say, my voice thin and high.

"Yeah, you look like crap." The girl covers her mouth, then whispers, "Um, not in general. But right now you look sick, is all. Bad-sick. Not, um. Rad-sick."

Rad-sick. I can feel the literal stars beginning to gleam in my eyes as history unfurls, and I discover the only person on the planet Earth who may have beaten me, Isis Blake, in making stupid puns. And having fabulous curves. And smelling like roses. But then I remember I'd been in the midst of undergoing a mild panic attack.

"You are really cute and all," I say quickly, "but I'm currently facing down the fact that my ex-boyfriend goes to this college, which is extreme grossness. You probably don't want to stick around for something that's the same level of gross as, like, a vat of Nickelodeon slime, so if you could just leave so I can get back in the mood of being terrorized helplessly, I'd appreciate it."

Glasses Girl frowns and searches the crowd. "He terrorizes you? I'm so not down with that, fry-slice. Which one is he?"

"Oh, he's the one with the hellish, menacing aura barely concealed beneath a mask of vague antisocial tendencies and abs, and he's currently walking into this very room and oh my God I have to go. To space."

I dart out the back door just as Nameless pushes into the cafeteria. I gulp twilight air and my steps are so big and frantic I almost trip. Glasses Girl steadies me by grabbing my elbow.

"Hey, um, seriously, do you want me to take you to the infirmary?"

I consider her for a long moment. "You know, that would be lovely. But first, I'm going to puke on your shoes, so you probably won't want to do that, or even be remotely nice to me anymore."

"Okay."

I unceremoniously puke on her shoes. When I'm not making attractive hurling noises anymore, the girl laughs.

"I'm Diana. These are my roommate's shoes. She's a bitch."

"Oh man." I wipe my mouth. "I love messing up bitch-shoes. I've done it so often. Mostly to this one stupid pretty boy. And now you. Not that you're a stupid pretty boy. Or maybe you are. Um."

There's a thoughtful pause. Diana looks thoroughly informed of her own gender.

"I'm Isis."

"Nice to meet you, Egyptian goddess of fertility." Diana smiles.

"She was full of magical spells and almost always naked, which is cool except for probably sand in her hoo-ha, but I'm not actually into marrying my own brother—side note: grody—and if I had Isis's banging magic powers—pun totally intended—I would be hexing dudes, not sexing them, and I'd definitely not stay here for four years to figure out what I don't mind doing to make money until I die and oh God I need to lie down."

So I do. On the sidewalk. Diana watches me with unmistakable morbid curiosity.

"Your puke puddle is right by your head," she points out helpfully.

I wrinkle my nose and scooch five feet sideways into the grass. And the grass turns into a hill and I'm rolling and it smells like earth and new fresh green sproutbabies, and when the world stops spinning and I stop moving and Diana teeters down the hill asking if I'm okay, bringing that soft smell of roses with her, I start laughing.

All the terror in my chest was spun out by the rolling fall. It broke the hard, icy grip of Nameless. The smell of the sun-warmed ground and the feel of grass tickling my butt reminds me it'll pass. He'll pass. He'll die, also, someday, and then I'll really be free, but it's not the end of the world. He's here. I'm here. But we're different people now. I'm stronger because of everything that's happened. Because of him, and the pain. But mostly because of Sophia and Jack and Kayla and Wren.

I want to be happier. Happy like Sophia is now. Happy like I want Jack to be now.

Even if they're both gone. Even if they're all gone.

Even if I'm all alone.

Diana watches me laugh, smiling, and sits beside me. It's then I confirm my suspicions—only a total weirdo would continue to hang out with someone who puked on her shoes, then rolled down a hill like a sugar-high hamster and laughed about it. Diana could be a serial killer. Or a genuinely nice person. Both the sort of people who shouldn't be hanging around yours truly.

"You're crying," she says offhandedly, picking a dandelion and blowing the fuzz away. I wipe my face.

"I've been doing it a lot lately. Because, you know. Crying is fun, if you think about it like Splash Mountain for your eyes."

Diana giggles. I stand up, brushing grass off my sculpted abs.

"Anyway, it's been great, but I must go and contemplate the fact that I might be losing my fucking marbles."

Diana shrugs. "I think you're just scared. It's scary—college. We can do anything. We can fail or flunk, or drink or smoke or have sex, and no one cares. We're not kids anymore. There're no parents here. Whatever happens in our future happens because of the choices we make now. That's really scary."

I watch her face. She hugs her knees.

"And seeing exes you haven't seen for a long time is scary, too."

I lose all will to leave and flop down beside her. The last thing I want to be right now is alone. We watch the sunset rip through the sky with fire and velvet.

"Boys are weird," Diana concludes sagely.

"I don't know anything about boys except they make weird noises sometimes," I say.

"That's called speaking."

"Oh."

Diana squints at me. "If he did something bad, I can punt him for you."

"You usually go around offering to punt people?"

"I have four little brothers. It'd be a shame to let my talents go to waste."

It's my turn to chuckle. Voices make me jump. I shoot a wary look up the hill, but it's just a crowd of loud, obnoxious girls shrieking as they pass.

"I really didn't wanna live constantly looking over my shoulder again." I sigh. "It was shitty in Florida, and it'll be shitty here."

"I would say ignore him, but I guess that's easier said than done, huh?"

I nod. Diana picks at a blade of grass. I'm about to say something deep and profound and possibly life-changing when Yvette's clear, strong voice cuts between us. A guitar case is strapped to her back, pink hair matching the sunset.

"Oyyyyy! You coming to the show or what, numb nuts?"

I stand, shakily. I shoot one last look back at the cafeteria. The choker of thorns around my neck is gone now. He's gone. I'm safe. Diana stands with me, and I smile at her.

"On a scale of one to duh, how much do you like music?"

chapter six

3 YEARS, 47 WEEKS, 1 DAY

WEIGEL HALL IS A MASSIVE glass-and-brick contraption built by rich, wrinkly alumni who wanted to see their name on something large and impressive before they kicked the bucket. The music majors and People Who Like Death Cab for Cutie Too Much™ hang around here 24-7, and they're the ones who put this whole thing on. It's a "battle of the bands" type of deal—handfuls of grungy college kids with aspiring indie bands performing on a stage to a likewise college crowd. Alcohol isn't allowed, but people sneak it in in soda bottles and flasks, laughing and sloshing about like waterlogged pirates. With trust funds. And essays due the next day. Not that pirates wrote essays. But if they did, they would be about singing parrots and knife-fights and fat booty of the not-woman kind, or possibly simultaneously of the woman kind and the treasure kind, because, well, *pirates*.

"Hold this for me. Take pictures of me on it. I want to see my own awesome live show in Technicolor." Yvette shoves a phone into my hand. Diana, looking a little lost but sweetly excited, giggles.

"Are you in a band?" she asks. Yvette looks at her like

she's just seeing her for the first time.

"U-Uh, yeah. Um. Major Rager."

"It's not that good of a party," I correct. "There aren't *nearly* enough people getting naked."

"Major Rager is the band name, dork." Yvette nudges me. "I'm late—we're next. If *someone* had been answering her phone instead of making me run around campus looking for her—"

"I told you! The government is listening to everything I say. I've switched to smoke signals." I pause. "Their texting plan is *obscenely* cheap. And arson-y."

Yvette rolls her eyes and wades through people, heading toward backstage. Diana and I watch the current band shred the hearts of the crowd as their lead guitarist rips out an ear-rending solo.

"She's cute," Diana shouts to me.

"Not as cute as me!" I shout back. "Wait, who are we talking about again?"

"Your friend. Yvette's her name?"

"Oh yeah. She's my roommate. I sort of infect everything I touch like that. She's going to get even cuter as my spores take over her body and turn her into my willing minion."

Diana giggles. I pause.

"I'm not actually that evil."

"I know," she says. "Evil people don't cry as much as you do."

I didn't used to cry so much, and I want to tell her that, but I realize the story would be too long. You could fit it in, like, at least three books. So instead I contemplate whether Diana meant Yvette's cute in the general adorable girl way or the *hey baby, you're 2 cute get in my bed* way. The sudden vastness of where I am hits me just as the enormous exhaustion of an emotionally draining day decides to punch me. It's a one-two combo, and I mumble an excuse and stumble through the crowd, finding relief outside, where people smoke and the music isn't quite as shouty. I hug my knees to my chin and watch the moon rise over the quieting campus. This is my home now, but it doesn't feel like home. When does it start to feel like home?

"When you start feeling all right," a voice cuts in. My ears know it before my eyes do, and I suddenly regret coming out here, coming to this school, and living in general.

Nameless smiles down at me, hands hooked casually in his jean pockets. He is tall and wrapped in shadow, and my fingertips go numb. He sits beside me, the paralysis creeping from him in static waves and flooding me up to my eyes.

"But you'll never feel all right here, will you? Not with me around." Nameless looks at me, straight in the eyes, and some deep part of me curls in on myself, waiting for the inevitable hurt.

"Why?" I manage through tight lips.

Nameless shrugs, brushing hair from his eyes. "My aunt and uncle—Wren's parents—are here in Ohio. Dad felt better about sending me here where there's family. I wanted to go to UCSD, but, you know. You can't always have everything you want in life. And even if you do get it, you might regret it. But you know that already, huh?"

He smiles at me, all teeth, and I start shaking, my legs and my arms and my neck quivering uncontrollably.

"I was sorry to hear about your friend." Nameless sighs. "He prodded at my firewalls for the longest time. Annoying bug. What was his name? John? Jake? Whatever, he's gone now. He hasn't poked me for months, and your high school's records showed he stopped going there toward the end."

"How do you know that?" I swallow.

"How do you think?" He laughs. "When all you've got is

a laptop and a dad who doesn't want you around, you learn to make your own fun."

My nails bite into my palm. Through my panic I remember his dad, a terrifyingly huge man who drank too much and worked on motorcycles. When Nameless's mom left him, his dad took it out on him. For the briefest of seconds I feel pity—old pity—but it evaporates with his smirk.

"Must've sucked, finally finding a boy stupid enough to like you and then having to watch him slip from your fingers."

"What do you want?" I manage. He sighs.

"I want you to know the truth, Isis. About Jack. About what he did that night."

I didn't think it was possible, but my stomach writhes even worse. "That" night. He's talking about that night in middle school—the one where Sophia lost Tallie. The one Wren caught on tape.

"You—" I swallow hard. "You sent me that screenshot of Jack's hand on the baseball bat months ago."

"Correct."

"How did you get that?"

"Simple. I have a copy of the video. The whole thing."

I can't breathe anymore, tiny shallow inhales are all I can manage. "But—"

"You might hate me," he says. "You might think I'm the lowest of the low, but I know you, Isis. I know how curious you are. If you want to see the tape—and you do—you'll come to me. You'll have to, sooner or later. And I look forward to that."

Nameless laughs, and quickly, too quickly, pats my shoulder. My panic tenses every muscle without my permission and, like it's being pulled by marionette strings, my knee juts out and hits him square in the side. He makes a winded, coughing noise, and the genial mask he keeps up fractures to shards, the smile turning cruel, the jovial light in his eyes twisting to malicious offense.

"You little—"

His hands reach for me, and I'm ducking, but neither of us gets to move any farther because someone steps between us.

"That's about enough of that."

And I recognize this voice, too.

Dark jeans, a flannel shirt with the sleeves rolled up. Shoulders I know—shoulders I slept against a long time ago. Tawny, gold-brown hair sticking up in the back. It's an illusion; it has to be.

"And who the fuck are you?" Nameless sneers.

"I'm hurt you don't recognize me, Will. All that prying into our school records, but no prying into my photos? That's lazy of you. Lax. I'd almost call it a mistake."

I see Nameless's eyes go wide, but he quickly adopts a neutral face, a smirk tugging at his mouth as he stands up, his full height almost level with the newcomer's.

"We're all here, then. Fabulous. The party can finally start." Nameless laughs. He looks at the newcomer, and then me, before turning and walking down the well-lit sidewalk. Like a spell, the paralysis lifts when he's out of sight, and I gasp for air.

"Shit, shit, rancid *shitmonkeys*!" I stand and brush myself off, willing the trembling to stop. It'll take hours. And it's not just Nameless that's causing it.

Jack Hunter turns to face me.

It feels like years, but it's only been months. A few months. He looks so much older—lines around his eyes that didn't used to be there. His face matured somehow, the sharp angles of pubescence rounded off in a handsome, hawkish way. His eyes are the same frigid, clear blue, brows drawn tight.

"Isis, I—"

I pull my fist back and punch him.

His head snaps to the side, and the people around us go even quieter. Someone murmurs "fight," but no one moves. Except Jack. He slowly turns his head to me, a red welt blossoming on his Legolas-high cheekbones. I expect rage to ice over his eyes, but it never does.

"Isis," he repeats, softer now.

"Who the fuck do you think you are, running off like that?" I demand.

Jack flinches—flinch? Jack? Never—but doesn't break his gaze from mine.

"You're shaking," he says.

"I know I'm fucking shaking! I'm a lot of things right now, and shaking is the least homicidal of them! You left all of us! You just...disappeared! Your mom, Wren, shit—everyone. You left everyone behind!"

Jack's frown deepens. I catch a glimpse of his hands at his sides—strong and spidery as ever. I want to hold them, I want to hold him, to lunge in and hug him until he can't breathe or leave again, to tell him it's okay, to tell him I forgive him, but the fury and Nameless's words mush together in my head and come out as acid on my lips.

"You left *me* behind."

"Isis, please, let me—"

"No!" I interrupt his soft, pleading voice. It's so unlike him it scares me. Almost as much as Nameless's hands shooting out to grab me did. Almost. "Did you think a fucking ticket to Paris would make me forgive you? On what fucking planet is a plane ticket a substitute for a proper goddamn good-bye, and how can I avoid said planet for all conceivable time?"

She is fire and rage, all claws extended, her hair swirling around her in the gentle summer night wind and her cinnamon eyes ablaze with light from the hall. She shines in the velvet darkness, a little thinner than I remember, and a little sadder, but burning all the same. Always burning. I warm myself on her fury, embracing the searing hot-sweet feel of her wrath and all the vibrant life behind it.

She is here; she is within reach. I thought I was seeing things when I came upon her there, looking uncomfortable and terrified with Will next to her. But she is real and corporeal and angry with me. Maybe she's never not been angry with me, and that's why it feels right. We have always been at odds. We have *always* clashed. After months of feeling wrong, this, staring down at my hellion—mine? No, I threw away the chance to call her mine—is the only thing that's felt right. The planets are in place, the last gear snaps into motion, and the world begins to turn again, as is proper and right.

"I thought you were going to Stanford," I try.

She bristles. "Don't change the subject, butt-lump."

"You should've gone to Stanford. It would've challenged you."

You would've been happier there. You would've bent the whole world to your will. You would've met smarter, kinder boys there. Boys who aren't me.

"Wow," she scoffs. "I didn't think it was possible, but you've somehow gotten even better at pissing me off. Call the pope, because we have a bona fide fucking miracle on our peasant hands."

Through the anger, I can see her shoulders trembling. I didn't think it was her at first. She was so quiet, her purple streaks all but faded. I recognized Will Cavanaugh, though. How could I not? I studied his face in the dossier for nights on end, memorizing every line and curve, planning out where and how I would hurt him most. The docile girl talking with Will couldn't have been Isis. But then came the kick to his spleen, wild and furious and all reaction, no forethought, and I knew instantly it was her. Here, of all places. My heart stuttered, the color and warmth flushing in where months of training and guilt had drained it out to grays and blacks. Fate is a terrible bitch.

"What about you?" she spits when I don't say anything. "Harvard get too snooty for you? Who am I kidding, the queen of England is less snooty than you."

"I started here. I never went to Harvard."

"Then where. The fuck. DID. You go?"

Her words are slow venom, her eyes narrowed. I can't tell her. She wouldn't understand. No—she would. She would understand best of all, and that's why I can't tell her. It would draw me closer to her. I was thrilled to take this job at first, if only for my planned retribution on Will, but now that she's here I regret it. This school brings us close. So close. Close enough for me to hurt her all over again, hurt her to the point of no healing, like I did to Sophia.

I savor the cuts her fury makes, the pain letting me know that yes—I'm still alive. Even after trying to kill the old me, the hurtful bastard me, to leave him behind buried in guilt beside Sophia and Tallie, a single flame from Isis's lips and I'm reminded of our war, our words, our bond. I want to kiss her. I want to kiss her as she turns me to ash.

But she is trembling. So I settle for words.

"I thought I'd never see you again," I say. She scoffs. Her armor is out in full force, tougher and spikier than ever, thanks to me. Thanks to Will. Thanks to bastards like the two of us.

"Did you get that line from one of Sophia's trashy romance novels— " She covers her mouth instantly, but it's too late. Sophia's name rings in the open, tearing apart the stitching on both our wounds. But where pain stops most mouths, it fuels Isis's.

"I hate you, Jack Hunter."

I want to hold her until she can't stand me anymore, until she runs away to somewhere safer. Somewhere without me.

I nod instead. "I know."

"No. You don't know. You think that immature war was hate. But this—this is—" She squeezes her eyes shut. "You left me. You left me like everyone else, and I can't forgive you for that."

"You don't have to," I offer. "You don't owe me anything."

She laughs, the harsh front breaking for just a moment, her old self spilling through the cracks.

"And you don't owe *me* anything, obviously. Not even a call. Not even a single goddamn text saying, oh, I don't know, *I'm not actually decomposing in a river somewhere after throwing myself off a bridge, still breathing, don't wait up for me*."

And that's when I see it. It's not anger because I've hurt her. Sophia's anger was always because I'd hurt her. This anger is because I made Isis worry. Because she thought I was dead, or rather, because she didn't know whether or not I was alive. She is too kind, too motherly for this fury to be anything but a protective instinct denied its full course. I held that sort of anger once, too. I took it out on Isis after I'd caught her in my room looking through my letters—in my mind, trying to get to Sophia.

I've known Isis long enough (not quite a year, but it feels like centuries) to know that when she shakes, she is far gone. When she trembles, her past is rearing its head, throwing shadows on her mind. I'd always refrained from touching her, from making it worse, and though I scream at myself to remain that way, I can't.

I can't.

I step into her, wrapping my arms around her weakly and resting my head against her neck.

"I can't do it anymore," I breathe. "I tried and tried, God—I tried to be the strong one. To do the right thing for everyone."

Isis goes stiff, and for a split second, I realize what I'm doing and frantically try to pull back. Something desperate and dark is eating away at my core, held back by Gregory's brutal training and my own dam of denial. And, like the bomb she is, the mere sight of Isis blew cracks in that dam. She's going to see me through the cracks, the real me. She's going to see me like no one else has, like I'm pretending not to be, broken and dead inside, and I have to leave, have to compose myself, but she doesn't let me pull away, wrapping her arms tight around my waist and keeping me pressed against her, against her warmth and smell and her understanding silence.

"I t-tried," I whisper. "I tried to protect her, and you, and everyone. But all I did was kill her. I failed. I failed and I killed her and hurt you."

I squeeze my eyes shut, hot moisture collecting in them.

"I don't deserve to live—"

Her arms tighten, squeezing the air from me.

"Stop," Isis says.

"It's the truth—"

"News flash: not everything that drops from your gorgeous, dumb mouth is the truth." There's a pause. "Ah, shit. I just called you gorgeous. Now I have to commit seppuku."

"Don't you dare," I mumble into her neck.

"See? That's how it feels. That's how it feels when you say you don't deserve to live. New rule: nobody gets to talk suicide ever."

A tear escapes, and I bury it in her shirt collar. She puts a hand on my head, petting it.

"If you really think you're so bad," she says, "then live. Live, and suffer. Live with the memories of all the bad things you've done. Don't take the easy way out."

There's a poignant pause. Then she adds, "Numb nuts."

The name is a tiny injection of reality, of light. The cracks in me relieve the pressure of the last year, of the year before the last, the water flowing through them slowly as my breath deflates in my lungs. I look up and cup either side of her face.

"I'll only say this one time, so listen carefully."

Her eyes are wide, her lips parted, and her cheeks flushed. Her eyes, too, I notice, are more than a little tearstained.

"You're right," I finish. "You're right for once, Isis Blake."

And then she smiles, and everything in the world is right, and bright, and better. We part, my body already missing her warmth.

"One sec!" She whips her head around to me. "So you're here now? You're living on campus like the rest of us peons?"

I nod. "Siebert hall. Three fourteen. For a while."

Her stare is flinty. "You have a lot of explaining to do. Due. A lot of explaining is extremely overdue. And you should call your mom. She's been really worried about you."

"I did. A month ago."

"Good. You still have my number, right? You didn't chuck your phone in a lake when you went to join the Empire or the seven samurai or the monastery of lame grossness or whatever?"

"I have it."

She chews her lip. "I still haven't forgiven you. But I've found, through eighteen years of vigorous experimentation, that I'm much more willing to forgive people if they interact with me on this physical plane. Talk to me. Text me. With cute cat pictures or winky faces— "

"I don't do winky faces."

"Aha, but you do cat pictures!"

"No."

"Yes," she argues.

"No."

"Ugh, look at us. Why can't we just talk like normal people? About, like, concerts and cake and our deep personal beliefs and the color orange and stuff?"

I stare at her blankly. She nudges me.

"Orange. C'mon, try it. A conversation about orange."

"It's…orange."

"Ding, ding, ding. Give the man a cigar. Orange is orange. Wow. This has been an excellent conversation. Your powers of observation are downright fearsome. Maybe we could work our way up to, like, purple next time. Except then you might disappear for years again—"

"It wasn't *years*."

"—and I would be lost and heartbroken, and then you would come back having spent fifty years thinking about purple, thinking, *oh yes, now is my chance to impress Isis with my deep and thorough knowledge of the color purple*, and you'd find me in a nursing home in a coma dreaming about hot men all vegetable-like, and you'd have to hurry to tell me about purple because one of my potential spawn might pull the plug on me. Maybe you'll pull the plug on me. Note to self: ugh, don't get old."

"Too late." I smirk.

She puffs out her cheeks and stands. "Anyway, I like you, but you're ruining my life. Bye."

chapter seven

3 YEARS, 47 WEEKS, 2 DAYS

EVERYTHING HAPPENS ALL THE TIME forever, and this would be a terrifying concept if I wasn't so enlightened and in tune with the natural forces of the universe, which include but aren't limited to: A) taco salad, B) taco salad, and C) my own glorious ass (glorioass). Which increases in size directly proportionate to how much taco salad is in the area. Science has come so far.

Regardless of how big my ass is, it won't be big enough to crush Nameless's huge fat head. Also, I would not touch him with any body part that is not spiked and/or doused in black mamba venom. Plus, he has the tape I've wanted to see for what feels like forever. I hate him, but he's right—I want to see what happened that night more than anything. I want to understand the source of Sophia's pain, of Jack's regret, of Wren's dismay. To do that, though, I have to stomach him. And I don't know if I can do that.

Now that Nameless is going to my school and has that tape, I have to devise ways in which to rid myself of him sans homicide. Maybe, like, a fortuitous black hole.

But first, I have to throw a tantrum. It's an area in which

I have great experience.

"Do I even wanna know what you're doing?" Yvette looks down as I attach myself to her leg the second she walks in the room. I whimper attractively.

"I'm taking the time to revisit your 'drop out of college in the first year' plan."

"Oh, stop." Yvette throws her laptop bag on her bed. She drags her feet to her desk. "While you're down there, untie my shoes for me."

"Like I was saying"—I untie with gusto—"I recently discovered someone that I really don't like goes here."

"That dude you were talking with the other night? Model McFartington?"

"Have I called him that? That sounds like something I would say."

"You say it a lot. In your sleep."

"Yvette!" I wail. "It's not Model McFartington. There is another person on my shit list. Model McFartington is on the shit list also, but he is not number one, and also he's got a bunch of red squiggly lines through his name, because sometimes I take him off the list and sometimes I add him back on."

Yvette raises one studded eyebrow.

"It's complicated," I summarize. "Let's drop out."

"No," she says simply.

"WhhHHHYY?" I inquire delicately.

"We gotta experience the whole nine yards of college agony before we drop out. We have to black out, drink a bunch, and swear off men forever and fail a bunch of classes and try cocaine. That's at least seven months' worth of work right there."

"Says who?"

"Says every poignant coming-of-age movie ever."

"Ugh!" I let go of her foot and roll under my bed. I see a moldy dick carved into the wood mattress slats and immediately roll back out. "Ugh."

"Look, I'm sorry about this dude, okay? Or…two dudes, or whatever you have going on. Point them out to me and I'll knock 'em out. But right now, I gotta finish this chem essay or I'm screwed. Metaphorically. I haven't actually gotten screwed in a while."

These are her famous last words, because when I go to get dinner and come back full of burrito and knock for her to let me in, there is groaning emanating from the door and I hear Yvette demand for something "harder." I trip over a dust particle with alarming grace as I make my way to calmer waters. Jack opens his door with sleep-mussed hair and no shirt, and it's then I realize these waters are about as calm as people who win free cars on *Oprah*.

"My roommate's being gross, so I live here now," I say as I push past him.

"You can't," he points out.

"They said that to Columbus, too, and look what happened there." I flop onto his bed. I know it's his because it's perfectly made, the covers just a little wrinkly from sleep. His roommate's bed is a mercifully empty nest of messy blankets. Jack pulls a shirt on and yawns, sitting beside me.

"You've got sleep boogers." I point at his eyes. He rubs them vigorously.

"You can stay here if you want," he says, still rubbing one eye. It is a drastically human, vulnerable motion I've never seen him do before. "But I'm leaving in fifteen minutes."

"You look like a little kid." I laugh. "With eye problems."

"Shut up," he growls, and rubs harder. His cheeks are sleep-flushed, and his hair sticks up every which way.

"Still got a duck's butt for a hairstyle, huh?"

"Still got the most infantile insults for a defense mechanism, huh?"

"At least it is not an animal's backside."

"The sounds are similar."

I flip him off with both hands, and he retorts by leaning against the wall and closing his eyes. The dusk-rose sky looms outside the window, sunset slanting in and painting the white walls peach-striped.

"What do you want to know first?" Jack asks finally.

A thousand questions erupt, but I pick the least confrontational one. "Where are you going in fifteen minutes?"

"A friend invited my roommate to a barbecue. He's dragging me along."

"Who's your roommate?"

"Charlie. An idiot, but a passionate idiot. I've heard that counts for something."

"Uh, you are looking at living proof of that right here." I point at my chest. Jack smirks and cracks his eyes open to look at me, the ice blue of them melted to faint purple by the red sun.

"You're not an idiot, Isis."

"I know. Duh."

"You're a moron," he corrects, and closes his eyes again, falling to lie on his side. I debate the merits of pulling his fingers off one by one and decide they are much too pretty to be removed. For now.

I hug my knees and try to remember how to breathe right, like normal people do. People who aren't chased by ghosts. Or in this case, chased by sadistic ex-boyfriends. And just as I start to spiral down into the darkness, where the monster lives and breathes and gnaws, Jack reaches up and pulls me down, and I squeak, and we're lying on his soft bed, him behind me. His heat and weight almost press against my spine, the careful space still there, the smell of mint and honey surrounding me like a blanket. It's the smell I longed for in the darkest nights alone, thinking about our war, and his hands, and what it would be like to kiss him, hard and for real and maybe more, because maybe, just maybe, he's the one person in the world who might kiss my stretch marks instead of calling them ugly—

"Stop," he mumbles just behind me.

"Stop what?"

"Stop looking so sad all the time."

I scrunch my face up, and I'm suddenly hyperaware of his breath on my neck. He moves closer, and my stomach starts to burn, and Will's voice is so clear and cold in my head.

But you'll never feel all right here, will you? Not with me around.

My heart suddenly decides it's an astronaut and attempts to do forty backflips in what feels like zero gravity. I immediately bolt off the bed. Jack sits up.

"Is something wrong?"

"I just—" I clench my shaking hands to still them. I don't want him to see. I don't want him to think he's making me feel like this.

"Isis." Jack gets up and moves toward me, but I hold out two hands.

"Stop. Just—just stay there."

He does, but his brows knit deeply. "I will. Did I do something wrong?"

"No!" I suck in a breath to try to stop the crushing feeling on my chest. "It's me. It's always me. Or, it's not all me. It's him."

It goes unsaid between us. Him. Will. Jack knows—I can see it in his ice eyes. Whenever Will comes up, those eyes turn to daggers, the anger in them not for me, but for him.

We stay quiet, and I rub my arms to work feeling back into

them. The panic was so strong, so fast, I was taken by surprise. It's been a while since it was that bad. Disappointment rages through me—I thought I was better than this. I thought I'd gotten better. Jack and I slept in the same bed at a hotel, for shit's sake! I should be better now!

The truth seeps into me slowly, like a black cloud. How can one night make me magically better? It can't. That's the answer—it can't and I'm still defunct, damaged, incapable of tolerating something as simple as lying next to someone. Was it the distance between Jack and me for half a year? Did my body forget who he is, how important he once was? Of course it did; I wrote him off for good. I did my best to black him out of my mind as a romantic option after Sophia's death. And now it's showing.

"Is there anything I can do to help?" Jack asks finally, carefully.

I make a huge exhale. "Let's just talk. About something else. W-Why are you going here for school?"

"Work."

The panic mutes itself, replaced with molasses and lead and spikes.

"Obviously. Frat boys just don't cut it; college girls need a suave and experienced undertaker of the vajayjay to relieve stress, because everyone in the world is obsessed with sex, apparently—"

"I'm not an escort," he says patiently. "I quit the Rose Club for good. I work for someone else now. Doing other things."

"Wow. That's so specific. I feel like I've gleaned a lot of valuable and specific information from this conversation."

"Remember the guys who were in that forest? The guy in the tweed suit? The ones who chased you in the woods where Tallie's buried?"

"Yeah, but—"

The door opens just then. Jack and I sit up hastily. In walks Tinyballs Mcsuitypants, he of the running-after-me-in-a-dark-Ohio-forest-because-his-boss-told-him-to. His black hair's in spikes, skin amber. He freezes, dark eyes catching on me.

"You!" he squawks, and points.

"*You!*" I shout. "How are you still alive? I FIFA'd your balls!"

"What the hell is she doing here?" he snarls at Jack.

Jack sighs. "Isis Blake, meet Charlie Moriyama."

"Already have," Charlie and I say at the same time. I glare. He narrows his eyes even farther.

"Look, we don't have time for this shit." Charlie looks to Jack. "We were supposed to be there five minutes ago. Let's not blow this, okay?"

Jack sighs and hefts himself off the bed, looking at me. "I'll be back later. We'll talk more then."

"Sure, yeah, just work with the bad guys. See if I care."

"Isis—"

"We're *going*," Charlie shouts, grabbing a towel off the end of his bed and slamming the door behind him. Jack frowns and follows reluctantly.

And I do the same. From at least five meters and two cars away. Charlie drives a white Nissan with a broken taillight. My mind runs circles around itself as they lead me down the highway and away from school. Why has Jack shacked up with Tweed-Jerk and Small Balls? Tweed talked about wanting to hire him, but I still don't know for what. I guess he succeeded. Let's be real, though—Jack let him succeed. Everything that happens to Jack is exactly because Jack lets it happen. Except me. But that's a different story, full of illegality and joy.

Jack said he's working, which means what? He's at school, but on a job for Tweed? What job, stealing good grades for the poor-grade people? What could Tweed's company possibly do for money, other than stand there and look dumb? It doesn't make any sense, and it makes less sense when Charlie pulls into a huge white-stone plaza surrounded by a posh apartment building. A security booth lets cars in and out of the massive parking garage. Charlie's Nissan disappears, and I pull up next. The security guard is a tan guy with a neat beard.

"Hey there, who are you here to see?" he asks.

"Um..." My brain scrabbles for a reason, and like all good brains, makes me blurt the first thing that comes to mind instead. "Jesus....? Christ."

He squints, and just when I'm convinced he'll launch a row of spikes under my car and into my tires, he smiles.

"Ah, yeah, you must be here for the North Presbyterian dinner."

"Yeah! That's right. Praise the Lord!"

He nods. "Go on in. Visitor parking is on the left."

Either the rest of the world is exceedingly dumb today, or I've gotten smarter. Thanks, college. Wait, who am I kidding? College hasn't taught me anything yet except how to have panic attacks and not pay attention to professors at all. Correction: thanks, *National Geographic*.

I park and walk slowly behind Jack and Charlie, who are waiting outside a fenced door that leads to the elevators. After minutes of silent agony in which I almost twist my ankle trying to hide behind a pillar when Charlie looks behind him, a redhead in a black bikini opens the door for them. She bats her eyelashes at Jack, and I pretend I did not see it, the same way I pretended not to see the end of *Sixth Sense*. Then again, she has titties up to her eyes and she has a wonderful smile, and if Jack's taste in women has changed then he should by all means bed her, because she looks fairly fun and also cute, and who am I to get in the way of true love? Nobody. Nobody should get in the way of true love. Not even well-meaning

Italian arch-nemesis families.

The three turn a corner and take the stairs, and as gracefully as an undercover ballet dancer, I make a mad dash to the door and manage to jam my pinkie finger in it just before it closes and locks me out.

"Banana shit-cake!" I whisper loudly, then nurse the tip of my finger in my mouth as I take the stairs. "What does a lady have to do to get a warm reception around here?"

"Stop her stalking habit, perhaps?"

I whirl around to see Jack leaning against the railing behind me. I look downstairs to my escape door, back to his calm yet irritated face, and then I peek over the railing.

"How many stories does it take before you break your knees? Medically? Asking for a friend."

"Don't you dare jump."

Jump. Sophia jumped. I flinch, but Jack is a tower of ice, murky and rigid and unreadable. I draw myself up to my full intimidating five feet five inches of height.

"I am out," I say with great dignity, "for a stroll. I wasn't stalking you."

"You were following Charlie and me. I saw your car."

"Oh. In that case, yes, I was stalking you."

"You should leave," he says without missing a beat. "Nameless might be here."

I grit my teeth but manage words. "So? I don't care about him. I want to know what you're doing in Tweed's company, and why. Is it dangerous? You said you wouldn't join them, you said—"

"I said a lot of things"—Jack sighs and rubs his eyes—"before Sophia died that I ended up regretting."

My stomach churns. Was saying he liked me one of them? I shake my head—selfish. *Stop being so fucking selfish and focus.*

"Since when is going to a barbecue 'work'?" I hiss.

"Since the one throwing the party is our target."

"Uh, hello? Earth to Zabadoobian Jack? This is reality, not *Call of Duty*. There are no 'targets.'"

"In my line of work, there are," he counters.

"And what, pray tell, is your line of work?"

Jack's frigid eyes harden, becoming clear and sharp as he answers. "I'm a freelance bodyguard who just so happened to be slotted into gathering intelligence. Now get back to campus and leave this to me."

I bluster about for ten seconds, squirreling my hands together. I say "sp" a lot but never quite manage to get the "y" out. Jack, ever sensitive to my plight, turns and leaves. I follow.

"S-Spy?" I choke. "What blind idiot died and made you a spy?"

"I'm not a spy. I'm a bodyguard who's been posted here."

"You're like…you're…what's the word for the opposite of 'subtle'?"

"Isis Blake," Jack offers.

"*Jack Hunter!*" I correct. "Jack Hunter isn't subtle."

"I'm very subtle when a girl shouting 'spy' isn't following me," he argues.

"You're a mobile, permafrost glacier with killer eyebrows and rapiers for eyes. People don't forget Jack Hunter so easily."

"I wish they would," Jack murmurs. It sounds so hollow and weak, so unlike him. I slap him on the back.

"Nonsense! You can never be forgotten. If you were, the last major glacier on planet Earth would fade from existence, and global warming would become a very scary reality. Scarier than it already is. And closer. And hotter. In the temperature sense, not the *let's sex it up* sense."

Jack stops walking and stares at me. I stare back. There's a profound quiet. Bikini Girl chooses that moment to run into the stairwell and give Jack a very drunk kiss on the cheek, accompanied by an extremely subtle drop of a pink condom wrapper as she runs back out. I pick it up and hand it to him.

"Wrap your willy before you get silly," I remind. Jack facepalms spectacularly, and I count it as a victory, because at least he is not sad-looking anymore. He is something-else-looking and it's not much, but it's better than sad. He comes up with the barest smile on his lips, but he quashes it quickly.

"Look, you can stay. But when Nameless gets here, you should leave."

"Yes, thank you for giving me permission to continue what I've been doing for the last three years."

Jack stops, hand against the stairwell door. "I apologize."

"Don't. It makes you seem nice."

"He's wanted by some very powerful people for helping some bad people do bad things."

"Good. Before you arrest him with your spy-goggles or whatever, let me punch him."

"Isis—"

"Just one punch. In the eyeball. With a spoon."

Jack considers it, then smirks. "Fine. On one condition."

"Name it, dork."

"I get the other eye."

I mull it over and nod. "I'm a generous god."

I'm more grateful than he knows. Or maybe he does know, because his eyes are soft and warm with the knife of his quiet blazing anger. I'd seen it pointed at me enough times to know that this time, it's not *me* it's pointed at.

It's Nameless.

I'm not the only one who knows. Jack might not know details, but he knows enough. He guessed enough. And he didn't pry. His eyes show no pity or guilt. They are clear and they see me, and my secret isn't a secret anymore. The weight is shared and divided, and I try to say thank you, but all that comes out is a wry smile.

I am half as dark as I used to be.

Jack turns and opens the door. We walk out of the stairwell, and my jaw pops like my old Beetle's shitty trunk. The apartment building is all white stone and marble, massive patio-style walkways intertwining between mounds of purple hydrangeas and autumn roses. People mill about, walking their dogs or sitting in fancy patio chairs near the covered glass fire pit, wood crackling and embers dancing. A hot tub and an enormous lit pool are surrounded by umbrella-covered tables and grills, drunk college students flinging burgers and nasty jokes like they're going out of style. Charlie is talking to the black-bikini girl, looking grumpy and munching on chips. People shove each other in the pool and shriek with laughter in the hot tub. Jack touches my forearm lightly and leans in to whisper.

"I'm going to socialize. I need information. Stay where I can see you."

"I don't need you to babysit me," I say. "Do your job. I'll just be over here, you know, having fun. You should try it sometime."

I grab a hot dog and sit on a lawn chair, near the hot tub. A blond guy with svelte abs and a friendly smile glances at me.

"Hey."

"Hi." I spew meat delicately onto the patio tile.

"No swimsuit?" he asks.

"Left mine back home. On Mars."

"Is that why you stand out like a sore thumb? Because you're an alien?"

"Or, or—and this is a crazy theory—I'm just hotter than everyone else here," I offer.

The guy laughs. "It's true. Your hair's awesome."

"So is yours. In that beachy, I'm-definitely-from-California-and-spend-five-days-a-week-in-the-gym kind of way."

He laughs again, louder, and gets out of the hot tub to sit by me, dripping wet.

"Three days, thank you very much. I'm not that much of a swole broski."

"Coulda fooled me." I nod at his stomach. He pats it like Santa after eating too many cookies.

"It's my one pride and joy. I've got no brains and no future, but I've got these babies."

"That's all you need," I say. "Take a picture and send it to Kim Kardashian. Marry her."

"I'd have to fight Kanye," he laments.

"Eh." I wave my hand. "Just tell him his sunglasses suck. He'll keel over and die."

The guy laughs. "I'm Kyle Morris. Nice to meet you."

"Isis," I say automatically. "Destroyer of hearts and dreams. And any cakes in a two-mile vicinity."

"Ravenclaw." He offers his hand to shake. I grab it with my greasy one.

"Hufflepuff," I say. He quirks a brow.

"Really? You don't seem all that nice."

"Oh." I point what's left of my hot dog bun at him. "Just wait until you see my friends. I practically run a charity show."

"The guy you came in with?" He nods to Jack, who's currently being exceedingly merciful and letting black-bikini girl cling to his arm and jabber at him, and she has a pierced belly button and probably a pierced vagina and her name is Hemorrhoid, by the way. The girls in the hot tub Kyle came from are slowly starting to notice just how good-looking Jack is, and they get out in a group, strutting past Jack and diving into the nearby pool with aching sexiness. The boys follow like hungry hounds.

"Yeah, the goober being goobed on," I say. "He's my friend."

"Just a friend?"

"Is that like, some subtle cue-slash-question I'm supposed to confirm so you know whether or not you've got a chance to sleep with me? Because if so, it's very not-subtle and lacking finesse, really, so next time maybe try a neon sign taped to your forehead that says LOSER LOOKING TO GET LAID. With the numeral two replacing 'to,' obviously, to save time, because that seems to be all guys really care about—getting laid as fast as possible."

Kyle takes it in stride, looking mock-wounded. "Hey, at least I'm being honest."

I roll my eyes and wander over to the pool, trying my darnedest and failing my darnedest to not glance at the way black-bikini girl is grinding her hip into Jack's as she leans on him. Charlie's off in the deep end of the pool with a bunch of girls, even his grin somehow grumpy as they splash him. Last time I checked, spying involved a lot more grappling guns and poison dart pens and a lot less giggling. I stand at the edge of the pool and watch the moon reflecting on the water in a wiggly silver medallion.

Kyle stands beside me. "So, what's your major?"

"I'm a freshman. Undecided. Nuclear thermophysics. Culinary arts. Depends on how I feel when I wake up that day." I hold two hands out and balance them like scales. "Destroy the world, or make a cake to celebrate destroying the world. The choice is so gosh darn difficult."

Kyle laughs. "God, you're cool."

"It's been said," I agree. "Screamed, really. By my enemies. Just before I decapitate them."

Suddenly there's a sharp pressure on my ass, a squeeze. I jump, my squeal entirely ugly and entirely necessary as I look to Kyle, horrified. My first grope ever. He smirks and shrugs. I ball my fist, but I never get the chance to punch him. Kyle goes flying, splashing into the pool with an embarrassing flailing motion. Jack stands at the place Kyle used to be, his expression cool.

"Oops," he drones. Hemorrhoid laughs, and the other girls start laughing, and so when Kyle comes up sputtering he has no choice but to laugh nervously with the rest of them.

"Ha-ha, nice one, bro!"

Jack quirks a disdainful brow at him. Charlie comes wading over and gets out, pulling Jack aside. Charlie's words are rapid and low and hissy, and Jack's are monotone.

Hemorrhoid stands with me, sighing. "He's so dreamy, isn't he?"

"Yeah," I agree. "If we are in opposite world, and dreams are actually nightmares."

She ignores me and latches back onto Jack the second he separates from Charlie, steering him toward the pool. Jack goes along with it, grimace obvious. Why is he doing it if he doesn't like it?

"You," a voice growls in my ear. I turn to see Charlie, anger etching his mouth.

"Me," I say. "Now that the introductions are over, we can finally move on to tea."

"You're distracting him," Charlie says. "You're a goddamn distraction he doesn't need right now."

"Excuse me?"

"You heard me," Charlie insists. "You see that redhead in the bikini? That's an important source of info we need on our side. Jack's gonna wind her around his pinkie, and he would've already, but you're here, and for some fucking reason he likes your dumb ass and is putting it off."

"You're mistaken. We hate each other. Platonically."

"You're cock-blocking him," Charlie snarls. "Now get the fuck out of here, before I throw you out myself."

"My, are you always this polite with the ladies, or am I the exception? Or perhaps it's the dudes you reserve your politeness for? Understandable. Dude-asses are polite-worthy as hell."

"Get. Out."

Over his tanned shoulder, I see Hemorrhoid lean in and graze Jack's cheek with her lips. Jack doesn't recoil, taking it like a frozen statue, inclining his head only slightly in response. I get the message. I always get the message, because I'm Isis Blake and I'm last choice for teams in gym, always, and whatever we had has been swallowed up by the void of Sophia, by the pain, by the ice-cold shield against it all that he calls "work." The little ball-light of hope I held in the darkness flickers, weakening irrevocably.

"I was already leaving," I say. Charlie watches me the whole way to the garage. My fury is the dull, aching kind, lingering even as I park and trudge up the stairs into my dorm. Yvette is, mercifully, not there. Her text from four hours ago reads: **staying at a friend's, don't worry**. Another booty call, maybe. I don't care. It's her life, and as long as she's safe and happy, I'm fine with it. I'm curious, but the throbbing hurt from the night beats louder against my skull as I lie in bed and stare at the ceiling, hot tears clouding my eyes.

I can't sleep. Not until I say something. I grab my phone and text.

Do you know how many times you've made me fucking cry?

His answer comes later, much later. It wakes me in two hours. I imagine him in her bed, sitting over the side of it, naked, and with her naked and sleeping opposite him. I imagine his tousled hair, his lean muscles, his blue eyes made silver by the moonlight.

Too many, his text says. Thirty minutes pass, and then: **Find someone who doesn't make you cry. Find someone better.**

Do you know how many times you've made me fucking cry?

I stare at the text, the sickly electronic light boring into my eyes like spears. Spears of guilt. Spears of regret. I shouldn't be here, and what's left of my heart knows that the second I read the words. I should be there, with her. I should be a normal college student, not playing at one while trying to catch a criminal.

Not sleeping with the criminal's ex-girlfriend so she'll give me dirt on him.

It had been boring and routine, the steps ingrained in me from my time at the Rose Club. I'd added every trick I could to satisfy her—satiate her so fully she'd be crawling on her knees for more in the morning, and next week, and the week after that. Her mouth is the only useful part of her—spilling the secrets of her ex-boyfriend Kyle, and consequently, his partner, Will.

It was the first time I'd slept with someone since spending the night with Isis at the hotel. Isis's smell surrounded me, vanilla and cinnamon, even when I hadn't touched her for very long. The hurt in her brown eyes haunted me as I finished, the silent name on my lips spilling from a place of heart-torn, guilt-laced pleasure, and if I shut my eyes I could pretend, if only for the briefest second, that it was Isis beneath me.

But the illusion faded quickly.

Use everything you can to your advantage, Gregory's voice resonates from training. *And that means your damn pretty face. Women will love it. Use them.*

The evidence we need is one step closer.

Redemption is one step closer. Redemption for Sophia. Redemption for Isis. Catching Will Cavanaugh, putting him away so that she never has to see him again, is the one good thing I can do for her. It got me through Gregory's training at the ranch. It got me this far. It's the one good thing I can do, period. The one thing that could put a dent in redeeming the hurt I've inflicted.

I pull on my shirt and button my jeans, leaving the posh apartment quietly so as not to wake her roommates. I pause at the door, looking back into the shadowed apartment that holds the evidence of my sordid manipulations.

I thought I was done with it, with this, with sleeping with people to get what I want—money for Sophia's surgery, information. But I got it backward—it was never truly done with me.

"Redemption," I murmur, and leave. The guilt sears me, gnawing at my insides. I need relief. I need distraction. I need something other than Isis's text, my phone burning up in my pocket with her sadness and disappointment.

What does she want from me?

I can't give her anything. I can't give anyone anything anymore. My heart is empty and broken and useless.

The neon lights of the college district flash with Technicolor temptation—pawnshops, strip clubs, liquor stores open late. I find what I'm looking for in a seedy club packed to the brim with sweat stench and greasy bodies. I watch the crowd carefully from the bar, then pounce on the one man who slips a roofie into a brunette's drink.

He is bleeding—his nose broken and his arm dislocated—when I am done with him. It takes forty seconds, and he punches back with equal fervor and splits my brow with his knuckles, hot blood oozing into my eyes. For those forty seconds it's all static—I am a blank canvas, moving like Gregory taught me, punching and dodging like he taught me. Nothing is in my mind but moves and countermoves, observations and rapid calculations of how fast my opponent's fist is moving, where it will land, how to sidestep and trip him so he'll eat a precise stone step of the club. I am empty. Isis is gone. Sophia is gone. There's only the taste of blood and anger and sweat, and the soundless roar of the beast in my head. But the roar is different now. It is sharp and honed and precise. It is softer, yet more chilling.

When it asks to be fed, feed it promptly, and in small portions. It will never rebel, and you'll never hurt anyone you don't want to, as long as it's fed. Gregory's words echo. *As long as it's fed, you are the master.*

The bouncers break us up, and as they lead me out I nod at the brunette, who gathered around to watch the fight with the rest of the club.

"Your drink was spiked. I suggest you take a cab home."

She looks shocked, and her friends sniff at the drink in her hand. Her horrified face is the last thing I see before they dump me onto the road. The beast gives me strength enough to stagger back to campus and collapse in bed, the blind rage fading rapidly, cooling like lava hitting ocean water.

I will never hurt anyone who doesn't deserve it ever again.

chapter eight

3 YEARS, 48 WEEKS, 4 DAYS

KAYLA UNDERSTANDS EVERYTHING because she understands nothing. She's like a dry sponge that I throw buckets of water on. And sometimes piss. With copious sides of vinegar.

It's a beautiful sight to see after a week of sporadic texts—her on Skype and me on Skype, both of us painting our toenails and talking at the same time.

"Isis, you're killing me," Kayla groans.

"Not literally, one would hope. Unless you want to be a zombie. I can dig being the only girl in the world to have a zombfriend."

"I am not actually dead," she declares. "What I am is disappointed. I can't believe you and Jack aren't just…like…"

I raise a brow, daring her to go on. She sniffs indignantly and then nearly tips over the green polish bottle with her sudden fist made of rage.

"He left, and you left, and now you're together in the same place, and I told you so, and why aren't you taking this very obviously predestined opportunity to hook up like crazy rabbits?"

"Because, sweet Kayla, there is more to life than being a

crazy rabbit. Bizarre, I know."

"Look, I just mean..." She grits her teeth and carefully adds a stripe of green to her big toe. "I just mean, even if he is doing some weird Jack-like stuff, that's never stopped you before! You were hitting on him constantly—"

"Actually hitting on him. With my fist," I correct.

"—when he was in the Rose Club, but now suddenly he's slept with a girl for info and you're all angry at him?"

"I—I—" I splutter concisely. "That was before!"

"Before what?"

"Before I—"

Kayla looks expectant.

I wail. "You know what I'm going to say!"

"Say it anyway," she demands.

"No!"

"Yes!" she shouts.

"You present a compelling argument."

"Isis, don't get smart with me!"

"Fine! I like him. I like him, okay?"

"So you like him." She leans back. "You want to make him lunch and hug him platonically once a year."

"No, because then we would be in seventeenth-century England."

"That's what *like* is," Kayla continues. "Like is just so-so. It doesn't really mean anything. Like...like me and you! I don't like you. I *love* you."

"Um."

"In the way where you keep your pants on, duh. I love you and you love me and you also love Jack. In a different way."

"Kayla—" I say warningly.

"In the hot way."

"No."

"In the *hug me until I run out of breath* way."

"Wrong."

"In the *invade me with your penis* way."

I screech like a horrified fruit bat and slam the lid of my laptop closed. I can hear my own flustered, angry panting. I fling the lid open again and argue at the screen.

"There are no invading genitalia thoughts going on here."

"Really?" Kayla asks airily, sanding her nails. "Because I can guarantee you Jack's thought about it. Repeatedly. While jerking it."

"Kayla! When did you get so—so—"

"Awesome? All thanks to your influence."

I'm silent and stare-y.

"And Wren's," she relents. "He's very informative and methodical. One time I got to hear a history lesson of the condom while I was putting it on him."

"Ugh," I gag. "I don't know what's more miraculous—the fact that he only did that once, or that Wren of all people in the conceivable universe has turned you into a sexpert."

"All I'm saying is," Kayla huffs, "if you want Jack to date you—"

"I don't!" I harp. "I don't, I don't, I don't, *I don't*. I'm not dating anyone ever again."

"If you want Jack to sleep with you—" she corrects.

"*I don't.* Why do people even say 'sleeping with'? There is no sleeping involved! Sleeping is peaceful and nice and sex is like…the opposite of that."

"You can't say that," Kayla fires back. "You've never had it."

"I've had it once," I defend, suddenly exhausted.

"That wasn't sex and you and I both know it."

"Look, it's great that you're all gung ho about sex and me and Jack all at the same time." I sigh. "But you're forgetting the part in which I'm never touching a dude again. And he's never touching me. Besides, Jack wouldn't even like touching me."

"He would."

"I'm fat."

"You are surprisingly not-fat."

"I'm not as pretty as like…any other girl he could get. You've seen his face. He got you. He could get freakin' Scarlett Johansson if he really wanted to."

"And I'm sure Ohio State is just teeming with Scarlett look-alikes."

"In black bikinis."

Kayla sighs. "It's hard, I get it. After everything that's happened… I don't know what it's like, but it's gotta be hard. And I'm sorry. But he really likes you, Isis. And you really like him. And you guys are like, really interesting together and you light each other up in a weird, symbiotic way. And life is short. Sophia taught us that. And I think you deserve a shot at each other before you write each other off completely out of misguided martyrdom."

"Wow. 'Martyrdom.' You might be the only one in the universe paying actual attention during college."

"Shut up." She flushes and leans in to close her computer. "And don't call me back until you've at least kissed him."

I slam my face on the keyboard of my laptop and roll it around, groaning. Yvette chooses that exact moment to burst through the door and collapse on her bed, likewise groaning.

"My life is over," she says.

I get up and collapse next to her on the bed. "Finally. Time to die."

There's a long silence of us just breathing into pillows, experimenting with suffocating ourselves. Yvette breaks first, coming up for air, gasping.

"I've been sleeping with somebody," she confesses.

"I know." I look up. "I heard."

Yvette goes red down to her skull earrings. "Sorry. I mean,

shit, I'm not sorry. It was damn good."

"Mind if I ask who?"

"Yes, actually. Very yes."

I welcome the distraction. "It's Steven. From socio."

"Wow." Yvette claps. "Ten points to you for saying the stupidest shit I've ever heard."

"Brett with the weird T-shirts."

"Yes, because I *want* to turn my vagina into a gonorrhea culture lab."

"Give me a hint. Like, at least seven hundred whole hints. In essay form, with citations and footnotes."

Yvette screws her face up like she's in genuine pain, and it's then I catch a whiff of something unmistakable. Something musky and sweet and floral. Roses.

"Dia—"

"I'm gay," Yvette whisper-interrupts, as though terrified someone will hear in the security of our own room. We stare at each other in stunned silence, and then I smile and punch her shoulder.

"Diana, right? You lucky piece of shit!"

Yvette's eyes widen, as if she was expecting something worse. Shouting, anger maybe. Her eyes well up with gratitude, and in typical Yvette fashion she shoves her face into the bed so I won't see it.

I stand. "C'mon, let's go get ice cream to celebrate."

She doesn't move. I tug on her boot. She groans.

"Get *up*," I insist.

"I can't get up!" Yvette's voice is muffled by her pillows. "I'm gay!"

"You're paying if you don't get up in the next five seconds, Gay."

Yvette peeks out of the pillow, looking like a scared child. "I haven't told my parents."

"You don't gotta," I offer. "Not right away. We've still got six months before we drop out. When they ask why you flushed their twenty thousand dollars down the toilet, tell them it's because you're gay. Trust me. They'll be more mad about the money than your girlfriend."

Yvette smirks, wiping her nose.

"Or. Or you could just drop the bomb now. Over the phone. Drop all the bombs. Blow up your own house."

Yvette laughs and punches me weakly on the knee. And then we share a sundae, and for a while I'm not the only one with problems. Yvette's bravery reminds me of that. I'm not the only one who thinks love and sex are all sorts of weird and hard and scary.

If Yvette could confess to me she's gay, if she could overcome that turmoil and life-changing revelation all on her own, then I can overcome what happened to me.

I can't be as strong as her, but I can try.

I owe it to myself, and everybody who loves me, to at least fucking try.

I visit Mom over the weekend. The drive is long, but the love is plenty—she comes out with a smile and wide arms that hug me close, and she's cooked dinner for once. Pasta. The house is clean. The windows are open and the air inside every room is fresh instead of musty. Mom's skin looks healthy; her eyes are bright. She can't stop talking about work and a new group of lady friends she met at yoga, and I just sit in my chair and eat quietly and absorb it all—all her happiness, all her change.

"Are you okay, sweetie? I'm sorry I've been blabbering, it's just—"

"No, I'm fine. Don't be sorry. I was just really hungry."

"Are you eating well at school?"

"Three square meals a day. Comprising doughnuts and regret."

She laughs, and I smirk into a noodle.

"It's been awfully quiet without you around," Mom says. "So I've been trying to get out more. Do more things, meet more people."

I flinch. "I'm sorry. I'm sorry I'm not here more, and I'm sorry I didn't come last weekend, I was—"

"It's all right. I don't want to hear excuses. But it was a promise, Isis. You *promised* me you'd come every other weekend. I know you're busy, and it's college, but I'm your mother. And I want to see you. I need to see you."

"I'm sorry!" I clutch my fork. "I'm so sorry—"

Mom gets up, sweeping over to pet my head and hush me in soft whispers.

"No, honey. I'm sorry. I'm sorry for needing you so much. You should be free. I have to let you fly away from me sometime. Other kids your age, other parents my age have all learned how to leave and let go but…but it's harder for me. And that makes it hard on you."

I swallow. Mom looks into my eyes.

"Sometimes I think bad things—dark things. And I go to Dr. Torrand and try not to think them so much. But they keep me up at night. And I don't sleep. And I start resenting everyone—your father, Leo, even you—and it's horrible. I'm horrible."

I hug her back, tight and unending.

"We're not horrible," I whisper. "We're just people."

I watch Charlie do his homework, hair greasy and his face eternally frowning. He's not the most intelligent bodyguard, and he doesn't think before he speaks. Where my style is to write lightly with a ballpoint pen, his is to press hard with a soaked paintbrush. We both get the job done, just in different ways. It's why Gregory assigned us to each other, probably—two radically differing methods double the chances of success. In theory.

In reality, we get along as well as two wet cats in a stewpot.

"What're you staring at?" Charlie grunts, never taking his eyes off his paper.

"I wanted to thank you," I say finally.

"Fuckin' doubt that."

"For sending Isis away at the barbecue. I was reluctant to do it myself."

"You don't say." Charlie rolls his eyes. "You and her got history or somethin'?"

"Something like that."

"Well, keep it out of this assignment. I don't need your fuckbuddies screwing this up for me. A job like this means a damn promotion."

I glance over at his desk. He doesn't keep a lot of personal items, but he brought a framed picture of his grandmother, an old Japanese woman with a wrinkled, smiling face, hugging Charlie in front of a tiny noodle shop in what looks like foggy San Francisco. He sends the money he makes back to her—I did some digging into his file and his bank accounts. Orphaned at the age of three due to a racial hate crime, he was taken in by his grandmother, and she raised him. Now that she's nearly eighty and unable to work the store, Charlie is the one who keeps it running with the money he makes. He used to be in a Chinatown gang until Gregory scouted him.

He's weaker than me, even if he doesn't act like it.

The people he loves are still alive, after all. And that is a weakness in and of itself. It's why I will always be a better bodyguard than him. Or I thought I would be. Until Isis stepped back into the picture.

"She wasn't a fuckbuddy," I clarify, tempering the soft fire of anger that flares in my lungs. He didn't mean it personally—his name-calling is a defense mechanism to keep from getting to know people and consequently, caring about them. It's similar to Isis's rampant jokes.

"Whatever she was to you, she was sure as hell jealous of Brittany that night. Kept giving her the stink-eye. Don't let her get in the way of pumping Brittany for info, you got me?"

Jealous? *Isis?* That can't be right. She's smart enough to know when she's chasing after a worthless cause. She would never pursue me. Not after what I've done to her.

Do you know how many times you've made me fucking cry?

I grab my coat and walk out.

The campus is quiet, night stars glimmering like discarded diamonds. My confused feet take me around the library, through the parking lot, and to a haughty granite fountain in the shape of a centaur shooting an arrow into the sky. I read the plaque—dedicated to someone's dead something. I sit on the edge. I'm not the only one there, I notice.

I could walk away. I could leave her, on this starry night, and walk away. I could choose not to form this memory, not to engage. But I long for it. I miss the fights, the blows, the wit. I miss her, even when my every perfect, lifeless, and calculated plan demands that I never speak to her again, in the interest of not hurting her further. But I am human. I am selfish.

And I let myself be human and selfish, like she taught me.

"Boo," I say.

Isis jumps, withdrawing her lazily circling hand from the water. "Fuckstick central! Are you *trying* to kill me before I attain my final form?"

"Do tell." I settle beside her. She's wearing a soft-looking sweater and jean shorts. "What's your final form? No, wait, let me guess—insane witch."

"Cyborg empress," she corrects with a dignified sniff. "Of a small yet filthy-rich country."

I laugh. "And what will you do when you've regained your kingdom, Your Majesty?"

"Oh, you know, improve schools, build better roads, form a harem of beautiful, delicate men, the usual."

I raise an eyebrow. "Really? I thought your type was more beefy."

"It was, until I learned it doesn't actually matter what people look like on the outside, duh. Don't you watch *Dora the Explorer*? Shit is straight informative. I've learned so much about treating people as equals. And like…backpacks."

I smirk, and she hides her twisted smile in the crook of her arm.

"Alone in the middle of the night and hiding behind a studly centaur's rump is no place for an empress," I say.

"I wasn't *hiding*." She frowns. "Hiding is for babies. And ninjas."

We graze our hands through the water, our ripples the only thing touching. Our fingers distort to albino snakes under the water, speckled by stars and moss.

"You wanna go somewhere with me?" she asks.

I look up. "Where?"

"Somewhere. Anywhere but here. Anywhere Sophia never got to go. Let's go to the moon."

I look up at the silver disc. "It'll be cold."

"We'll bring jackets."

There's another quiet.

Isis huffs. "Where'd you get that thing on your eyebrow?"

"I ran into a doorframe," I answer smoothly.

"Where, at Samwise Gamgee's house?"

"Samwise lives in a gardener's shack, not a house."

"Oh my God, who cares?" She throws up her hands. "The point is that scratch looks nasty."

"Yes. That's what I've been doing all along. Nastying up my face so no woman will ever look twice at me again."

"Impossible," she scoffs. "All it'll do is heal and make you look badass, and then you'll have girls *and* their moms running after you. More than you do now. Distant aunts, maybe. God, life is so unfair."

She pushes her chestnut hair off her shoulder. It's gotten so long—past her shoulder blades—the faded purple streaks now lavender with a touch of white from the bleach. Her bangs are messy, in dire need of a trim, shading the warmest of brown eyes and gracing her flushed cheekbones. Her lips are still endearingly small and pouty. A year has changed her. She's grown taller ever so slightly, a mature sort of beauty sending out its first roots into her face. Her lashes are as long and dark as ever, and only when she blinks four times do I realize I'm staring and look away quickly.

I owe her the truth. I owe her at least that much.

"I left Northplains because I couldn't stay," I say. "Because I didn't know what to do with myself. Because I was hurting, and I was afraid I would hurt people with my own hurt. People like you."

Isis is quiet, hand slowing in its caress of the water.

"I took the car and drove for days. I don't even remember most of it. When I snapped out of it, I was in Vegas. I spent weeks there, in a motel room."

"Doing what?" she asks softly.

"Fighting. Fighting and drinking. There was a club in the lower east end, and I'd go there every night, beating up tourists or seasoned veterans or whoever wanted a piece of me. I got beat up more than I did the beating, unfortunately. But I wanted to be hurt. I wanted to feel pain, to feel something, anything. Anything other than the horrible nothingness that closed in after the funeral."

I see her swallow, her fists clenched in her lap.

"The guilt drove me like a demon. It still does, a little. But thanks to Gregory, it didn't swallow me alive."

"What do you mean?"

"The guy who chased you with Charlie in the forest—Gregory. He found me. God knows how. But he tracked me down, and just as I was running out of money, he offered me a job and training. Something to devote my energy to, to strive for, to pour myself into. I'd been so afraid of losing control for so long. But it's been that way since my father died, I think. That's when it started. I lost control in the forest and caused Joseph's death. Terrified, I tried to control myself even harder, keeping people at arm's length so they wouldn't get hurt. But then you came along."

She flinches, and I slide my hand into hers under the water and hold it, lightly.

"That's not a bad thing. Leo was, objectively, a bad thing. And I lost control then. But you—I lost control in a more pleasant way around you. In a way that was healthy and supportive. Losing control showed me the intricate web of emotions I'd been denying for so long. You teased them out, like the sun does to spring sprouts."

The flush on her cheeks grows redder, and I smile. But then I realize I'm holding her hand and disengage quickly. Motions like that are not helping her move on to a better man. None of this is. And yet I'm too selfish to stop talking, to walk away. I want the sun. I want to be warmed again by her heat, if only for a fleeting moment.

"Gregory taught me to control myself in a deeper way than I was doing alone. He took me to the desert, a ranch house he owns in the middle of nowhere, and he made me work. I hauled water and firewood and struggled with the stallions. Horses hate me, by the way. And they hate snakes. But primarily me."

"The difference between you is marginal," she muses, grinning. I flash her a smirk.

"Gregory made me fight—him, mostly, and sometimes his ranch hand, a giant of a man. Gregory showed me that control isn't suppression—it's expression, expressed when and where you choose and with deliberate purpose. After three months, he said I was ready to join his team. And I did."

"Spying," she says.

"Bodyguarding," I correct. "With a side of information collecting."

"So you're spying on Nameless."

"He's very secretive, and more clever than I gave him credit for. But with enough time, we'll get solid evidence."

"What's he done? Other than ruin a girl's life?" she asks.

"He's helped some people involved with opium, meth, human trafficking. The list isn't pretty. My employers aren't after him, just the people he knows. He probably didn't even know exactly what he was doing at the time, but he knew it was illegal."

Isis is quiet. She puts her hands between her knees and rocks on the edge of the fountain, a nervous gesture.

"I'm scared. Every corner I turn—I'm convinced he'll be on the other side, waiting for me."

"Then why come out here alone at night?"

"He doesn't like the dark," she says.

"Fascinating," I say, filing away the information for later use. "Not that you're scared," I correct quickly. "But that someone so terrible could have a fear so mundane."

She shrugs. "His dad locked him in the closet a lot when he was a kid. For hours."

We're quiet. Isis tries to break the tension.

"So, you and Bikini Girl going steady, then? Charlie said it was to get info out of her, but I mean, c'mon, look at her. No living thing with a portable piss tube could *not* feel something while dating someone that hot."

"She's boring," I say, my voice acidic. "If you must know."

"I do say, I must know." Isis takes on a faux-British accent.

"Why? Why would you care?"

"Because, idiot," she snaps. "I like you. I told you that a long time ago. Not that you'd remember—you get confessions like that all the time, why would you remember one from an annoying, angry little girl—"

Even after all the hurt, she still likes me.

"I've hurt you," I interrupt. "You deserve someone better."

She wrinkles her nose. "Oh my God, I forgot how arrogant you are. Who are you to decide what people deserve?"

It goes unsaid between us, but even she can tell what I'm thinking.

"And Sophia…Sophia loved you. She would've wanted you to be happy. That's all any of us can do in this short-ass life. Try to be happy. And I know it's killing you and I know you blame yourself, but you're not the only one blaming yourself—"

She stops, a choke ending her words.

I'm not the only one. How could I have forgotten that? What kind of selfish prick had I become—running away and leaving her to bleed over my shadow, and the shadow of all the things she should've done? She waited alone in silence and fear, bravely holding together the pieces of my life that I abandoned because I was too selfish to stay. Even after I abandoned her, she held on to the memory of me, to her feelings for me, guarding them carefully so they wouldn't start to rot. Any other girl would have given up. Any other girl would have sown hatred for me for the rest of her life.

But not Isis. Not my stubborn, courageous, kind Isis.

"It's okay." She looks up, smiling, though her eyes are waterlogged. "It's nice of you to pretend you still like me, but… But I understand. If you don't really, you don't have to say I should find someone better. You should just tell me. I know I'm not—I'm not all that ladylike, and I'm weird and loud, and I'm inexperienced, and I know that isn't your type. And I've got a lot of huge, dumb issues, so. That's too difficult for someone to deal with, I think. That night in the hotel was months ago, so it's okay if things have changed. You don't have to feel bad about not wanting me anymore. It's okay to just like someone as a friend and not want to sleep with them. We can be friends. Just friends."

I want you. I want you as more than a friend. I want you in my arms, in my bed, where you'll be safe and ecstatic and all mine. I want to show you how good a kiss can be. I want to show you life isn't always suffering—it's pleasure, too.

My brain screams it, but my mouth never moves, condemning me to silence. I have to be stone. The slightest crack and I'll spill my every secret at her feet—that I crave her like a parched plant craves the rain. That the only time I feel alive—honestly, radiantly alive—is when I see her purple streaks, the outline of her shoulders, her smile.

But what kind of barbed love could I offer her? I'm broken, shattered like a mirror of lies. She would try to pick up my pieces and only cut her fingers on them. Any love I could give her would hurt her more, when all I want to do is heal her. I want to build her back up, not tear her down with me. She is too important. Any further hurt by a man could tip the scales of her heart irrevocably, and send her into the place of no return, where no light or love could ever reach her. I'd ruin her for good. And I could never live with myself if I ruined her.

Not after Sophia. Not after ruining a girl once before. Once is an accident. Twice is malicious and unforgivable. I'd be no better than Nameless. If I put my own wants and needs above her safety and well-being, I'd be no better than him.

So I put my best mask on. The lifeless one. The one Isis practically destroyed. There are only shards of it left, but it's so familiar I fill in the blanks quickly and make my expression unreadable.

"I apologize," I say. "For leading you into thinking we were something more than friends."

The light drains from her eyes instantly at my words, something deep and bright dying within her. Hope. But she hides it in a split second, sweeping it under a rug of sardonic exasperation. For all the things she is miserable at, she is very, very good at hiding her pain.

"Ugh, stop that. Apologizing looks *so* gross on you."

"I'm sorry."

She stands up, putting her hands above her head and stretching, making a satisfied noise. But I can read her easily—it's a farce. It's a moment for her to regain control over her emotions, to hide them from me. She turns and smiles.

"So, I mean, just a casual question between friends is okay, right?"

I nod.

"What you said about liking me…that night in the hotel. Was that true?"

I swallow and form words carefully. "Yes. But something changed, and now—"

"No, I get it." She laughs. "Really, it's fine. Feelings change, hormones, experiences, all that good stuff just mixes everything up in our brains. It's a wonder people are stable at all! Shit, sometimes I'm surprised I feel the same way about somebody for more than a week, you know?"

To anybody else, she'd seem fine. But to me, the pain in her offhand words is palpable.

"Isis—"

I stand, and she takes an abrupt step back, holding her arms up.

"Hey, whoa there. I'd really appreciate it if you wouldn't come near me right now. It's night, is all, and you're a guy, and, you know. It just freaks me out. Nothing personal."

My throat tightens, something heavy sinking in my stomach. I'm like all the other men to her now. I'm just another one who's disappointed and hurt her.

"Right. I'm sorry."

"Again with the apologies!" She grins. "Get a hobby, or like, a better word for sorry. 'Pancakes.' Yeah, that's it. Replace every 'sorry' with 'pancakes,' and watch your life become a thousand times better. Also, fatter."

I'm trying to piece together the right words for her, words that won't hurt her, but I can already tell I have. There's no taking back what I said. The damage has been done. Isis, always the faster one, smiles and salutes me facetiously.

"All right, I think I feel sleep coming on. Going on, actually. I'm sleepwalking right now. You're talking to a not-awake person. Ooooh!" She makes a creepy noise and then coughs. "Uh. Right. So. I'll see you around, James Bond. Try not to shoot anyone you don't have to. Shit hurts."

"I could walk you to your dorm, if you'd like."

"Nah, I'll be fine. Ears like a hawk. Except hawks don't have ears. Do they? I dunno! That's why I'm in college. Good night."

Isis leaves, and I remember, with painful regret, what it's like to be cold again.

chapter nine

3 YEARS, 50 WEEKS, 0 DAYS

I GO TO PARTIES IN COLLEGE for the same reason I did in high school—to forget.

In the two weeks after my and Jack's meeting at the fountain, I realize just how important parties are. I'm not one of those people who like big crowds, but I don't hate them, either. They're useful—when there are so many people around you, talking and laughing and living their lives, you start to forget your own. You can get lost in them, in their energy, in the crowd itself. For all of the seven hours the party is going on, I don't have to think about Jack, about his voice saying, *I apologize for leading you into thinking we were something more than friends.* For a brief moment between shots of vodka, I forget he ever said that, and the seed of hope in my chest that he still likes me can glow warmly. It's an illusion, a fake, but it's so pleasant and soft I do everything I can to live in it. And that means lots of parties.

If you asked high school me if I was thinking about becoming a college party girl, she would've laughed in your face. High school me was smarter than that. She was smarter than I am now. But pain does funny things to people, and denial is the only sweet release, no matter how temporary.

So yeah—I dance. I drink until I puke. I sleep on someone else's bed, or floor, in someone else's locked room to keep the wolves out. And when I wake up, I do it all again. For as long as I can, until classes start or a worried Yvette calls.

After two weeks, I'm starting to feel okay. Numb, but okay.

But God must've heard my prayers for something good to happen. And Buddha. And frankly every god ever worshipped on this green earth, because Kayla texts me with incredibly great news on Thursday.

Wren and I are back in Northplains for fall break! Let's meet up!

With all the controlled grace of a choking mule, I make excited noises and text her back. We agree to meet up at a coffee shop nearby, and I'll give them the grand tour of my campus. Wren—always the quiet, calming presence—asks me if Jack will be there. Kayla's told him he goes here, of course, so I don't bother denying it. But affirming it makes my insides roil. Yeah, he's here, and Wren knows it. He has to know Nameless goes here, too. I hope he isn't planning to hang out with him. It'd ruin my life forever. Or maybe just my appetite.

The next few days pass like molasses on an igloo in December, until Friday finally arrives in all its weekend-ish glory. I throw on a pair of comfortable jeans and a very fluffy sweater so I can pick at it while I wait. The coffee shop is practically empty, and I try and fail to sit still. The double shot of espresso doesn't exactly help, but I thought it would, and I'm so very wrong, and what if Kayla and Wren are way more mature than me now? What if they're studious and serious and full of Worldly Information I'll Never Understand™, like how to balance a checkbook or how to order takeout without getting an anxiety attack, and what if Kayla's made new girlfriends, better girlfriends who don't say "butt crack" and think out loud—

"There you are!"

A Kayla-shaped blur launches into my chest, hugging me fiercely. I hug her back tentatively, and she pulls away, her sheet of silky brown hair longer than I remember. Her smile is the same, though, so infectious and golden I can't help but smile my biggest right back.

"Holy shit, you look great!" I state the obvious in an excited voice. She laughs and looks me over from head to toe.

"And you look way better! I love that sweater! Did you get taller?"

"I think so? It's hard to tell when everyone around here is the rough height of a frost troll."

"Frost trolls don't live near cities." Wren's patient voice comes from behind Kayla. "They hate technology."

"Wren!" I throw my arms around his neck. He adjusts his glasses and smiles when we part. His pale hair is slicked back smartly, just like I remember it, and his sensible khaki pants and button-up shirt never cease to amaze me with the sheer amount of absolute boredom contained in one outfit. But it suits him. It always has.

"It's good to see you, Isis," he says.

"You, too!"

"Seriously, though, you'd be more likely to see a forest troll—"

"All right, Mr. Dungeons & Dragons, give it a rest."

"He joined MIT's campus club for it." Kayla winks at me, and Wren goes pink.

"I did not!"

"And the math club, and the chess club, and the Helpful Hand charity club, and a bunch of others, but he kept looking longingly at the D&D application." Kayla laughs. "So I filled it out for him and turned it in."

Wren rubs the bridge of his nose. "I just didn't think an impractical club like that would look good on résumés."

"It's okay to have fun once in a million-year cycle," I chime. He shoots me a small grin.

"All right already. I'm in it, I'm a half-elf paladin, and none of you can make fun of me for it, period."

"Ugh, seriously Wren? A half elf? Everyone and their mother and their mother's grandmother wants to be a half elf! If you're going to indulge in a little fantasy role-playing, the least you could do was be less obvious." I roll my eyes. Kayla laughs again and goes to the counter to order her tea.

"What would you be then, Madam Rebel?" He smirks.

"A dwarf warrior. With a giant hammer. If I'm the most awesome person alive in real life, I'm sure as hell gonna be the most awesome in the realm of Dragonsville, too."

We fritter away hours in the coffee shop, eating cake and catching up on one another's lives. Kayla's slogging through her calculus class, but acing everything else. Wren tutors her off and on, when he isn't volunteering for a hundred club activities and doing every piece of extra credit he can get his hands on. For once, he doesn't have the highest grade in every single class, and he says it's more freeing than anything, like the pressure to be the best all the time and keep that number-one spot is gone from his chest. Of course, he struggled to let that "be the best" urge go, and it was painful, but he managed.

I tell them the abridged version of life at Ohio State—I'm keeping up in most of my classes, nearly failing two, and my roommate is fantastic.

"I'm so jealous." Kayla sighs. "Mine is awful. She leaves her dirty underwear everywhere—even on my bed!"

"You live with a goblin." I make a face. "And not the gold-hoarding D&D kind."

"We're planning to get an apartment together after the

school year is over," Wren says, and he and Kayla share a tender look.

"Seriously? That's fantastic! Can I come visit you and eat all your food?"

"Only some," Kayla insists.

"Most," I barter.

The bells over the coffee shop door ring, though I'm so lost in bargaining with Kayla about how much of her bubble bath I'll get to use when I visit them, I don't notice who comes in. Wren gets up, making some excuse about the bathroom. Only when Kayla looks over my shoulder does she gasp.

"Oh crap, is that who I think it is?"

I look behind me. In black jeans and a jacket stands Jack Hunter, perusing the pastries. But he isn't here alone.

"Can I get that one, *puh-lease*?" a girl begs at his arm. I recognize the voice—how could I not? It's Hemorrhoid, the chick from the pool party. I try not to look at where they're touching, something about it making me feel sick to my stomach. Thankfully they can't see our table; the mottled glass partition is right in front of us, and I shrink behind it more.

"Fine, Brittany." Jack sighs. "But just that one, and then we get out of here."

Kayla looks to me, then her, then to Jack, and then back to me, and her eyes narrow.

"Is Jack…*dating* that girl?" The way Kayla says it, it might as well be poisonous, with how much hate it's steeped in.

"I guess?" I shrug and try my hardest to play it off cool, leaning heavily on all the numbness I've built up over the weeks. "Who cares?"

"You don't?" She frowns. "Isis, what the hell happened? Last time we talked, you were pissed at him but still willing to insult him. You can't just 'who cares' this!"

Kayla's voice draws Hemorrhoid's attention, and I pull at her arm.

"Hey, please, let's not do this here."

"You can't just—"

"Jack," Wren says, coming out of the bathroom. "Fancy meeting you here."

Kayla and I freeze, watching Jack and Wren. Jack can't see our table. All he can see is Wren, his icy eyes suddenly hard.

"Wren," he says. "When did you get back into the state?"

"Just today. Here for the weekend, for fall break. It's weird how Ohio and Massachusetts schools have completely different schedules." Wren smiles, and Kayla and I look at one another warily. Since when is Wren able to talk to Jack face-to-face?

"I wouldn't call it weird so much as typical," Jack says. Hemorrhoid is too busy with her croissant to butt in. There's an awkward pause. I spot Wren's hands behind his back, balled up and slightly shaking. He's nervous, but he's trying.

"Who's your friend?" Wren asks innocently. Jack narrows his eyes.

"It's really none of your business."

"Where did you go?" Wren says quickly, never missing a beat. "After Sophia's funeral?"

Jack's eyes flash with the briefest spark of anger. "Away. Obviously."

"Right." Wren exhales. "Well, any time you want to stop being a prickly bastard and start talking to me like a normal human being who loved the same girl you did, albeit in a different way, you let me know. You still have my number."

Wren walks over to our table, Jack's eyes following him. I duck farther behind the partition, desperately hoping he doesn't recognize the sweater arm he can see as mine. He doesn't, leaving with Hemorrhoid after she's gotten her croissant. Wren watches them go, and Kayla stands up, her chair squeaking with the sudden effort.

"Where are you going?" I ask.

"To punch him." Kayla smiles, but Wren puts his hand on hers.

"Kayla, let it go."

"Let *me* go! He can't just date someone other than Isis!" Kayla stamps her foot.

"He can," Wren says quietly. "And he is."

"But—" Kayla looks to me. "Isis, are you okay with it?"

I start to say no, the word half formed on my lips. But that would be wrong. I'm just fine with it. I have to be. I have to be, or all the effort, all the parties, all the other boys, all the drinking—all the work I did to put distance between Jack and me will crumble and leave me right where I started: alone, and sad, and tired of being alone and sad.

"It's fine," I say. "It's his life—he can do whatever he wants."

"Not when it hurts my best friend!" Kayla snaps, and starts to move, but Wren grips harder.

"Kayla, please."

"Look at her, Wren!" Kayla gestures to me. "I've never seen her this quiet and amiable in my life! She's like…she's like almost *normal*! Something's seriously wrong!"

"I'm still here, you know," I say.

Kayla deflates. "Look, Isis, I'm sorry, but I'm also not sorry because this is seriously a fucked-up situation."

"I'm okay," I raise my voice a notch. "I'm okay. Right now, with you guys here, I'm just fine. And you're only here for two days. Let's not ruin our time together with shit like this, okay? Please. For me."

Wren and Kayla share a look. Finally, Kayla sinks into her seat and breathes deep.

"Okay. I'll try to not punch Jack through the stratosphere

while I'm here. All bets are off for when I come by during winter break, though."

For once in my life, I don't say what I'm thinking. I wait, and I listen as Wren tries to cover the awkward silence with chitchat while my heart sinks heavy in my chest. Is this what it feels like to be normal? So disappointed with yourself and everyone else you can't talk at all? I should've said something. I should've gotten up and walked over to Jack and Hemorrhoid and said exactly what was on my mind, that I'm sad he's with her and not me. But I didn't. Who even am I? Is the real Isis with the body-snatching Zabadoobians? How can I get her to come back and replace this lifeless clone I've become?

No—I'm not lifeless. I'm doing everything I should be doing; I go to parties and smile and drink and do my assignments and essays. I kiss. I don't tell. I do everything a girl in college should be doing.

So why does it feel so *wrong* when I catch the barest glimpse of Jack?

He knew me before college. He knew me during one of the most chaotic years of my life. He knows me. Maybe that's why it feels so wrong. No one else has known me like he has—seen through me, to the person inside me, so truly and quickly. Maybe that's why it feels wrong when I see him with someone else, when I see him, *period*. We should be together. Every time I see him, that's just drilled into my head harder. But then the thought of Nameless pops up, black and oozing bad memories and telling me I'm the worst, and I recoil into my instinctual shell.

Sometimes looking at Jack feels like reaching out to the horizon—I'll never touch it, never hold it, but it's the prettiest thing I've ever seen.

After Wren and Kayla and I have fueled up, I show them

around campus and my dorm. Yvette is inside, studying for once.

"Yvette!" I slap my hands on both her shoulders. "These are my fantastic friends, Kayla and Wren. Fantastic friends, this is Yvette, my other fantastic friend."

Yvette smiles half awkwardly and shakes equally awkward Wren's hand. She blushes when Kayla hugs her.

"It's great to meet you guys. Isis won't shut up about you."

"She won't shut up about you, either!" Kayla laughs. "I'm gonna be totally honest with you—it made me kind of jealous."

"Yesss," I hiss. "Now fight over my love in an arena death match!"

"Not happening," Yvette says. "Unless there's a battle-ax. In which case, yes."

"Two-handed or one-handed?" Wren asks.

"Two-handed, obviously, for maximum badassery."

"Perfect," Wren agrees. "Although if it's one-handed, then you can have two. Twice the chopping."

She smiles. "I like the way you think."

"Oh my God." Kayla darts over to Yvette's impressive collection of lipsticks on the windowsill. "Those are such nice colors!"

"You like 'em?" Yvette walks over to her.

"Definitely! Where did you find this shade? I've been looking everywhere for it."

While they discuss the finer points of colored wax, Wren and I linger outside the doorway. I put my head on his shoulder tiredly, and he pats it.

"How are you doing?" he asks.

"Fine. Dandy. Dine and fandy."

"Even with Wi—my cousin here?"

I blow my bangs out of my eyes. "You can say his name. I've been trying to. Weee-illl. Weeeeeel. I've seen him more times around campus than I ever wanted to. And it's helped.

Sort of. If you see something enough it becomes normal, you know? So I figure if I say his name enough, it won't hurt as much anymore."

Wren's hand is gentle on my head, but his other hand tightens into a fist.

"I'm sorry, Isis. I'm sorry he's here. If I'd known, I could've warned you—"

"So I could've what—not gone here?" I stand up straight. "No. I'm not gonna let him have any more control over my life than he already does."

"But—"

"No buts. Okay, maybe some buts. But only the kind in jeans, and only nice ones."

"Isis, seriously..."

I take his hand off my head and hold it with the best smile I can muster. "I've spent almost two years running away. And I've started to hate it."

Wren squeezes my hand wordlessly, and I squeeze back.

"I just wanna walk forward, like everybody else is, instead of running away."

"I'm just...worried." Wren sighs. "Just take it at your own pace, okay? Everyone's different. And if you try too hard, too fast, you could end up hurting yourself."

"It's sweet you're worried. But I can take care of myself, Wren. We aren't kids anymore."

Wren's quiet. Suddenly my phone buzzes with a text from Heather, a girl in my sociology class I'd made kind-of-sort-of friends with after we realized we both loved mobster movies. Since then, she's been my party hookup, inviting me to as many as she can. And that's what she's doing now, too.

I don't want to go. I want to stay in with Kayla and Wren, watching stupid cat videos and catching up on all we've missed. But after Wren's run-in with Jack, I feel like I have to show them I'm okay. I have to move forward. I have to show them I'm moving forward so they don't worry about me.

"Hey, do you happen to feel like drinking copious amounts of cheap booze?" I ask Wren. He sigh-chuckles.

"I suppose. Any excuse to stay out of my parents' house for a bit longer is more than welcome."

"Is that where you're staying?"

"Yeah."

"In that case, let's tear ass-phalt. Kayla! We're going to a party. You wanna come, Yvette?"

"Is it one of Heather's?"

I nod, and she shakes her head.

"No thanks. Those are a little wilder than I'm used to."

"If you're sure!" I singsong. "Don't wait up for me—I'll be late."

We take my car, the backseat cramped with textbooks and changes of clothes I forgot to take in. I'm so excited to be going to a party with Kayla again like old times that Wren has to remind me to keep my eyes on the road.

"—and you've got to meet Kieran," I insist. "Heather's fine, she's just not that funny, and Tyler's a jerk, but Kieran's a pretty nice guy. We've been hanging out a lot lately at Heather's parties, and he's super chill."

"'Hanging out'?" Kayla air-quotes. "Back in my day, that meant making out."

"*Por que no los dos?*" I ask. Kayla rolls her eyes, and Wren laughs.

"Since when did you start taking Spanish?"

"Since I realized it's the second-most-spoken language in the world. Also, Spanish dudes are beautiful."

Kayla tosses her hair. "I've seen better."

"It's true, you *are* the fairest in the land," Wren chimes, and she smiles brilliantly and all but flounces in her seat.

"Thank you, sweetie."

"Hold on, I need to pull over and vomit," I say.

"Why?" Kayla asks.

"Because you two are too cute."

Kayla immediately punches my shoulder.

We pull up to Heather's boyfriend's frat house after everyone's arrived. I used to think parties in high school were huge, but I realized how small they are the second I saw my first frat house. An entire house, bigger than most families', filled to the brim with people? It's insanity. But it's become my insanity, my own personal brand of alcohol-induced forgetting. The music alone makes the windows in the other houses on the street shake in their frames. I lead Kayla and Wren inside, awkwardly shuffling through the boozed-up crowd.

"Do you know any of these people?" Kayla calls.

"Uh, not really?" I try to laugh it off. "I know Heather and Kieran, he's on the wrestling team, but that's about it. Oh hey! There's Tyler. He tried to make out with me once, and shortly thereafter learned the meaning of absolute pain."

I point at a boy with a buzz cut and skinny jeans. He gives the once-over to Kayla as we approach, and whistles.

"Well hello, hello. Who's the friend, Isis?"

"She's taken," Wren says instantly and with a hardness that surprises me. Where's meek Wren? Not here, that's for sure. Then again, I'm sure he's had to beat off the other guys with a stick since he and Kayla went official.

"Whatever, man," Tyler scoffs.

"Listen, Tyler," I say. "I'd really appreciate it if you could stop being such a primordial ooze for one minute and tell me where Kieran is."

Tyler shrugs. "Somewhere upstairs, I think."

We push past him—well, I do. Kayla and Wren sort of lag behind, Kayla looking bewildered and Wren looking slightly more off-put than when he came in. I feel like an absolute dog turd knowing they aren't having a good time.

"Drinks!" I announce as we pass a hastily set-up table upstairs. Drinks solve everything. I've learned that well since Jack started dating Hemorrhoid. I grab two Jell-O shots and shove them in Kayla's and Wren's hands, pouring myself a shot of vodka and yelling "Cheers!" as I down it. I spot a dark head of hair over the crowd and dash toward it. I slap my hands over the person's eyes.

"Guess who?" I chirp. Kayla and Wren catch up to me, watching us.

"There's only one person with that annoying of a voice," Kieran deadpans. "Isis."

"He got it right!" I take my hands off and pinch his cheek as he turns. "He's growing up into such a smart boy. Eats his veggies and everything. Kieran, these are my friends Kayla and Wren. Kayla, Wren, this is my barely friend Kieran."

"Gee, thanks," he drawls, then flashes a smile at Wren and Kayla. "I've only known her for two weeks, but sometimes it feels like twenty years of unending torture."

"Welcome to the club!" Kayla laughs. "Isn't it great in here?"

"Practically palatial," Wren agrees with a small grin. "You're luckier than most, Kieran. Jack got punched within the first hour of—"

Kayla jabs her elbow in Wren's side, and he falters, shooting me a look. My stomach churns a little, thinking about Jack right now.

Kieran looks confused. "Um, did I miss something? Who's Jack?"

"More shots!" I crow, forcing a smile at the three of them.

"I'll go get some. You guys stay here and mingle."

I take the stairs two at a time.

"Isis! There you are!" I turn to see Heather, a black-haired girl with the biggest lips ever. She throws her arms around me the second I walk in the kitchen. She smells like tequila and reminds me of Kayla; when the real Kayla isn't here I can sometimes squint and pretend she's her. Tonight, at least, I don't need to pretend at all.

"Hey, Heather. What are you up to?" I ask as I pour shots.

"Playing beer pong, obviously." She holds up her red cup and winks. "I'm glad you came, though; this party was just getting boring." She grabs my hand and pulls me toward the dance floor.

"Heather, wait, I've gotta—"

"Just one dance, please?" she begs. "That'll get tons of people dancing, and then you can go do whatever! But this party is super dead! We need you—no way I'm dancing on my own!"

I want to say no, to go back to Wren and Kayla, but then I remember Jack's name coming from Wren's lips. I love him, but he managed with a single word to crumble the wall I worked so hard to build. Kieran's going to ask questions about who Jack is, and everything will be ruined. He was such a nice distraction, his emerald eyes and easy laugh and our similar sense of humor a great way to bury my memories. But now the doubt of who Jack is will filter in between us, and I'll be forced to tell him, forced to confront it all.

It's ruined.

So I go with Heather, and I dance my heart out with her on the carpet. I will the bass to blast my thoughts clean from my head. People start dancing with us, around us, and Heather gets happier and happier with each person. And I get sadder and sadder. None of these people know me, and they never will. None of them care about me. The ones who do are upstairs. That's where I belong. But it's so much easier to dance down here than it is to go up and face them. So I keep dancing.

Because I'm a coward.

Because I've done enough hard stuff to last a lifetime.

Someone, Heather maybe, passes me a shot. And another. The music is so loud my ears are starting to ring, but I like it. I need it. Eventually, just as I'm getting out of breath, I feel a tug on my arm. I look over to see Heather pointing at a distant figure.

"Hey, isn't that the girl you were talking about? The one you hate?"

She's right—in the kitchen stands Hemorrhoid, red hair practically luminescent and her black dress classy.

"I don't hate her," I shout back. "She's just—she's just a girl, okay?"

"No, I remember! You told me when you were throwing up at the Rho Delta Kappa house! You said you hate her because she's dating someone you like!"

"People say a lot of things when they're drunk, Heather. The Greeks even made a saying for it: *in vino veritas*!"

"Harass who?"

"Ugh, never mind!" I yell.

"I'm gonna go talk to her!" Heather shouts, her eyes glassy. She's clearly had too much. "Someone's gotta tell her to back off!"

"Heather, no!" I snatch her arm. "Just leave it, okay?"

With a surprising amount of force for someone so drunk, Heather tears away from me and stomps toward Hemorrhoid. I dash after her, but the dancing crowd is so thick I have to push people aside.

"Sorry, excuse me, minor social apocalypse incoming, sorry!"

Heather gains distance, and my queasy stomach goes into full-blown panic mode. If Heather confronts her about me and Hemorrhoid says something about it to Jack—what will he think of me? As much as I dislike Hemorrhoid, I don't want her involved in anything negative because of me. Heather's already talking to her, if I run out of the house now maybe everything will stop forever and I—

"She said what?" Hemorrhoid scoffs, eyes pointed like daggers directly at me. "If you've got a problem with me, say it now."

I put on my best smile, Heather looking satisfied with her misguided work.

"God, I'm really sorry about my friend," I say. "She's drunk, she has no idea what she's talking about. I don't have a single problem with you, Hemorrhoid—"

"What did you just call me?"

I freeze. I'd said that name for her so many times in my head and to other people that my booze-loose idiot mouth just blurted it out. Her pretty face twists with anger.

"Repeat what you just said, bitch."

"I'm sorry! That was a mistake! We all make those sometimes, right?" I falter. "I didn't mean to—"

Hemorrhoid advances on me, all painted nails and anger, and Heather pumps her fist in the air.

"Get her, Isis!"

People look and start to wander over. I back up to the wall, my eyes darting around for someone, anyone to save me. I need an escape, and I needed it yesterday.

"I don't want to fight." I hold up my hands. "This is a misunderstanding, okay?"

"You called me something!" she snaps.

"Yeah, I did! And I'm sorry!"

"You still said it, bitch!"

She lunges for me, and I duck past her. She stumbles into the arm of a couch, and people make an "oooh" noise. She rights herself and pivots, now looking even more pissed.

"Hey, relax." I use my calmest voice, even though it shakes. "Let's not—"

Stars burst in my eyes, my cheek screaming in pain. Her knuckles are so bony, like daggers into my flesh. The punch is so hard it knocks the wind from me, and as I crumple to the floor, some tiny part in the back of my brain laughs at me, at the irony of it all; she's punched me at a party, just like I punched Jack so long ago.

Faintly, through the crowd jeering, I hear someone call my name.

"—sis? Isis? What happened to you? Oh my God, you're bleeding!" Kayla's voice.

"Stay away from her!" Kieran barks.

"We have to get her out of here," Wren commands.

I rub my eyes to clear them of their watering and feel someone with strong arms help me up. It's Kieran, and he leads me out of the house, Wren and Kayla hot on our heels. I can hear Hemorrhoid's shouting faintly.

"Come back here! You're such a fucking bitch!"

I'm still too dazed to pull away when Kieran puts me in the backseat of my own car. Wren kneels and inspects the damage.

"Jesus, she got you good."

"Do you have a first-aid kit in your car?" Kayla shouts, already rummaging in my trunk, with my keys in her hand. When she swiped them from my purse, I'll never know.

"No," I moan. "I'm fine, seriously."

"Seriously? You're bleeding, Isis," Kieran insists. "We were wondering where you went. Turns out you ditched us for a half hour to get in a fight."

"That was toward the end of the dance." I wince as Wren dabs away the blood on my cheek.

"Who even started it?" Kieran asks.

"I didn't," I say. The three of them share a moment of silent suspicion aimed at me. "What? I'm telling the truth! I definitely didn't punch first. But I did call her names first."

"Isis!" Kayla sighs.

"On accident!" I insist. "My mouth just does that go-fast thing, you know? I didn't think about it and bam! A second later I called her Hemorrhoid out loud. Thanks, me."

"That's a fairly bad name," Wren says. "But it's still no excuse to punch someone this hard. She must have something against you."

"Ugh, that girl is awful!" Kayla stomps her foot. "I knew it the second she walked into the coffee shop! I'm telling Jack about this so he can dump her ass—"

"Don't!" I stand. Wren eases me back down.

"Relax," he says. "We won't."

"We won't?" Kayla scoffs incredulously. He turns to her.

"This is between them, Kayla. Not us."

"But—"

"Who is this Jack guy, anyway?" Kieran asks. Kayla inhales, ready to spill everything.

"He's Isis's—"

"He's no one," I say quickly. "Kayla, please, just give me my keys, and let's go back to the dorms."

"But what about—"

Wren puts an arm gently around her shoulders. "It might be better to get Isis somewhere quieter, don't you think?"

Kayla very plainly fights the urge to say more, practically wiggling under his arm. Finally she exhales and hands the keys to him. Wren flashes me a smile.

"We'll wait over there. It was nice meeting you, Kieran."

"Same to you." Kieran nods, a grumpy Kayla saying nothing as Wren leads her away. I turn to Kieran.

"Sorry you had to see all that," I say. "You should go back in and try to have some fun."

"Can't." He smirks. "Not while you're not there."

"Try anyway, smooth."

"Take care of that cheek, will you?"

"The next time you see me, I'll be growing a third arm from it."

"Fantastic." He laughs as he walks back toward the party. I wave.

The ride home is silent, Wren doing his best to get Kayla to stop pouting. He's the only person I know to stick that mission out for more than ten minutes. Once Kayla's in pout mode, she's there until she's fallen asleep. Wren and I both know she'll wake up much happier, but for now we suffer her beautiful mug glaring at us with nary a complaint. When we get back to my dorm, Kayla makes an excuse about the bathroom, and Wren and I wait outside by her car.

"She'll get over it," Wren says as we watch Kayla walk away.

"I know she will. But I won't."

Wren chuckles. "First time being on the receiving end, huh?"

I cup my cheek gingerly. "The core of all disputes can be resolved without violence."

Wren quirks a brow at me.

"Fighting is wrong?" I try. "Hate can't drive out love. Um. Hold on, I learned like seven different famous quotes last week and they're all mashed up right now, like some awful deep house DJ who also happens to be into protest literature lost total control of his life in my brain."

We enjoy the silence for a moment. Well, for as long as one can enjoy something while suffering a broken face, anyway.

"Your face isn't broken," Wren insists without taking his eyes from the starry sky.

"Build me a castle and give me a rose—I'm a beast."

"Build your own castle."

"I'm trying!" I throw my hands up, then instantly get tired of doing that. "I'm *trying*."

"We did miss you," Wren says. "At the party. We thought you forgot about us."

"I just—" I flinch. "I didn't forget. I'd never forget. It was just more like I didn't want to remember."

"Remember what?"

I tilt my head this way and that and mouth words I can't say. Wren makes an "oh" face.

"I brought up Jack. Right," he muses. "I'm sorry. I didn't think he was a sensitive topic."

"He's always been a sensitive topic," I scoff, and Wren laughs, his eyes crinkly behind his glasses.

"That's true. But in a different way from Nameless, right?"

"What do you mean?"

Wren shrugs. "It just seems like…he's not on the same level, right? He hasn't done anything too bad, other than date that Steroid."

"Hemorrhoid," I correct. "And I'm going to be using her real name from now on, which is"—I think hard—"Mildred."

Wren and I share a look and bust out laughing.

"Of course." I calm down mildly. "Of course he's not as bad as Nameless. It's just the only way I know how to put something behind me, you know? Not say it. Not think about it."

"I used to do that, too," Wren agrees softly. "If I worked hard enough at school, I thought I could put the loneliness behind me. The loneliness from losing Jack as a best friend, and Avery and Sophia. All of them were gone from my life after what happened in middle school that summer. My mom and dad were never home, either. And when they were, all they seemed to care about was my report card. And that would just make me try harder. My life was keeping busy so I didn't have to think about things honestly and seriously."

"What changed?" I ask.

Wren smiles. "I met you. Sophia gave me that math badge from when we were kids. Kayla kissed me for the first time. Slowly, I started to learn what it meant to slow down. To stop being busy and just enjoy the moment. Those are my most important memories now. They're burned in my mind forever. Maybe they always will be. I hope so, at least."

He's so honest. He always has been. More honest than I'll ever be. What are my most important memories? My brain flashes with images and scents and feelings just below the surface: eating at the Red Fern with Kayla before we left for college, laughing and trying to be so brave; Sophia hugging me and thanking me for bringing Tallie back to her, her hair soft; Jack's smell, mint and honey and sleep, and his ice eyes opening groggily, beautifully, in the bed at that hotel and smiling when he saw me.

I can't run away from them. They'll always be here, with me, inside me, making me who I am.

This time, Wren puts his head on my shoulder.

"No matter what happens between you and Jack, or you and me, or me and you and Kayla," he says, "we're here, right now, together. We could be anywhere else, anytime else, on any other planet in the universe, but we're right *here*. If anything at all had changed in our lives, we might not know one another. But we do. And sometimes I can't help but think that's a miracle. It's a miracle I know you. It's a miracle I'm alive at all."

He smiles at me, brighter than the moon.

"I guess what I'm trying to say is…thank you, Isis."

"For what?" I feel my throat tighten, my eyes watering.

"For being my friend. For being born. For being right here, right now."

Wren isn't Jack—he doesn't let me cry quietly. He puts his arm around my shoulders, and he asks what's wrong, over and over, until I manage words through the tears.

"T-Thank you, too, you big idiot."

Kayla sees me crying and jogs over, her pout gone as she demands to know what's wrong, if my cheek hurts, if she should drive back right now and punch that girl in the esophagus, if a piece of gum might help. We bandage my cheek together with a first-aid kit, Kayla reveling in telling the story to an outraged Yvette. Ever worried, Kayla insists she and Wren stay for the night, and Yvette pulls her mattress down, and I pull mine, and all four of us lay sideways under a pile of blankets, our toes dangling and our words hanging as we interrupt one another, make jokes over one another, finish one another's sentences.

One by one, we fall asleep. I'm the last one awake. I watch the dawn light peek through the blinds, over the soft planes of our blankets and skins, and try to make a memory of it.

chapter ten

3 YEARS, 51 WEEKS, 2 DAYS

I CRY PROFUSELY for approximately two decades after Kayla and Wren leave. And then I get over it. People are way too dramatic all the time.

Just look at Hollywood—there's drama around every corner. And kale. Hollywood really loves kale. And like, babies. God forbid science ever makes a baby out of kale within five hundred miles of Los Angeles, because then it will be war, with Gucci guns and heavily armed limo drivers and I would put all my betting money on Vin Diesel and the Rock, who would obviously team up and become the ultimate kale-baby rescue team, with me as their outfit coordinator–slash–witty sidekick.

"Isis, I feel the need to inform you that you're being weird out loud again," Diana says, picking a daisy and putting it in my hair.

"Having friends who love you for who you are must be so cool," I muse. Diana laughs and picks another daisy, weaving together a chain.

"I'm just glad you're talking to yourself again. You seemed kind of down the last few weeks. Even Yvette noticed it."

"No." I act shocked. "Our very own blockheaded, emotionally stunted Goth grump? Noticing how I feel? *Preposterous*."

"You haven't been eating a lot."

"Debatable. Some very enlightened yoginis consider air food."

"You stay up all night."

"Studying! For midterms!" I protest. "Unlike you, some of us have to prepare to get our asses kicked."

"And you've been hanging around with—" Diana frowns. "Well, with people who don't really seem your type."

"Oh pishposh." I wave. "Heather's a perfectly nice girl. Except for the part where she started a fight for me."

She stares at me expectantly. I throw my hands up.

"Fine, and the guys! John, and Tyler, and Kieran, and Erik! They're all nice guys! And it's just hanging out!"

Diana frowns. "I just thought…what happened to that guy Yvette told me about? Model McFarter or something. The one we saw you talking with at the concert?"

"Who?" I ask airily, inspecting my fingernails.

"You know who." She glowers. "Dark blond, really neat blue eyes, tall. Made you laugh."

"I had a flu in my throat," I correct. "That was coughing, not laughing. Remind me to never take you to a comedy club."

Diana sighs and puts the finished daisy crown on my head. "We're just worried, that's all. I mean, if you *like* going to the frat parties every night, be my guest. More power to you, girl. But…"

I smile and slap her back. "It's nice of you to be worried about me. But look at me! I'm a big girl. I'm *huge*. I can take care of myself."

Diana knits her pretty lips together, but before she can say anything Yvette comes up from behind her and pounces, wrapping her arms around Diana's shoulders.

"Surprise, motherfuckers!" Yvette crows, then looks around to make sure no one is watching before pecking Diana on the cheek. "Hi, sweet thing."

Diana flushes. "Hey, you."

I keel over in the grass. Yvette sniffs under her armpits.

"I don't smell *that* bad, do I?"

"I'm dead," I rasp hoarsely. "From the cuteness."

Yvette goes red. "Shut up! You wouldn't know cute if it bit you on the ass!"

"It's true." I laugh. "I'm not all that cute!"

Diana frowns. "You are plenty cute."

"Well." I fluff my hair. "We'll let the ladies and gentlemen at the Phi Omega house tonight decide that."

"You're going to another party?" Yvette sighs. "Shit. Remember to be safe."

"Remember to eat my ass." I pause thoughtfully. "I take that back. I'm not into that. I don't even actually know what I'm into yet! But I'm pretty sure eating poop is not one of the things I will be into in the foreseeable future." I see Yvette glaring and throw my hands up. "Okay! Okay. I'll be safe. I promise."

Hanging with Yvette and Diana is fun, but there always comes a part where they stare into each other's eyes a little too long or their fingers lace together too tightly, and I instinctively know I should leave. So I make a little excuse about getting ready for the party and wave as I head for my dorm. They are obviously in love. Even Yvette's paranoia at being found out doesn't stop them from being publicly and purely in love. Diana seems less paranoid, but is careful just for Yvette's sake. It's cute and a little gag-worthy, but most of all, painful. Every second I watch them touch is a second the darkness drills into my head further. No one will ever look at me like that. No one will feel that deeply for me. No one will treat me that tenderly. No one will ever love me like that.

Ugly.

Ugly, ugly, ugly.

Not even Jack.

Not even the boy who got the closest, the furthest through my bitter shell. Not even the boy who stood in the doorway of my heart could bring himself to take that last step.

Something made him turn back. Something in me. Something wrong within me. And I'll never know what it is, because I can never ask him. I don't even see him often anymore. I catch glimpses of his face in the hall, but that's all I permit myself to look at, and only for mere seconds. The rumor about Hem—uh, Mildred—and me "fighting over him" circled through campus like a hungry vulture over a corpse. People I don't even know whisper about it sometimes! Isis Blake caught fighting over a boy? It's shameful. I want to crawl inside myself forever. I pray to God Jack didn't hear about it, but knowing what blabbermouths were at the party, he definitely did. So I can only look at him for seconds. Anything else is dangerous. Anything longer would mean a closet, and quiet, and tears, and more darkness, more holes I tear in myself so the darkness can crawl inside and live there like it always has.

My mirror makes me look a little taller. It also makes me look like I'm about to cry, and I really don't need that again. It's only been a few days, but my bruise from the fight has all but faded. I put a smile on instead and rummage through my closet. I pick a black skirt and long black socks. My fingers glance over the pink blouse, and I pull back like it's lava.

The memories are the worst part and the best part, all at once.

Jack's smile, his voice saying I was beautiful, the way he wrapped his arms around me in his bed, his breath on my neck. His smell, mint and honey. His rare, sonorous laughter. Our conversations, our fights, the way his hand grabbed mine under the fountain water for the last time—

I swallow nausea and bury the blouse under a hoodie. I pull on a red shirt instead, and brush out my hair.

He came so close.

But in the end, he ran away. Like they all do.

I pucker my lips, applying pink gloss. It's my fault, really. I was stupid for thinking Jack was different from any other guy in the world. They want things that are easy. They want girls who are cute and fun and experienced. None of this angry, bitter, sarcastic, virginal nonsense. Who I used to be was just too much work for Jack—for anyone! I don't blame him at all for turning tail. I certainly wouldn't want to be faced with the daunting task of loving someone that difficult.

I check my eyeliner one last time, ignore the fact that my foundation doesn't cover my dark eye bags entirely, and make sure no tags are sticking out anywhere. I grab my phone and stuff a twenty down my bra just in case I need to bribe someone.

My phone vibrates, and before I take it out I wish it's a text message from a certain icy someone.

But it's Mom. Calling. I brace myself.

"Hey, Mom. What's up?"

"Hi, sweetie. How are you?"

"I'm..." I catch a glimpse of myself in the mirror. I'm a bruised skeleton with a bit of meat on her. "I'm fine. How are you doing? How's work?"

"It's just fine! I mean, it's been slow, but I've been going every day. Dr. Torrand gave me these wonderful pills, and they're doing just the trick. I'm sleeping like a baby again."

Relief loosens some knot twisted up deep inside me.

"That's...that's really great. I'm so glad."

"What's wrong, sweetie? You don't sound too good yourself."

"I'm just glad, that's all. For a while there I thought—" *I thought you hated me.* "I thought you would get worse. But it's good. Sleeping is good. Sleeping is the best thing, really."

"It is. I'm about to do that right now, actually."

"Did you eat dinner?" I ask.

"Lasagna." She chuckles. "Although it was nowhere as good as Jack's. I do miss that boy. Whatever happened between you two?"

I gnaw the inside of my mouth, a little hurt to distract from the big hurt threatening to swallow me whole.

"He's dating someone else," I force out.

"Oh, that's too bad. He was quite the catch, but there are always better fish in the sea, sweetie, and you deserve only the best. Sweet dreams, you. Don't stay up too late studying."

"I won't. I love you," I say.

"Love you, too."

I ditch my car to walk instead—the night is too cool and pretty to be stuck in a tin box. Mom is actually wrong—I don't deserve the best fish. I deserve whichever one will put up with my bullshit the longest. Fish that actually understand and accept and care for me won't look twice at someone so fucked up. Jack taught me that.

I hope he's happy with Mildred, at least a little. Wren reminded me that it's okay. It's okay if he isn't with me, as long as he's happy and alive. That's all I wanted earlier this year—I burned to know he was okay, at least. And he is.

That's all I can ask for.

The Phi Omega house is a few blocks from campus. It's a big blue multilevel house, old as dirt and probably full of history. And corpses. Hopefully both. The music is already booming across the toilet-paper-strewn lawn. I knock, and a familiar boy with dark hair and green eyes grins down at me.

"Isis! There's my girl!"

"Kieran!" I squeal, and punch him in the gut in our customary greeting. He doubles over in mock-pain, and when he lifts his head I peck him on the cheek. "Where's the booze?"

"Down the hall and to the left. Dance floor's boring without you. Get some girls grinding. Preferably without starting a fight this time."

I wink at him. "No promises."

Girls and guys are already sloppy-making-out on the couch, and the beer pong game is well into its seventh round. That's how I know I'm really late.

"Isis!" Heather shouts. "It's about fuckin' time! I was gonna text you to get your butt over here but…but I forgot my lock code thingy!"

"It's 5429, girl, we changed it yesterday," I remind her. "Where's Tyler?"

Heather sniffs. "Tyler and I aren't talking. He's a douchebag."

"But you *are* making out with him tonight," I say.

"Duh." She rolls her eyes. "You were right. He's hells my type."

After a very drunk Tyler once tried to suck my lips off my face, I knew exactly who to set him up with—the girl on campus with the legendary lips. They'd been going out ever since with the fervor and rough visual resemblance of two crocodiles eating each other's faces. I like playing matchmaker almost as much as punching jerks. Almost. It warms my heart to see two people happy—even if that happiness is based on torrid and repeated sexual encounters versus, you know, an actual relationship. But who am I to judge? I've never had an actual relationship. Or an actual sexual encounter that wasn't awful.

A song comes on with booming bass, and Heather squeals and grabs my hand, dragging me to the wood dining room that's been converted into a dance floor. Once I make sure

Mildred or Jack isn't here, I get lost in the music, laughing when Heather tries to twerk drunk in six-inch heels. She leans over and kisses a guy who isn't Tyler, and it's then I realize I'm not special. A lot of the people here—heck, maybe most of them—are kissing a guy, or a girl, to forget the kiss of someone else. We'd all rather be kissing that one special person, but for some reason, we can't or won't. So we're here.

I'm not special. It just took me a while to come down to everyone else's level, is all. It just took me a while to get desperate enough to forget.

That's all.

I wade off the dance floor and pour myself a rum and Coke, downing it as fast as I can. It burns. But, hell, everything burns nowadays. A headache blindsides me, so I go outside and sit on the steps where the cool air can calm my throbbing head.

"You really did a good job," a voice says. Nameless, in a sweatshirt and jeans, sits beside me with a grin. "Losing weight, I mean. That was a lot of meat to lose. I'm impressed."

"I didn't do it for you," I snarl. When did he get here? The urge to run consumes me, but I stand fast. No, not this time. I came here to have a good night. I won't let him ruin it, or drive me off, or influence my actions in any way, really.

"Oh, we both know you did, Isis." He chuckles. "You picked at your food in the cafeteria. We used to take bets on it—if you'd eat the single celery stick you picked out or not. It was pretty gross."

I'm not as weak as I used to be, and I'll show him that. He can't taint me with any more darkness. There's no light to snuff out in me anymore. I'm all shadow now. He's just hosing down a campfire that's underwater.

"Remember when you fainted?" His chuckles get loud. "Oh shit, that was good. It was in the middle of PE dodgeball, and you just—"

He goes stiff as a board and falls to the side, coming up laughing.

"What do you want?" I ask coldly.

Nameless shrugs, putting his hands in his pockets. "Just wanted to say hello. I know Tyler, and I wanted some whiskey, so I came down. The girls here aren't half bad. You're a different story."

He's lying. He used to be better at it, or maybe I've just gotten better at reading liars?

"What do you *really* want, asshole?"

He looks surprised and starts clapping. "Oh, wow. *Asshole*. You haven't had the guts to say my name for three years, let alone insult me. I'm impressed. My compliments to your shrink."

"I never went to one. I didn't need one."

He chuckles.

"You can fool them, but you can't fool me. Anybody with half a brain could see you wanted to die. No one stopped you." He leans in and whispers. "Maybe they wanted you to die. Ever think about that?"

A volcanic vent oozes from my heart, spilling hot lava on my lungs, my stomach, my liver, and charring them instantly. This isn't me he's talking about. Mom loves me. Aunt Beth loves me. This is his dad talking through him. This is not about me. This is about him working his frustrations out on me. Nameless smiles wider.

"It's weird—I've been hearing rumors about you. Isis Blake is turning into quite the party girl. She was a nobody, and all of a sudden she shows up at parties, blacking out drunk and starting fights."

I try to breathe, to keep breathing and not let the memories overwhelm me. Nameless pulls a cigarette from his pocket and lights it, and my heart rate skyrockets and all

I hear is a high-pitched white noise. My hands start shaking, the scar on my wrist aching with a phantom burn. Nameless smirks, blowing the smoke in my face.

"What's the matter? Did that stuck-up pretty boy refuse you? Is that why you're throwing yourself down the bottle?"

I'm frozen, rooted to the steps as echoes of pain sear my skin all over again. The smell of cigarette smoke, the way it curls around my face and lingers in my hair—I want all of it to go away. To stop existing. I don't want to be here. I want to stop existing, right now. I want to black out. If I hold my breath long enough, I'll black out and everything will stop.

Nameless chuckles, my silence all the affirmation he needs. "He's a smart, talented, handsome guy. You tried to step above your status, and he put you back in your place. What a great guy. My opinion of him has done a total one eighty."

He leans in, and the bile in my throat moves to my mouth. "Or maybe…maybe it's more than that. Maybe you told him what happened between us. And maybe he just doesn't want to fuck you. Not after—"

"Isis? What's going on out here?"

The horrid black spell cracks, and I can move again, think again. I turn, Kieran's huge frame blacking out the door. Nameless smiles at him, turning on the charm full-blast.

"Oh nothin'. Just a little talk between old friends. Do you know where Tyler is?"

Kieran glares at him, then jerks his thumb. "Upstairs."

Nameless gets up and pats him on the shoulder. "Thanks."

When he's gone, Kieran sits on the steps with me. "Hey, you okay?"

"Yeah." I clear my throat, the pain fading. "Old friend."

"You didn't *look* very friendly with him."

"It's…nothing. Don't worry about it."

Kieran lets out a breath. "Well, look. Me and Ulfric and

a few of the girls are going into town. There's a club that's got a rave night. You wanna come?"

Kieran might be big and on the wrestling team and flunking all his English classes, but he's got cute green eyes, like a puppy, and he's weirdly sensitive. He asked me to tutor him when he saw my test scores in English, and we've been hanging out ever since. He knows exactly what to say and do to help a person feel better, and he's got a sixth sense–slash–invisible insect antennae for how people feel in general. He's like Wren in that way. He can tell I don't want to be here anymore now that Nameless is around. I nod.

"Yeah. Sure. Who's driving?"

"Me." Kieran smirks. "I'm the DD, but you may call me Sir Chauffeur. You get shotgun."

"I wish I had a shotgun," I grumble as I follow him to his PT Cruiser. Two girls in form-fitting dresses and a massive blond guy who looks slightly like a Viking king are waiting by it.

"Oh yeah?" Kieran laughs. "What would you do with one?"

"Go on a picnic. Start an indie band. Kill a certain someone."

"We're killing people?" The girl in the red dress claps her hands. "Let's start with Professor Summers. We'd be doing the world a favor."

"He's not even that bad." Kieran rolls his eyes and starts the car, backing out.

"He looked up Tessa's skirt with a mirrored pen yesterday, I totally saw it." Red-dress girl nudges green-dress girl, who must be Tessa, because she meekly withdraws into the seat. Red-dress flashes a smile at me. "Hi, I'm Livy."

"Isis," I say, and look at Tessa. "Did you report him?"

Tessa shakes her head, not meeting my eyes. Livy scoffs.

"You know campus won't do shit about it. They take reports and then file them away in a huge cabinet that no one ever touches. I've seen it. You might as well go scream at a brick wall."

Tessa finally looks up, voice meek. "Even if I do, they never believe girls. They'll ask me what I was wearing. It won't be his fault. It'll be mine."

I ball my fists. Kieran sighs in a weary, resigned way.

"Das not fair." Ulfric, with his rich accent, frowns. "In Denmark, my old university fire all creep."

He punctuates the word "fire" with a savage karate chop to the air.

"Yeah, well, welcome to America." Livy shrugs. "Land of the free to harass girls and home of the brave on the outside, cowardly on the inside."

"Professor Summers, huh," I whisper. Kieran flashes me a warning look.

"Don't you dare."

"What?" I play innocent.

"I know it was you who put the spaghetti in Sarah's purse last week," he adds.

"You did that?" Livy leans forward and laughs. "Holy shit, Tess, she's the one who messed up Sarah's purse!"

"Sarah?" Tessa looks confused.

"The girl who was cheating on her tests in our calc class! Isis was the one who put the noodles in her bag!"

I gasp. "How dare you accuse me! Slander, slander I say!"

"You smelled like sauce for four days after that," Kieran offers, irrefutable evidence.

I smile. "When you put it that way, you make me sound so bold. Possibly even...*saucy*."

There's an awkward silence in the car. Ulfric groans.

"You like pranking people who you think deserve it," Kieran says. "You Silly Stringed the whole inside of Tyler's car when he tried to make out with you. And now you're thinking of pranking Summers."

"What kind of outlaw do you peg me for, Sir Chauffeur? Look at me! There's no way I could ever think up something brilliant like rolling dung bombs under office doors or coating toupees with Crisco or putting spiders in desk drawers."

There's another silence.

"Or eye drops. Replaced with pepper spray."

Livy makes a thoughtful, approving noise. Kieran sighs and pulls into the parking lot of a flashy club with a neon sign that reads ETERNITY, and we all pile out. Livy grabs Tessa's arm and skips ahead. Ulfric looks at me like I'm a hungry tiger.

"You are very scary woman," he says.

"Coming from you, Leif Can-Decapitate-You-with-My-Forearm-Son, that means a lot." I pat his shoulder.

He looks appropriately offended. "I have never decapitate any people!"

"You should try it. It's very relaxing."

"When you're done planning murder," Kieran drawls, "let's get some drinks."

"How could we forget our Viking priorities?" I slap Ulfric on the back. "Booze first, blood second, boobs third."

"Boobs first, booze second, blood never," Ulfric corrects.

"Ahhh, don't be such a stickler, Ulfie. The gods demand revelry! Onward to Valhalla!"

Like all people who've had the extreme luck to meet me in this lifetime, he looks bewildered, but he follows me anyway into the booming club. We flash the bouncer our IDs, and he looks at Tessa's a little longer than he needs to, and then he squints at one of my (many) fake IDs, all of which I bought from Yvette.

"Vanessa Gergich?" he asks. "And you're thirty-one?"

I start to sweat. This is the one downside of twelve fake IDs.

"I'm very healthy?" I offer. "I eat my vitamins. I moisturize. I moisturize *constantly*."

"She's with me," Kieran cuts in. The bouncer glances between us, then sighs.

"All right, Kir, but if she fucks up I'm telling the cops it was you."

Kieran flashes him a smile, then pulls me past the bouncer and toward the bar.

"One rum and Coke for the lady," he yells over the music, then turns to me. "That's what you like, right? I've seen you drink it a bunch."

"Yessir." I nod. "But you don't have to buy me anything. I'm a strong, independent—"

He shoves the chilled glass in my hand and slides a five across the counter to the bartender. I swirl it a bit, checking for dense foam that would indicate a dissolved pill. I mean, I trust the bartender, and Kieran. Sort of. But you can never be too careful. I sip slowly, and we stand like that, watching the writhing masses in short skirts and polo shirts grind on each other. Tessa is dancing with Ulfric, still a little shy but smiling more now. Livy is dancing with some Italian-looking guy four years too old for her. The smell of sweat and cologne practically chokes the air. Strobe lights pierce our eyes and poke holes in our patience for overused EDM music.

"Is this just..." I pause and listen to the speakers. "Is this just someone saying 'ass' on repeat?"

Kieran stops, looks up, and starts laughing. "Holy shit, you're right. What's happened to music?"

"Money," I say. "Money happened. But personally, I blame spandex and Auto-Tune."

He laughs. Livy detaches her ass from Italian guy's crotch long enough to walk over to us, breathless and smiling.

"Hey, you guys. Come over here."

We follow, curious, as she leads us to the bathroom hallway, covered in graffiti and bits of toilet paper. Livy pulls something out from her bra. She presses one into Kieran's hand, then mine. It's a small white pill shaped like a playboy bunny.

Kieran quirks an eyebrow. "Where'd you get these?"

"Heather, duh." Livy huffs. "She was practically handing them out like candy at the house."

"Is this what I think it is?" I ask.

"Molly?" Livy asks.

"*Illegal?*" I stress.

"Chill." Livy rolls her eyes. "It's just one tab. It's not gonna kill you. And Heather always buys from a reliable guy, so nothing weird's in it."

Kieran pushes it back at her. "I can't. I'm DD tonight."

"It's in and out of your system really fast," she insists. "Like, way less time than booze."

"Seeing giant red elephant monsters isn't my idea of a good time." I glare at it, but Livy smiles and pats me on the shoulder.

"Hey, it's okay. It's not a hallucinogen. It's really safe, I promise. I've done it a hundred times."

I stare at the white pill. Nameless's ugly words rear their head.

Did that stuck-up pretty boy refuse you? Is that why you're throwing yourself down the bottle?

And maybe he just doesn't want to fuck you.

No one else is going to want you.

No one else is going to want you.

I put the pill on my tongue and chug the last sip of my rum and Coke, drowning the words in their tracks. Kieran swallows his, too. I head to the dance floor and wait to die. Or have a good time. Whichever comes first. Kieran shadows behind me, dancing with me, and even if he's a little stiff in the legs and too white-guyish in the sense that all he does is rock on his feet, I still catch myself smiling. Life's been shitty, but dancing has always been good to me, for me. I can just drift and think about nothing and everything with the music keeping the darkness at bay.

I didn't know Heather bought drugs. I didn't know she supplied them to frat parties, either. On the ladder of bad things to do, that's nearly drug-dealer-level status. Or is it? I don't know shit about drugs, and even less about the people who deal them. I just know a lot of people take them, and more power to those people, but they're dangerous. Then again, I've been drinking nearly every day since that night at the centaur fountain, so who am I to judge? Who am I to get angry? I'm drinking away the pain, and that hasn't been working. So I have to try something else. No danger is as bad as the things waiting for me in my own memories.

The bright strobe lights get brighter, more colorful, greens turning into red-blue, two colors at once. I blink, but the colors keep fracturing. They flash off girls' makeup and jewelry, spots of gemstone color burning pleasantly onto my eyelids. Everyone looks so happy, so nice, so kind. No one will hurt me here. I'm surrounded by good people. The darkness can't get me here.

Kieran smiles when I smile at him, and that's a good sign, and he's much more handsome than I thought before—sort of swarthy, pirate swarthy, ~~Jack~~ Sparrow swarthy (*we don't speak that name*), strong and big-shouldered and he could protect me from the darkness, couldn't he? Someone as strong as him could fight off anything, protect me from anything. I tried to protect myself for all this time, but it was so hard. I'm so tired of doing it all alone. It would be nice to have some help. Kieran could help. Jack didn't want to help anymore, which is okay, because I'm hard, and not really worth all that effort, even if he was the only one who touched me in the good way where my heart peeked out of its shell, but it was stupid, I was so stupid for thinking—

No one else is going to want you.

I wince and lurch for Kieran, hugging him around the waist. He stops dancing.

"Isis?" he shouts. "Are you okay?"

"I'm...I'm...I'm not okay." I laugh. "I'm not. I'm just not."

"Hey, whoa, okay. Let's get you some air."

I hang on to Kieran's arm as he guides me through the crowd and out to the front of the club. I shoot a look at the bouncer as we pass.

"I'm not thirty-one," I blurt.

"I know." He rolls his eyes.

Kieran eases me onto the steps. I shiver when my eyes catch on the lit cigarette ends of a circle of smoking people. Kieran sees it and moves us away from the circle, farther down the curb. I gasp for air, choking on nothing and everything at the same time. Kieran waits patiently, staring at the star-studded sky. When the pressure is a little less and the world isn't so bright, I form words.

"I'm sorry," I say. "You should go...back in and have fun. This is not fun. This is me dying."

"You're not dying." He laughs.

"Yeah I am. A little faster than most people."

Kieran's face is blank, but Sophia's words ring in my head, a welcome relief from Nameless. Where his sound is the bark of a mad dog tearing my throat out, she's all crystal bells and raindrops.

No wonder Jack loved her.

No wonder Jack broke when he lost her.

No wonder he doesn't want anyone else ever again. No one else can compare.

I laugh, but the laugh turns into something weird, and I start biting my arm to make it stop. Kieran pulls my arm away from my mouth, and I see the ring of darker red on my shirt sleeve but only faintly.

"You're really freaking me out, Isis," he says softly.

"I freak a lot of people out. I'm freaky. Halloweentown loves me. But nobody else does. Except my mom. My mom's great, but sometimes I feel bad for leaving her behind."

Kieran is silent. I feel the darkness start ebbing away, the streetlights bright and swollen like giant amber fireflies.

"There's a guy," I say, and laugh. "But that's the story with every girl, isn't it? There's always a guy. Some guy. Some guy who hasn't done something. And I like him."

"If you like him, just go up and kiss him," Kieran says.

"You do not know how things work very well, do you?"

Kieran laughs, and I clutch my head and lean on his shoulder. The night is too dark and he is too warm and I need someone, something solid beneath me. Someone to keep me from disappearing into the shadow half of my life. Or maybe it's too late. Maybe I've already disappeared, and the darkness will be here always with only brief flashes of light, instead of the other way around. Guilt works its way into my stomach; Kieran shouldn't be dabbling with a girl full of shadows. Why does he bother? Why does anyone bother?

It hits me then: there's only one reason a guy would bother.

"Do you like me?" I ask Kieran. It's forward, but I'm nothing if not forward and stupid.

Kieran coughs. "Well…uh…"

"It's a yes or no question."

"Yeah," he says. "I do."

No one else is going to want you.

"Do you want me?" I press my chest into his shoulder like I saw Hemorrhoid do to Jack. Kieran clears his throat.

"Yeah. I mean, since I met you, I— "

I lean up and kiss him, and he kisses back with a soft, fierce edge to it. It's not Jack. It's never Jack, but it will never be Jack again, and I don't want to cry so I kiss harder, and longer, and Kieran's hand slithers up my shirt and I let it—

"You!" A voice shouts at me.

"How do you listen to this crap?" Charlie snarls, turning off my opera music.

"I take it you aren't a fan of Italian men singing their heart out over a woman?"

Charlie runs a hand through his spiked hair, rearranging it. "If I wanted to listen to assholes complain about bitches, I'd listen to Biggie Smalls. Or Nas."

"Ah yes, because referring to women as 'bitches' will get you very far in life," I say, and take a left turn at the stoplight.

"I don't care about bitches, okay? They're all whiny, and they want your money and they want you to dress nice and pick them up ice cream and huge diamond rings and I'm done with it. Just gonna focus on hustling for my mansion, and then I'll buy me some bitches."

"You won't buy bitches or a mansion. You'll buy a house for your grandmother."

Charlie shoots me a sharp look, going red. "What kind of stupid shit is coming out of your mouth right now? I swear you get dumber every day."

I park in front of a seedy club called Eternity. I can hardly bring myself to lash out at him with my usual ice. He's so soft on the inside and trying to be so hard on the outside.

He reminds me of someone.

"Well," I muster. "Hopefully you're getting smarter, because one of us has to be coherent enough to interrogate the club's owner."

Charlie just grumbles, pulling a pair of brass knuckles on under his sleeve.

"You don't need those," I say. I set my phone to record at the push of a button, in order to get hard evidence on tape.

"I make it a policy to bring them to every club I go to," Charlie scoffs. "Especially ones with drug-dealing scumbags."

"His name is Terrance," I say. "Not drug-dealing scumbag."

"I don't give a shit what his name is; let's just beat the hell out of him."

"No one beats anything." I make my words steel, permafrost. "Brittany told me about him—Terrance is a businessman. He doesn't like violence. He's easily persuaded in a number of logical ways I'd be more than happy to enlighten you with."

Charlie groans. "I don't *care*. Let's just do this. You can chat his ass up all you want, but if we ain't getting anywhere with that, I'm moving to plan B."

"The threat of violence is often more effective than violence itself. Someone soft and rich like Terrance will cave without a single punch." I get out. He follows suit, a thoughtful look coming over his face.

"You might actually be right for once." Charlie flashes his ID, and I do the same. The bouncer waves us through. "How're you and Brittany doing, by the way?"

"Fine," I respond automatically. "She's very insistent."

I don't tell him about the rumors, because he's heard them, of course. Brittany picked a fight with a girl at a party over me. She's territorial to the extreme. I don't tell him she is a thing, a means to an end I feel constantly sick about, the same way I always felt constantly and faintly nauseous working for Blanche and the Rose Club. Brittany's a puppet stand-in I mentally paste over with forbidden memories of a girl I gave up for good.

"Is that what you call it?" Charlie barks a laugh, and we weave through the edges of the club crowd. "She's banging down our door 24-7. She can barely hold herself back from jumping on your icicle dick before I'm out of the room."

I shrug. Charlie studies me carefully.

"What was it you said you did before Gregory found you?" he asks. "Because I've seen ladies' men, and even the best ones don't got girls salivating over them in broad daylight like you do. What makes you so special?"

"I know how to treat women," I say. "Step one—don't call them bitches."

"Unless they're into that," Charlie attempts to correct.

"Select few women are into degradation, and even then they only appreciate it in the bedroom. Never insult them out of it."

As Charlie's brain struggles to absorb this, I approach the VIP lounge door. Two bouncers flank it. One of them puts a hand out to stop me.

"Who're you?" he asks.

"Step aside!" Charlie juts out his chin. "We're here on business."

"Give me a name or get out," the bouncer insists.

"Jack Hunter," I say. "We're here to see Terrance. He's expecting us."

The bouncer turns away and touches his ear, speaking into an earpiece. After several seconds, he turns back and opens the door with his meaty hand. Charlie salutes him as he walks in, and I slide in after. The music dulls, champagne cooling in an ice bucket on the black glass table. The couches are leather—real and shining sleekly under the lights. Two other bouncers are sitting on them, drinking champagne and tapping away on their cell phones. They are huge and beefy, but it's nothing Charlie can't handle with an element of surprise—he's a furious Tasmanian devil in a fight, and all I ever have to do is mop up the pieces.

They look up when we come in and pat us down quickly. Charlie complains, but I silence him with a look as another man walks in and sits down. His pin-striped suit is impeccable—though he's overweight, it fits him very well. His hair is thin and gray and balding on the very top, his eyes watery and his skin a nut-brown from obsessive tanning sessions. Dozens of rings are stacked on his fingers—real gemstones, as far as I can tell. Clear, no flaws. This man is very rich and very well connected.

"Gentlemen!" Terrance smiles, sweeping his hands out and then offering one to me. "Welcome to my office. Glad you could make it on such short notice."

"It's good to be here," I say, and shake his hand. We sit, and Terrance starts pouring champagne.

"Need a drink?"

"We'll pass, thank you," I insist. "We wouldn't want to waste any more of your time than is necessary."

Terrance raises an eyebrow, then laughs a full belly laugh. "Concise and ready to get down and dirty right away. I like that. You rarely see that kind of single-minded dedication in your generation these days."

Terrance drains his glass, then claps his hands.

"All right, so what's your offer? I've already got guys on campus giving me cuts on my supply. What do you think you have that's better, huh?"

"Information," I say.

"Yeah? You know somebody better?"

"First, I'd like you to fulfill your end of the bargain. The names, if you will."

"Oh, see"—Terrance clicks his tongue—"I can't just do that without any assurance I'm gonna be getting something good. It's not right. I like those guys. Giving them up for bad info would go against my business practices."

"Listen, buddy—" Charlie snaps. The bouncers lean in suddenly, and I put my hand across Charlie's chest to stop him.

"Terrance." I stare into his eyes. "Our boss has told us much about you, but this excellent club tells us more. You're very good at what you do."

Terrance relaxes, and his bodyguards relax with him.

"I am. Thank you. Always good to get a little recognition where it's deserved."

"So I know that a businessman as skilled as yourself is very keen on gaining assets, not losing them."

Terrance narrows his eyes. "Go on."

"There are some people who have suddenly become very interested in 'your guys.'"

His eyes flash, and his fist tightens, but he keeps his voice cool and level. A true professional.

"Yeah? How important are these people we're talking about here?"

I smile. "I'm so sorry, Terrance. But without names, that's all I can tell you."

I watch the gears sync up in his mind—I've told him law enforcement is looking into his MDMA suppliers. These Gatekeeper suppliers give him a huge discount, and with a booming college town party scene right here in his club, the profits are no doubt enormous. But without knowing who exactly the authorities are, he's reluctant to give us the names and therefore lose the discount. If it's just the local police, he could bribe them. But if it's the less corruptible DEA—

"Bill," Terrance finally says. "I think one of them is named Bill, or Will, or something like that. His last name is complicated, C-something. Caraway? Carlsbad?"

"Cavana?" I try, feigning innocence.

"Cavanaugh, that's it." Terrance points. "Now, you tell me who's after them, and I'll give you the other name."

"How do we know you won't just tell them and they'll split?" Charlie snarls. Terrance smiles at him like he's a child.

"Oh, I wouldn't worry about that. We cut all ties with the ones who are being investigated, for our own safety, you understand."

Terrance looks back to me, and I lean in, lowering my voice with the lie that comes out.

"DEA. Cyber-crime ops. Your boys help out a larger group on the internet black market. Hackers, mostly."

Terrance nods, putting his fingers to his lips. "Hacking isn't my thing—the internet isn't my thing in general. I prefer to conduct business old-school."

"Which is why you'd do well to cut them off," I say. "This is far bigger than club drugs. We're talking meth. Human trafficking."

"You don't have any proof," he shoots back. I pull out one of the three USB's Vanessa supplied with the dossiers, containing any and all material on Will's misdeeds.

"If you need some time to look at it, I understand," I say as I hand it to him.

Terrance studies the USB, then looks back up at me and inhales sharply through his teeth before he hands it back to me.

"Dammit. I *knew* it was too good to be true. They're always a little more crooked than you'd like, aren't they? You've got your name—Kyle Morris. Easier to remember than the other one. Now, if you'll excuse me, I have some phone calls to make."

We get up, and he shakes my hand before we're escorted

promptly out of the lounge. The music blares again, the smell of sweat and cloying perfume practically assaulting me. Charlie follows me to the door, and he doesn't ask questions until we're on the curb.

"Why'd you lie? We ain't DEA."

"We aren't *anything*," I say. "We're third-party contractors hired by someone we don't know the identity of. We had to bluff."

Charlie makes a face but doesn't argue. "I guess Gregory was right to put you on this shit. You know some things."

It's as close to a compliment as I'll get from him, but I only barely hear it. My eyes are riveted to the curb, where two students are kissing fervently. The boy has dark hair and huge arms and is sliding his hand up the girl's red shirt, a shirt I recognize very well from a certain day in a certain high school after certain photos were posted around, and her makeup's darker and bolder than I've ever seen it, and she looks so skinny, so small against his huge hands and face as their lips meet, her hair wild around her cheeks—the passion in the kiss so bright, so tangible—and my body stops responding, my blood pumping hot and hard through every vein as the beast in me begins to growl.

"You!" Charlie shouts. The boy pulls back, and Isis Blake looks up with surprised eyes.

I yank on my own chain, pulling myself inward so I won't explode outward. I bring up every lesson of Gregory's in rapid time, his advice and the steps and methods colliding in a desperate attempt to regain control. She is kissing someone else, but I have no jurisdiction. I have no right. I broke her and I left her, and she is free to kiss whomever she wants. She deserves to be in love with whomever she wants, whenever she wants. I have no right. *I have no right*. She is not mine and I have no right, I gave up that chance, he is better than me, he is kind to her, he has to be kind to her or I'll rip out his throat—

Isis smiles, holding a hand up. "Hey, Tiny Balls," she says to Charlie. "What's up?"

His hackles go up. "Tiny what? Fuck you, bitch!"

I'm about to lunge for him when the dark-haired boy does it for me. He gets in Charlie's face, his green eyes furious.

"What did you just say to her?"

Before Charlie can throw a punch, I step between them, staring into the boy's eyes. He's the same height as I am, but his shoulders are much broader, and his core radiates muscle and power. A jock. Surprising—I didn't think she'd go for one of them.

"I apologize," I say icily, "for my friend's behavior. He doesn't know how to rein himself in sometimes."

I dare to glance at Isis over the boy's shoulder, and our eyes meet, the thorns digging in until she looks away first. The thought of her kissing him, kissing someone who isn't me with genuine want, makes me sick. But I swallow it. I have no right to feel this way.

"Kieran," Isis says. "It's okay! Really. I know them. He's just kidding around."

Kieran's breathing evens out, his eyes never leaving mine as he steps away.

"Fine. But if he says it again—"

"He won't," I add. Charlie opens his mouth to argue, but I shoot him the deadliest look I can, and he falls silent. I turn back to Kieran and Isis. "We'll be leaving. My apologies for interrupting your evening."

It's the first time she and I have been within speaking distance in weeks. Her cheeks are thin, though she tried to cover them up with blush. The dark circles under her eyes are so obvious it's painful to look at. But through all the pain she is lovely, more lovely than any girl I've seen—all red silk and dark-lined, catlike cinnamon eyes. The purposeful deadening of my senses I practiced in order to endure Brittany shatters, crumbling as every muscle begs to hold her, to stroke her wild hair, to kiss away her frown lines.

Charlie breaks the moment first, snarling some swear words as he trudges toward the car. I put a hand on Kieran's shoulder and soften my voice so only he can hear it.

"Please," I say. "Be gentle with her. Be good to her. She's a very special girl."

"To you?" Kieran murmurs.

Yes. To me.

"In general," I say instead. "She means a great number of things to many people. We all want to see her happy."

Kieran is quiet. Isis shuffles nervously behind him, hugging herself. Kieran finally speaks.

"You're the guy, huh?"

"What?"

"The one she talks about." Kieran sucks in a breath. "Damn, dude, do you know how fucked up she is? How much you've fucked her up?"

I spot it then, through the guilt his words punch into me. I stride over and touch her left wrist.

"What happened to your arm?"

Isis shivers, looking everywhere but at my face. "It's nothing."

"Nothing? Isis, there's blood—" I swear under my breath as I gingerly pull back the stained sleeve and reveal the indented teeth marks, welling with dark blood. "Who did this to you?"

"No one!" She whimpers. "I did it…I think? I don't know—it doesn't hurt. I didn't know it was that bad—"

"Look at me," I say. She twists away, but I use a harder

voice. "Isis, look at me."

She turns her face slowly, eyes meek and so un-Isis-like I barely recognize them. But I recognize the enlarged pupils, the way she's sweating, and her breathing.

I round on Kieran. "What did you give her?"

"What?" Kieran holds his hands up. "Wait a second—"

"Tell me." I stride toward him, and Kieran, a good seventy pounds heavier than me, suddenly looks nervous. "Now."

"Nothing! Shit, *nothing*! Livy gave us some molly! That's all, I swear."

"And you took it, too?" I shout. "You let her take it and took it yourself? What kind of idiot are you? What if she had a worse reaction? How could you help her if you're doped up, too?"

"She's fine!" he yells. "We were all okay before you guys came along!"

"Fine?" I roar. "Look at her arm! *Look at it!*" Kieran flinches. "She bit herself, you moron! She's far from fine, but you ignored that so you could slip your tongue in her!"

Kieran's eyes spark, and I see his muscles twitch before his fist flies toward me. Gregory's training is all but automatic—I sidestep him and hook my ankle under his, pulling back. He eats cement hard, groaning as he rolls over.

"Enough!" Isis's shout rings out. I turn and look at her, and her glare is a bonfire on the coldest winter's day. "He didn't 'let' me take anything. *I* decided to take it. So lay off him."

I still my heavy breathing. Kieran glowers from the ground, nursing his nose, but it's a muted, ashamed glower now. I dare him with my eyes to make a move, but he just sits up and swears. I pivot back to Isis.

"You have to get that looked at. Come on, there's bandages in my car—"

"I'm not going anywhere with you," she says evenly. "I'll

get it looked at on my own."

"Isis—you're injured. You have to—"

"Don't pretend to care about me now, Jackoff." She laughs.

"This isn't pretending. I do care about you."

"Well, cut it the hell out, okay? I'm not your girlfriend. I'm not even your friend anymore. You shouldn't waste your energy on me. I'm nobody important to you—" She shudders, hugging herself and laughing harder. "I'm nobody important."

You are the sun, I try to say. *You are the most important. You are the only light that's ever truly pierced my armor. You are the happiness and the spark and the one girl who never ran, who never cowered, who saw through my facade. I will never meet another girl like you; I will never want anyone as much as I want you.*

But all that comes out is self-censoring silence. Kieran gets up and puts his arm around her shoulders.

"We should go," he murmurs. They pass me, Isis refusing to meet my eyes as they turn the corner and go back into the club. Her smell lingers around me for a brief second, and I try to hold on to it as long as possible with shaking fingers as the clear, volatile truth wells up in me, past the walls of lies I've built around it (*you're not good enough for her, she never really wanted you*), past the excuses I use to deny myself happiness (*you'll hurt her, you've hurt her, all you do is hurt her*), past my own self-loathing (*you should've died instead of Sophia*). The realization shines bright, quietly exploding, blowing them all away and leaving a single truth behind.

"I miss you," I whisper to the empty curb.

chapter eleven

3 YEARS, 51 WEEKS, 6 DAYS

IN MY IMAGINARY BUT STILL VERY REAL *Book of Things That Aren't Okay with Me*, I've bumped drugs up to the number five slot, right between applesauce and jorts. In all my years of being an idiot, which is nearly two decades—as we all know, two decades is practically decrepit—I've never done anything worse to hurt myself than that molly. Except, you know, develop a mild case of an eating disorder for a few months.

All right, fine, so in my imaginary but still very real *Book of Things That Aren't Okay with Me*, developing an eating disorder is number one, and doing drugs is number two. Number three is seeing Jack Hunter's gorgeous yet infuriating face looking hurt, like I've wounded him, when it's clearly the opposite.

After straightening all this out for a whopping two days in which I sleep and skip class and visit the infirmary and Jemma, one of the main nurses, for bandages and antibiotics, I decide to reenter polite society.

Taking one step into English class, however, makes me want to take three steps out.

I arrived early, so it's not weird to see an empty auditorium, but it's super weird to see an empty auditorium and the testing room door closed. It's a tiny room only for people who've gotta do makeups, and it's never closed unless it's being used.

So, like the proper, not-nosy lady I am, I peek into the slit of a window on the door. And I immediately regret it.

There, on the other side, is Professor Summers. He sits on the desk, his floppy hair and sweater vest slightly rumpled. He's talking to someone, and when I tilt my head I can see them—his hand is around a girl's waist, and he's pulling her into his lap. Or trying to. She's fighting it, and the pleasant smile on his face makes my stomach turn. The girl in question clearly isn't happy; her expression is all screwed up. I know that look—it's utter disgust and helplessness.

I fling open the door and Professor Summers quickly stands up. The girl takes advantage of his moment of slack grip and ducks around me, dashing out of the classroom. That's all the confirmation I need that she wasn't into it. Also, she's his student! He's like, nearly forty and she's a freshman! I quash the urge to yell *you're nasty!!!* and stutter instead.

"Oh crap—I'm sorry, Professor. I didn't know anyone was in here, I just—"

He smooths his vest and coughs. "It's fine, Ms. Blake. Anabel and I were—looking for her missing pen. Very expensive. Her father gave it to her."

"Oh." I let him hang, the nervous gleam in his eyes somehow satisfying. I have to play dumb. I smile again. "Okay. Did you guys find it?"

"No." He sweeps past me and returns to his desk. "But I'm sure it'll turn up eventually."

Yeah, in your pocket. Which you'll ask her to reach into, you sicko.

But I don't say any of that. I make an excuse for the bathroom and look around wildly for the girl. I spot her in a courtyard, hiding behind a pillar and texting madly on her phone. Her eyes are a little red, but they widen when she sees me.

"I wasn't doing anything—" She chokes. "It was nothing, okay?"

"Hey, it's okay." I use my softest voice. "I'm not blaming you. That guy's a creep."

She gnaws her lip. "I should've listened. My friend told me all these rumors about him, and I just ignored it. I thought I could talk to him about my grades, try to get some advice for writing the essays he assigns, since I suck so bad at them, but then he—"

She shudders, shoving her phone in her pocket and looking at me. "You saved me."

"Naw. I was just in the right place at the right time."

She hugs herself. "He wanted me to—to blow him. So he'd give me a better grade. And I hated myself because for a second, a split second, I considered doing it. I need that grade. My mom worked so hard to send me here, and I can't let her down, and now he's going to flunk me—"

I put my hand on her shoulder. "He's not. If he does, I'll go to the office and tell them what I saw. He can't do that. It isn't fair."

"Haven't you heard?" She wipes at her eyes. "All the rumors say people have told on him before, but no one's done anything! This school doesn't give a shit, or he must be connected somehow, or—or they just don't believe what we say."

"It's probably all of those," I say. "Look, you don't have to go to him. Here, let me give you the tutoring center's number. They've got great people there. My roommate is one of them, and she's super smart in English."

"Thanks," she says once I've entered the number on her phone. "You're really nice. I'm Anabel, by the way."

"Isis." I smile. "I put my number in there, too. You ever

need anything, or if he's creeping on you again, just throw me a text. I've got ways to deal with tools like him."

She waves and starts toward her dorm, and I inch back to Summers's classroom, listening to his lecture while stabbing a pencil into my notebook.

It's not fair.

It's not fair that people with power get away with abusing it. Someone has to stop them. If the school won't listen, then someone will just have to scream too loudly to ignore and not stop ever.

My mind begins ticking away like it used to, plots and plans forming like angry frozen ghosts in my head. My old plans used to be playful, not-serious. But now I'm angry.

Now, I'm older.

Yvette is not impressed with my new diet.

"Are you eating…Doritos with ice cream?" she asks.

"My mind is strong, but my flesh is weak," I mutter through a spoonful.

"Well, at least you're eating *something*." She throws her hands up. "What happened to the Isis who could put away a pizza on her own?"

"She got bored," I say. Yvette looks appropriately scandalized. "Of eating! Not of pizza. God no. The only people who get bored of pizza are evil at their very core."

"How's the war wound holding up?" Yvette collapses on her bed. I pull my sleeve up and inspect the bandage on my forearm with a shrug.

"The nurse gave me antibiotics that taste like butt, and I have to change the bandage every two days, but so far it's like a walk in the park. If said park was covered in infectious zombies and land mines. Kieran got the worst end of the deal—broken noses hurt like a bitch."

I told Diana and Yvette my wounds were from a bar fight that broke out in the club. The last thing I want is for cool-ass people to think I take party drugs on the reg.

"Yeah, but they're quicker to fix," Yvette says. "Only hurts for a second."

"Oh yeah? How do you know that?"

"I got in a fistfight," she says proudly. "At a concert."

"What concert?"

"Does it really matter? I think you are missing the point here, the point being that I have also broken my nose." I stare at her until she mumbles, "Taylor Swift."

"*You went to a Taylor Swift concert?*" I screech.

"*I was taking my little sister!*" she shrills defensively.

"Why does it sound like a cage of birds in here?" Diana winces as she walks in.

"Di, she's making fun of me," Yvette whines. I courteously flip her off.

"If you met me at the pizza place, like I *asked*," Diana sniffs, "you wouldn't be here, getting made fun of."

Yvette groans and rolls off the bed, riffling through her closet for a jacket to wear. Diana sits on the bed beside me, all smiles.

"Hey you."

"Don't look at me, I'm hideous," I whisper, shoveling more soggy Doritos into my mouth. She laughs and smooths her low-cut shirt that makes her impressive rack all the more bouncy.

"And what are you doing on this lovely Friday night?"

"Eating. Sleeping. Sacrificing a goat to Mantorok, the god of corpses."

She looks over at the stack of fake blood packets on my desk and raises an eyebrow. "Riiiight."

"Those are for a sociology experiment!" I defend. "Called

'see how many people run away from me when I squirt fake blood at them.' Prediction: many."

"Okay but…just don't get punched out, all right? Getting a new injury every weekend is sort of a new thing with you, and I'd like for it to kindly stop forever."

"You and me both."

Yvette flaunts her army surplus jacket; Diana and I applaud. They're gone before I can blink, Yvette crowing about pepperoni and jalapeños. My stomach makes a disagreeing noise, and I put the ice cream bowl aside and bring out my laptop. I get on Skype, looking for Kayla's photo, but she's offline, the little gray "inactive" dot taunting me.

It's nice Diana's worried. It's only been two months, but she and Yvette treat me like they've known me for years. Sometimes it makes me feel better, but right now it only makes everything feel worse. It makes me miss Kayla more. I hadn't gotten to tell her about what happened that night at Eternity, but part of me doesn't want to. Part of me hesitates to blab everything like I usually do. What would she think of the fact that I took molly? She's already seen me get in a fight. I didn't tell Diana or Yvette the truth. I haven't told anybody.

Would Kayla be disappointed? Would she hate me? I'm still disappointed in *myself* that I took it. And she wouldn't be happy to hear about Jack and how we're still strangers. And I know for a fact she'd hate my stories of drinking at frat parties. She wouldn't understand it. I'd just disappoint her. My life isn't exciting and romantic like hers, all neat and organized. My life is just a series of fuckups and sadness.

There it is again. Jealousy. I swallow it whole and try to convert it into exactly what it is—poop.

I get up and stretch, tracing the bandage on my arm lightly. Jack touched me there, and it's stupid to think about, but sometimes in the quiet moments I touch the same place and wish things were different. But tonight is not the night for self-pity. I pull on jeans and a loose T-shirt and stuff a side bag full of the fake blood packets, some gum, forceps, and a credit card.

Tonight is the night for revenge.

Granted, as I walk through the sunset-washed campus with happy couples clinging to each other and excited, dolled-up girls on their way to parties, I have the minor revelation that I probably shouldn't be doing this. I brush off the nonsense—*of course* I should be doing this. Doing possibly illegal things that would get me kicked out, such as breaking into Professor Summers's office and sending him a message, is going to be hells more fun than sitting around another frat party waiting to die. People stare. But then again, people have always stared. I smile and wave.

I've done my own independent study on Professor Summers—asking around parties didn't exactly make it hard to find the girls he'd previously harassed. He'd do it quietly—dropping reflective pens, coming up behind them after class and pinning them to whiteboards, asking them to come in on Saturdays and offering A's for a hand job. He's 100 percent scum. And the worst part? He doesn't look like scum. He's almost cute—mousy hair, a thin beard, blue eyes. But the worst people rarely look like the worst people. I learned that from Avery.

Professor Summers's office is in the Denney building, which is about as ironically fitting as we can get for a Friday night in a Midwestern college town. Denney closes at seven, but I manage to sneak in at six fifty and hide in a bathroom. The janitor comes around checking the stalls, and when she asks me to leave I groan and empty a blood packet into the toilet. It makes a satisfying plop noise, and she sighs and tells me to get out when I can.

I hiss in victory as she shuffles with her cleaning cart down the hall. I pack everything up and flush the evidence before tiptoeing out of the bathroom. I pass Ferguson's office, and then Vacroix's, and as I turn the corner—

My ringing phone scares my intestines out of my anus.

"You scared my intestines out of my anus!" I say when I pick up.

"Where are you?" Kieran asks on the other end, the distinct muffled boom of bass in the background. "You said you were coming to Rho Alpha Alpha tonight, but I can't find you."

"I am currently engaged elsewhere. Minus a ring. And a bachelorette party."

Kieran's quiet, then his voice lowers. "Isis, you aren't doing what I think you're doing."

"I'm not, don't worry!" I chirp.

He groans. "You are. You totally are. You're gonna get busted and thrown out. Just forget about Summers and come to the party!"

I check my phone. "Oh my, is it that time already? Shut up o'clock? I must go, farewell, sweet prince."

"Isis—!"

I hang up and slither down the corridor with the grace of an oiled sidewinder. Summers's office is the last on the right, and I crouch and immediately begin assessing my foe. It takes me three minutes of strenuous lock-jiggling to find out these locks are much, much sturdier than anything I picked during high school. There's no way I'm getting in.

This is where most people would paste a giant GAME OVER in their heads.

Thankfully, Isis Blake is not most people.

I pull as many blood packets as I can out of my pack and start decorating. I'm halfway through when the janitor calls into the same bathroom for me. My heart jackrabbits around in my throat and I squeeze out the last few words as quick as

I can. I hear her footsteps about to turn the corner just as I jam everything into my pack and skid around the opposite one.

She squints, her eyesight obviously bad, but she can't see the wall I defaced—parallel to the windows—from that angle. She sighs and trudges back the way she came, and I jam on the gas full blast and beat her to the front door, taking the steps two at a time as cool twilight air washes over my victorious face.

If she sees it, she'll get rid of it, and it'll have been a glorious adventure all for naught. But if she skips it over, then tomorrow—

I smother a laugh and reinstate myself as best in the world at everything. The high is so familiar, so enthralling, that all I can think about is it—just *it*. Just my victory, just my near-busted status, just the retribution a pervy scumsucker like Summers will get if anyone other than him sees what I did. It might not be proof, and it might not convince anyone fully, but it'll breed doubt in their minds, and doubt's the most insidious thing there is.

Tonight, I don't need any parties to keep away the yawning chasm of silent pain. Tonight I'm high on my own brand of drug—pure, stupid recklessness. I wash fake blood off my hands and head to the nurse's office for my bandage change, laughing under my breath.

I'm crazy and going crazier, and I don't know how to stop it.

I don't know how to stop this horrible darkness from eating me alive, and no one in the world is going to help me.

I'm alone.

Tonight I don't need any parties, but I go to the Rho Alpha Alpha party anyway, because it's become habit. Because it's who I am now, who I always was. Who I used to be. Because once upon a time I was a stupid fourteen-year-old who drank and smoke and spat with the best of them in a desperate attempt to look cool, and I did anything to look cool back then, because when you're big like I used to be, people only see how huge you are and forget you're a person with feelings, but if you're huge and you party, you're a little cooler than not cool at all. Letting them make fun of how big you are (*whale, fatso, piggy*) makes you a little cooler than not cool at all.

I look around at the faces at the party, skinny and tan and glittery with makeup and good looks, and I know they'd be the first to call me fatso if I was the old me. They smile at me *now*, Heather and Livy and Tessa smile at me *now*, but they'd change so fast, become mean and ugly so fast, if I were the old me. They don't like me for who I am—they aren't Kayla or Wren—but I'm trying, trying to make them fit in the spaces left behind, and I hate myself, I hate that they left me behind—

I hate them. I hate every single person here and I don't even know them.

Kieran comes up to me, a rum and Coke in hand. His frown is obvious, but I smile and take the drink with the practiced grace of an alcoholic marquise.

"Don't give me that look, Kir." I sigh. "Do you know how many professor dudes like him get away with shitty stuff? I mean, he was gonna get what was coming to him. I just sped up the process a bit."

"You put a brick on the gas pedal," he corrects.

"I put a brick on the gas pedal," I cheerfully agree, then sip. "God bless America."

Kieran waits for a lull in the music before he speaks. "My sister used to pull crazy stunts like you."

"*Used* to?"

"She's in a mental hospital now."

"Awful place," I say. "Really sorry. You should bust her out."

He stares at me, and I shrug.

"Well, if you won't, I will."

"You don't have to save everyone, Isis."

His words trip me, my thoughts skidding to a halt.

"I'm not saving anyone," I say carefully.

Kieran shakes his head. "You try to. You try to stop all these injustices and save people from them. But you never try to save yourself."

I'm quiet. Kieran slides his hand down to mine and squeezes.

"What are you waiting for?"

I look down at our joined hands and whisper, "For someone else to do it, I guess."

Kieran leans in and kisses me, tasting like tequila and lime and salt, and for a moment his lips aren't his, they're Jack's, and we aren't at a fraternity house, we're at Avery's, and there's less glitter and heels and experience but just as much booze and swearing—seventeen isn't so different from eighteen, and this kiss drives away the darkness, makes it scuttle back under the rocks—but then I open my eyes and see Kieran's green ones and flinch. I have to tell him. I can't keep using him like this, but I am, because being with him is better than being alone, and I'm a coward. Before either of us can break the awkward silence, Heather runs up and grabs my arm.

"There you are! I've been looking so hard for you! C'mon, one of your friends wants to talk to you."

I follow her lead, glancing one last time back at Kieran. She leads me with impressive force up the stairs and to a room.

"Uh," I offer eloquently. "Who wants to talk to me?"

"This guy." She hiccups. "He was really insistent. He said he's your friend."

I can tell she's trying hard to make up for getting me into that fight by doing this. A friend wants to see me. Jack?

No—he's written me out of his life. There's only one person left. Nameless. I face the door down like it's an angry bear. Behind it, there will be his face, the face that triggers so many of my awful memories.

He has that video.

I've never seen it. I've always wanted to, ever since Wren told me he had a camera that night when they were in middle school and Avery forced him to film "it." Whatever "it" was. It's solid evidence of what happened that night, that awful night that haunted Sophia until her death, and haunts Wren and Jack still today. If I can see it, then I'll know what happened after practically two years of not knowing.

Nameless might have it. But my need to know burns hotter than my panic. I swallow hard and open the door. Nameless sits on a bed, smiling. He opens his arms to me.

"There you are, Isis. Care to watch a movie with me?"

Heather giggles, then pats me on the shoulder with a wink and flounces off downstairs.

Nameless clears his throat. "In or out, Isis. It's your choice."

"I'm not going to walk in there," I manage.

"You will," he says. "If you want to watch a certain video."

He's going to trap me in there. I just know it. He wants to see me squirm above all else—he toys with people like they're inanimate objects moved for his pleasure. And me? He's always enjoyed tormenting me. Especially now. Especially after everything.

I watch him hold up a tablet, the screen flickering in his eyes.

"It's a very interesting video," he says airily.

It's right there. It's less than ten feet from me—the answer to all my questions. I cross the threshold, leaving the door open behind me. Nameless chuckles.

"Ah, ah, close that door, if you would."

I hesitate. For the briefest moment, he ups the volume on the tablet, and I hear Sophia's voice crying out for Jack, and it rips my heart in two. I shut the door behind me with shaking hands, and he smiles.

"You look tense. Relax," Nameless says. "I'm not going to do anything."

My eyes dart wildly around, and I grab a nail file off the dresser, clutching it like a knife at him. He just laughs harder.

"I forgot how funny you are."

I tighten my grip and back up as far as I can against the door. I briefly think of flipping the light switch to freak him out, but he's got a lamp on by the bedside.

Nameless stares at me, thinking, and finally he claps his hands, applauding me slowly. Each clap is a bullet that pierces the building hysterical tension in my chest.

"I'm congratulating you for taking on such a dangerous person as a nemesis."

I narrow my eyes. "Jack?"

"Jack," he confirms.

"I know you stole that video from the Feds."

He laughs. "Steal? Don't be stupid. Even I can't hack into a federal vault. They gave it to me. Well, not me, but some friends of mine. We work together, you see, on the internet, as freelance digital consultants. The Feds contacted us and gave it to us. They wanted us to enhance the video quality as much as we could, so they could identify exactly what happened."

I swallow hard. Nameless smiles.

"And we did. But we never gave it back to them. Not yet, anyway. I wanted you to be the first one to see it, in all its enhanced glory."

"Why?"

"So you can see exactly who you're dealing with," Nameless says smoothly. "Jack isn't a nice guy. It's a good thing you two aren't speaking anymore, otherwise you might've gotten hurt."

A sick, dark fire flares up in my lungs. *He* hurt me. Not Jack. Nameless smirks at my impotent silence, then throws me the tablet with the play button smack-dab in the center. My finger wavers, hesitating.

"Go on," Nameless urges, smiling even bigger.

After months of wondering, infuriating hints, and half truths, I have the whole story beneath my index finger.

I press play.

There's two seconds of darkness and then the sound of rustling leaves. The time in the lower corner reads 21:45:01, making it roughly ten at night, and 8/15/2011. I do the math—Jack was thirteen.

"Take the fucking cap off!" a voice that can only be Avery's mutters. "God, for being such a huge nerd you're kind of an idiot."

There's a muffled grumble I recognize instantly as Wren, a younger Wren with a higher voice but definitely Wren. The camera cap comes off, unveiling a leafy ground and tall trees that are so familiar. Avery, a young Avery with no curves yet, wears a tube top, a white skort, and jelly sandals, looking imperious and bratty as ever. She grabs the camera and huffs.

"You hold it like this." She points it at Wren. He's so skinny and short, his glasses practically swallowing up his entire terrified, innocent face. His cheeks are still round with baby fat. He wears cargo shorts and a striped shirt his mom obviously picked out for him, and a massive watch twice the size of his tiny wrist.

"I don't know if this is such a good idea," he whispers. Avery zooms in on his face.

"If you chicken out, I'm going to tell everyone at school about your mom cheating on your dad. So you're gonna stay here, and you're gonna be the cameraman, if you know what's

good for you."

Wren goes an even paler shade of white. The camera focuses on Wren's face, then goes dark. It starts back up again, reading a new timestamp: 22:07:15, or ten at night. It's much darker, and Avery swears.

"Shit. What's taking them so long?"

"Does this thing have a…a light?" Wren asks timidly. Avery rolls her eyes but you can barely see it.

"Yeah, because we're going to film secretly with a giant camera light."

"Then how—"

There's a jostling of the camera, and suddenly everything is night vision—green and shades of black and gray. Avery's pupils are white, glowing eerily as she hands the camera back.

"Just stay focused on her, okay?"

The camera shakes, like Wren's hand is unstable. "Avery, I don't want to. I don't want to do this anymore—"

"Shh!" Avery hisses, lying flat on the ground and pulling him down with her. "There she is. Just film."

My breath catches. Wren zooms in on a pale figure cutting through the forest trees.

Sophia.

Thirteen-year-old Sophia.

Her hair is short, but the same color of winter moonlight. She carries a flashlight. She's skinny, but much plumper than when I knew her—her cheeks are robust and filled out and her blossoming curves are noticeable. A flush dons her face, and she skips. Skips! I never once saw Sophia go any faster than a floaty, leisurely walk. She's wearing a sundress, floral and wavy around her calves. She looks around, calling out.

"Jack? Jack, where are you? C'mon, you're freaking me out."

"J-Jack's not really here, is he?" Wren whispers.

"Of course not, idiot," Avery scoffs. "I just forged a note

from him and stuck it in her purse. They're soooo in love, she'll believe anything."

The camera focuses on Sophia, now looking very scared. It's eerie and heartbreaking all at once to see her alive on camera, and so happy. So different.

Her flashlight beam bounces around, landing in the bushes Avery and Wren are hiding in. They duck lower, and the beam passes as Sophia does a slow turn. She freezes and then starts backing up.

"W-Who are you?"

The beam illuminates a bearded middle-aged man with a cruel smirk. He wears overalls, and an oily rag sticks out of his pocket.

"They're just gonna scare her, right?" Wren whispers frantically to Avery. Avery doesn't say anything, her attention rapt on Sophia. "Right, Av?" Wren presses. He swings the camera back to Sophia, his hand shaking harder and the camera shaking with it. Another man walks out of the trees, and another. Five of them. One of them has a baseball bat; another has what looks like a crowbar. The one in overalls talks in a low voice to Sophia as she backs up, into the trees, her face twisted with horror. Only Sophia's high, panicked voice can be heard.

"Leave me alone! My friends are in the house! If I scream, they'll call the cops!"

This earns a laugh from the man, and it spreads to the other men, until it resembles a ring of hoarse hyenas. She is so defenseless, I tremble with the urge to reach in and pull her out, pull her to safety.

"Av!" Wren hisses. "Call them off!"

Avery's smile just gets wider. "Not yet. They haven't really scared her yet."

"They're going to—they're not going to touch her, are they?"

Avery glowers. "No. I ordered them to just…just scare the shit out of her. But they can't touch her. I told them they can't."

Wren swings back to the men, now so close they've formed a ring around Sophia. She tries to run, but one of them catches her and throws her to the ground in the center. There's more laughter.

"Leave her alone!"

That voice is young, strong, angry. I've never heard it sound that way before, but I know whom it belongs to by heart. Jack, proud and tawny-haired, draws all the men's attention. His blue eyes aren't icy, instead burning with white-blue fire. He still has baby fat on his cheeks, but the rest of him is tall, lanky; a boy-growing-too-fast kind of lanky. And he's just as infuriatingly handsome. But he's not the Ice Prince I know now—his expressions boil over, his emotions clear and legible in his every tensed muscle and flexing fist. He is a lion, a little king, angry and righteous and true.

Two of the men start toward Jack, but he ducks under their grasp and bolts for Sophia. One man throws himself on Jack, slamming them both to the ground in a spray of pine needles and dirt.

"Jack!" Sophia screams. Jack swears, kicking and punching and thrashing like a wild animal, but the other two men catch up and put his arms behind him in a lock, forcing him to his knees.

A soft fog starts to roll in through the trees. The other men turn to Sophia, who screams and curls against a tree trunk like it'll offer her some protection.

"Leave her alone!" Jack screams, a piercing scream that rips my heart into jagged pieces. "You fucking bastards, pick on someone who can fight back! No! No, Sophia! Sophia, run!"

"N-No," Avery's voice is clear, though Wren seems to be paralyzed, focused entirely on Sophia and Jack. "No, this isn't

how it's supposed to— Back off. Just back off."

Her whispered commands don't work. The men close in, and Sophia puts her head in her hands.

"Help me, Jack," she cries. Some of the men sway, obviously drunk, as they close the gap and start pulling at Sophia's dress. I choke back bile but Jack reacts quicker—the man holding him cries out and collapses, and Jack jumps up, scooping the aluminum baseball bat the man dropped and swinging it into the man, over and over and over. Avery swears. Two men dive for Jack, but Jack slips through their meaty arms and swings for their skulls, a hollow, sickening thwack *resounding through the trees when metal meets bone. The fourth man fumbles with something in his jacket, a gun maybe, but Jack ducks behind the first man who's hauled himself off the ground, and the bullet cuts into the man's shoulder, the force of it pinning him to the ground again. Jack takes the moment to lunge in, slamming the bat over the gunman's neck. He crumples like a rag doll, the gun dropping into the leaves.*

The whole time, Jack is grinning madly, his mouth and face blood-spattered.

The fifth man, the one who'd pinned Sophia to the tree, frantically backs up. Jack slams the bat into his side, and the man staggers into the leaves, reaching for the gun. But Jack swings again, and Sophia screams. Something cracks, and it isn't the bat, and the man holds his hand up, and against the night vision it's a cluster of broken bones and mangled meat and dangling skin. The man looks at it, stunned, and then the pain catches up to him, and he starts crying and crawling away and begging.

"Please, man, we didn't mean— We weren't gonna—"

The man gets up and starts running, and Jack throws back his head and laughs, and then chases after him. They disappear into the gloom, the night vision losing sight of them, but not of the sobbing Sophia, who staggers to her feet and tries to pull her dress back on. She's shaking too badly. She tries to walk away, but trips on something, and her fall isn't far but she rolls down the hill, hitting trees with vicious momentum until she rolls to a stop. There's a stunned silence, minutes ticking by as Sophia squirms and there's a squelching noise and then she goes still, her white-blond hair splaying in the pine needles.

"Holy fuck," Avery whispers. "Holy—"

From the darkness, Jack returns, and a shiver runs through me; his grin is gone and an even more terrifying expression is in its place—one I've come to know very well.

The mask.

The ice mask is wearing him.

But it lasts for only a second, because when he sees Sophia he makes a choked noise and runs to her, dropping the bloodstained bat and cradling her in his arms.

"Soph," he whispers. "Sophie, Sophie please—"

He holds his hand out, sticky and wet with blood. Sophia doesn't move. He pats the pine needles around Sophia's body and chokes again, the sound of a wild animal shot through. Blood. A pool of blood around her pelvis, her floral dress stained with it.

There's a noise, like Avery shifting and her shoe breaking a twig. Jack's head snaps up, eyes glowing an unholy white with the night vision, and he grabs the bat, face twisting with rage. Avery swears and takes off running, and as Jack advances, Wren's paralysis breaks and he drops the camera, the lens barely catching his shoes as they flash by. Jack's bigger shoes pass just a split second after.

"I'll kill you!" His screams echo. "I'll fucking kill you all!"

He keeps screaming, the sound fading and coming back, like he's walking in circles. The metallic noise of a bat splintering wood resounds, and his screams are deep and strong and furious and riddled with pain, and over them,

Nameless finally speaks.

"He keeps screaming. Then he calls 911. And then the tape cuts out."

The tablet screen goes blue, then dark. My hands want to shake, but I compose them. Nameless is watching me for a reaction. I can't give him that satisfaction. I'm disturbed and on the verge of tears, but I won't show him that.

"So?" I ask. "What was I supposed to learn from this?"

Nameless quirks a brow. "You weren't terrified? He beat four men to a pulp and killed the last one— "

"The last one ran off the cliff because it was dark," I say smoothly. "Jack didn't push him. Joseph, the man he thinks he killed, killed himself."

"He wouldn't have been running if Jack wasn't chasing him," Nameless counters. "Don't defend him. He killed a man, and he's going to jail for it once we turn this tape in to the feds."

"He didn't, and there's no body anyway," I retort. "You can't prove anything."

"Belina Hernandez. You know her, don't you? You went to visit her."

"How do you know— "

"It wasn't hard to dig up facts. Belina Hernandez is the wife of Joseph Hernandez, the man who ran off the cliff. Your bloodthirsty nemesis has been paying her child support under the guise of federal funds because he's so guilt-ridden. How do you think it'll look when the jury sees that? He's practically convinced he killed Joseph, and that'll convince the jury."

"He was protecting Sophia!" I snarl.

"Protecting is one thing. Mindless violence is another. This tape shows the difference very clearly."

I clutch the tablet and weigh the pros and cons of throwing it into an incinerator, but Nameless laughs.

"I know what you're thinking. Don't try it. I have many copies on different hard drives. You'd just be ruining a perfectly good tablet."

Nameless stands, and I shrink into myself, fully aware again of how close we are to each other in this room.

"I wanted to show you just who you think you're in love with. He's not me, that's for sure. He's worse than me. He's a killer. He'll hurt you more than I ever did."

He ducks just in time as I throw the tablet at his head, my chest heaving. It clunks against the wall, leaving an indent in the pink paint.

"Fuck you," I spit. "No one will ever hurt me more than you did. I won't let them."

The door behind me suddenly unlocks, and a wild-eyed guy with an afro walks in.

"Oh, u-uh, shit. Sorry, wrong room."

I lunge for the door, but Nameless calls me back.

"It's been nice talking with you. I know you don't like it, but you'll have to do a lot more of it."

"Why?" I whisper. He smiles.

"I saw you defacing Summers's office. Even took a video of it for myself. What will the dean think of that, I wonder?"

"Why?" I repeat. "Why the fuck are you on my case all the time?"

"Because"—he cocks his head like a mildly interested bird—"you're mine."

My stomach goes cold, and he laughs.

"You've always been mine, Isis. You know that. And no one, not even a pretty boy in shining armor, can come between us. Not after what we've shared."

I run as far as I can from the room, from the house. When Nameless's voice finally fades in my head, I collapse onto the lawn and throw up on the grass.

chapter twelve

4 YEARS, 0 WEEKS, 0 DAYS

SEEING AND TALKING to Nameless is one thing.

Seeing and talking to him the day before the anniversary of his evildoings is too coincidental. He had to have planned that. Or not. Maybe I'm the only one who remembers the exact date everything went to shit. He probably couldn't care less.

In the last few years of my short yet brilliant and extremely fucked-up life, I'd take the day off from school in Florida, play hooky. I'd walk down to the beach with McDonald's and count crabs and collect little jewel-colored rocks. I tried to go easy on myself, since on that day no one had gone easy on me. Last year I hadn't done anything at all, because I was so wrapped up in the war with Jack.

Looking back, I should've realized the only boy in the world who managed to distract me from my pain was special. Special and worth keeping around. Maybe I knew that subconsciously, because I tried to keep him around in my own way, in my "ha-ha I planted fake drugs in your locker and pried into your past" way, which admittedly probably wasn't the *best* way. But I was so out of practice asking people to be my friend, asking them to stay, it was all I could do. Be annoying. Be loud, and people will remember you and maybe hopefully stay.

Maybe hopefully.

You try to. You try to stop all these injustices and save people from them. But you never try to save yourself.

I shake Kieran's voice out of my head and make a quick damage assessment. Nameless is gonna give the feds back the video, and Jack will be in a whole new world of shit. Even better—he has footage of me defacing Summers's office. Has he been stalking me? My unquenchable zeal for justice blinded me, and I went completely overboard and into the sea, but that is honestly nothing new; the only new thing is this time I could get kicked out of college for it.

College! Collagen! Collage! This isn't high school. This is the Real World™ waiting for me to slip so it can open its mouth and swallow me whole. College is the end-all-be-all, the big, cool thing you're supposed to do so you can get a degree and put it on your wall or use it as kindling when your student loans eat the money for your heating bill, I guess, and sometimes it helps you get a job, but all the upperclassmen at my old high school went to college and got a degree and then worked at American Eagle or Starbucks anyway, so I'm fairly certain it would be more useful as toilet paper, or, if you're feeling particularly vindictive about your college experience, a maxi pad. I worked hard to be here, didn't I? I think I did. I can't exactly remember; it's a blur of school assignments and "your mom" jokes and bad fish sticks. If I get kicked out of college, I'll bring shame to my entire family and Dad will be disappointed and Mom will be happy I'm back, probably, and I'll be sinking my future into the ground with a jackhammer and condemning myself to a life of flipping burgers, and blood will probably start raining from the sky or something. *Everyone goes to college*. That's just something Middle America does, and I'm definitely privileged Middle America.

If everyone goes here, why do I feel like I'm a seal in a fishpond?

Why do I need to go to college again? To figure out what I want to do? But I already knew what I wanted to do, and that was to get out of this state. Get away. Go to Europe. But I couldn't leave Mom, so I compromised.

I put my feet up on my desk and frown.

Getting kicked out of college is nothing compared to getting arrested for murder.

The tape lingers in my mind, Wren's young face and Sophia's healthy face and Jack's furious, heartbroken one. I wandered right into all that without even considering their feelings. I forced my way down the shittiest, darkest rabbit hole, their rabbit hole, and they somehow tolerated me for it.

If I close my eyes for too long, I hear Jack's screaming again.

If I close my eyes for too long, Nameless's laughter mixes with it and makes thinking impossible.

My arm throbs, and I remember I have to get the bandage changed, so I head to the infirmary.

"Isis?"

I recognize the voice. It was shouting at me last time I heard it. Sure enough, Mildred stands there, a bunch of textbooks in her arms. Her eyes are softer than I remember.

"Oh God, hi, look, I'm really sorry about that night at the party—" I start, but Mildred holds up her hand.

"Don't. I don't really feel like talking about it. I don't like you, and I don't want to like you. I just wanted to say I'm sorry."

I frown, and she sighs and flips one wisp of red hair over her shoulder.

"I'm with Jack, right? The hottest guy on campus, pretty much. The hottest guy I've ever seen, that's for sure. And so I thought I was super lucky or whatever, but then this guy starts talking to me at this party—another one, not Jack."

"Guy?" I narrow my eyes.

"Yeah, sort of cute. Dark hair, really intense gray eyes."

That sounds like Nameless—why would he do that? No, I know exactly why he'd do that. To hurt me. To make me suffer in any small way he could. To make someone else hate me as much as he does. I let my guard down, and he shot at me from another angle, and I didn't even see the bullet this time.

"Anyway, he starts telling me about you, and how you and Jack used to fool around in high school. And I was so drunk, I guess I— " She gnaws her lip. "He kept telling me all this shit, and I believed it. So the next time I saw you, at that party, I just— I just lost it."

"It didn't help that I called you a colorful name," I remind her, then kick myself for reminding her. But she just shrugs.

"I guess. But it was shitty of me to listen to some stranger and go wild off whatever he said. He was just so persuasive, and I was super fucked up. Anyway, I've felt really bad about it these last few weeks and I wanna stop feeling bad, honestly. So. I'm sorry."

"Me, too," I say.

Mildred sniffs. "I'm Brittany, by the way. So you don't have to call me names anymore."

"Okay. Hi, um, Brittany."

"Hi," she says, looking me up and down one last time. "Bye."

I watch her go, opening my mouth a few times. I want to say something, but it gets blocked each time, until finally, "Brittany!"

I run to catch up to her, and she mercifully waits.

"What is it?"

"Is Jack—" I swallow hard. "Is Jack doing okay?"

Brittany frowns. "What do you mean?"

"Is he… Does he smile? Is he— Is he eating okay?"

"How should I know? We don't like, live together. And yeah. He smiles, like every normal person."

Some tight knot I didn't know I had in my throat loosens, and I grin. "That's great. Thanks. Have a good day."

She turns and leaves again, and I watch her go. She's very pretty, and very honest and straightforward. She's the opposite of me, and maybe that's what Jack wants. Maybe that's what he needs.

I swallow what's left of the knot and head toward the infirmary again.

Jemma is a pretty woman with brown hair and big dark eyes like a deer. She sits me down the second I walk in and peels the bandage on my arm back carefully. The smell is rotting flesh and stale cotton balls. She doesn't even wrinkle her nose.

"Well, it's looking good. You're taking those antibiotics I gave you, right?"

"I made a candy necklace out of them and I've been chewing it in class."

She fixes me with a stern gaze, and I sigh.

"Two a day with meals."

Jemma smiles. "Good. You can't imagine how dirty a human mouth is and what it can do to a wound."

I fidget as she dresses my wound, my eyes catching on a fishbowl full of condoms she has on the counter. She unfortunately catches me staring.

"Are you sexually active?" Jemma asks.

"Nay, madam."

"Do you plan on being sexually active?"

"In the entirety of my future as a living human being I would certainly hope so. But, you know. Things could change. Meteors could strike. The sun could go cold and peanut butter could stop being gross and I could get smart."

Jemma stares at me forever. Fivever. Her brown eyes are huge and knowing and for a second I could swear she knows me, knows what I'm all about in a creepy crystal-ball way. And then her eyes soften, and I know she knows. She knows what happened without my saying much at all.

And it makes me angry—angry that I'm so obvious. Angry that I'm too weak to hide it anymore. The bruises and the booze and the flurry of make-outs have only made me weaker, and I didn't want that shit. I wanted to be stronger. Better. More experienced.

"I've been having some problems," I say carefully. Jemma takes out a clipboard slowly, like she knows she won't be able to take notes on this at all.

"Where does it hurt?" she asks.

There's a moment, a moment where I could get up and walk out and leave her to less complicated problems, problems that pills and casts and shots can fix.

"I tried shots for my problems, too," I say finally. "Vodka shots. But it didn't work because that's not how it works. You can't just shoot things over and over and expect them to get better."

Jemma's silent, writing fluidly.

"Bad things happen, and you tell yourself that's life, because you've lived a while and you know bad things happen, and they'll keep happening, but you try to stay alive even after they do because you know it isn't all bad, so you keep moving, keep going, try to put space between you and the bad things so you forget about them, but they always catch up, and then they sit on your back and make you trip while you try to move forward and it sucks." I knead my forehead with my knuckles. "It just fucking sucks."

A couple sits outside the window below us, holding hands on the bench, and I want to be them and barf on them at the same time.

"And sometimes you get tripped so much and so hard you just feel like staying down, you know? Like, maybe you deserve to stay down, maybe it's meant to be. Maybe it's just easier to stay down. You don't have the energy to haul your ass off the ground again, anyway."

"It sounds terrible," Jemma says softly.

"It's the worst!" I laugh. "It's everything you don't want to happen to you. You think you're strong and that you'll always love living and want to live, but sometimes you get so tired..."

"You're tired a lot, then."

I shrug. "Sometimes. But I'm Isis Blake. I'm the opposite of tired. Derit. Being tired just isn't something I do."

"We all do it once in a while, Isis," Jemma assures me. "No one is an exception."

"But I'm special!" I whine. "You don't understand! Crazy shit is my forte and I *do stuff*, the best stuff, and I never stop moving ever except when I am peeing and even then sometimes not. Side note: the janitor hates me."

Jemma tries to hide the laugh-snort behind her hand, eyes twinkling, and suddenly I start laughing, too. But it's a different laugh from the angry, short laughs I've been making lately—it's loud and happy, and it only gets louder and happier, and it's light, the lightest thing I've done in a long time.

"That wasn't even my best joke." I sigh when we both calm down. "And I broke rule numero uno."

Jemma wipes away a tear. "Which is?"

"Never laugh at your own joke, because that means it's probably not a very good one and also you look like an easily amused, self-absorbed asshole."

"I see what you mean now," she says. "Someone like you, so vibrant and funny, is rarely tired. It must be so strange for you when you are."

"It's like...like losing a leg but trying to run a race anyway," I say. Jemma nods, then inhales.

"I know this isn't going to sound very sensitive, and please don't take this to mean I'm diagnosing you with anything, because I'm not qualified to do that, but does anyone in your family have a history of depression?"

I melt all over the chair dramatically and grumble. "My mom. But I don't have it!" I protest, sitting straight up. "I swear to you I definitely don't, because I've worked really hard to not have it and I'm happy all the time so I don't have it. Ever. And I never will."

Jemma nods and writes on the clipboard, but my words are so hollow and wrong-sounding I burn to fill them up with the truth. I squirrel my hands and clutch them together tight.

"I had it. Maybe. I think. When I was fourteen."

"What made you think that?"

"I didn't like myself. I still don't a little. But I really didn't like myself because I was huge and I thought being huge was wrong, but it's not, but when you're in love and a guy tells you you're ugly and fat you start to believe it, you know? Also it wasn't love. Maybe it was. But probably not, because it made me feel horrible, and love's supposed to make you feel good."

"Some people say it's supposed to make you feel good and horrible at the same time."

"Well, those people are dumb and wrong." I jut my chin. "That's just...that's just the old-man-poetry-romanticism of it. People like to sound deep, so they say pain is a part of love, but it's not. Love is—"

"There is nothing about it that is ugly," Jack says. "May I?"

I hesitate, then nod. He reaches around and brings my

forearm up, gently running his fingers over the cigarette burns on my wrist. He traces around each circle with his thumb gently, so gently.

"It looks like a galaxy." He smiles. "Full of stars and supernovas and conductive cryogeysers and a lot of wonderful science things I could go on to list that would probably bore the hell out of you."

"—Love is being accepted and adored for who you are, scars and all."

My eyes get wet and my lap gets wet and I curl in on myself, hugging my arms.

Now I know the difference.

Now I know what love is and what it isn't.

Jemma puts the clipboard down and her arms up, enclosing me in them as the darkness comes rushing out of my mouth and into her sweater.

"I w-was…I was r-raped. When I was fourteen. By the guy I thought I loved."

It pours out of me; it falls on the floor and pools on the tile and slithers down my cheeks. Four years of carefully silent suffering floods her office, and her lap, and I'm a stranger and she must hate me for it, but all she does is hug me closer, and I hate myself, I hate who I used to be and I hate who I'm trying to be, and the people I loved betrayed me, and I betrayed myself. I hid it away instead of telling—telling somebody, anybody—I stayed quiet instead of asking for help from somebody, anybody, and all the hurt is being pulled out of me sideways, the thorns scraping my mouth and eyes and this must be what it's like to die, except the pain doesn't end, not for hours and hours, and Jemma just holds me and cries with me and whispers *I know* over and over again, because she does know, because she went through it, too, and I'm not alone, not anymore.

chapter thirteen

GREGORY CALLAN MIGHT BE A BUSY MAN running a successful bodyguard firm, but that doesn't stop him from enjoying the finer things in life, like dropping in on his employees on the job without a single warning. I open the dorm room this morning to find him with two cups of coffee, a fresh-pressed suit, and a jovial smile.

"Good morning, boys!"

I groan, and Charlie dashes to the door to greet him like an eager puppy. It's almost endearing, how much Charlie's all but crammed Gregory into the male-parental-figure-hole in his life. Gregory doesn't seem to mind, smiling and patting him on the shoulder more than anyone else.

Except this time, before either Charlie or I can say a word, Gregory orders us to get dressed and come with him to breakfast. The diner he chooses is small and drowned in vinyl and a fine layer of grease, so run-down and sketchy even college students tend to avoid it—the sort of place I desperately begged for a job at the tender age of fourteen when I found out about Sophia's illness. The waitress delivering our meal can't even muster a tired smile, but

Gregory thanks her profusely anyway.

"So why the visit, boss?" Charlie inquires with half a plate of eggs already stuffed in his cheeks.

"Did your grandmother teach you how to chew?" I quirk a brow, and Charlie robustly flips me off as he shovels bacon in his mouth. Gregory finds it amusing, however, and chuckles.

"See, Charlie? This is why none of your old partners stuck around for more than a week. Generally speaking, people don't like it when someone is rude."

Charlie swallows. "Generally speaking, people can kiss my ass—" He pauses, then finishes quietly, "Sir."

Gregory just chuckles again and looks to me. "He's even starting to snark back with more substance than four swear words. I'd say you're rubbing off on him."

Charlie looks me over warily and scoots his chair a few inches away from me. "Gross."

"He has a point." I look at Gregory. "Why come all the way out here to visit us? We could've easily texted or emailed whatever information you needed."

Gregory clears his throat. "I was just—curious."

"Curiouth?" Charlie asks through toast.

"How you two were getting along."

Charlie and I freeze, and we both scoff at the same time. Gregory smiles at that, like it's particularly amusing.

"But I can see my worries were unfounded," he says. "What's the status on your project? The last we spoke, you managed to cut off one of the heads of the serpent, at the very least."

He's talking about Terrance, at the club. Cutting off one of Will and his friend Kyle's drug connections here on campus meant significantly reducing their income, and therefore, their ability to have enough money to do drastic things, like move away quickly or buy new and updated technology to hide their doings better.

Charlie looks confused for a moment, then his eyes widen.

"Ohhh, you mean Will Cavanaugh's club guy! Yeah, we totally took care of that."

"Here's an idea," I say stonily. "Maybe don't announce names out loud for everyone to hear."

"Everyone?" Charlie looks at the tired waitress wiping tables in the corner and the man behind the steel counter in the kitchen. "This place is dead."

"Jack is right, Charlie," Gregory says. "This is a small college town. Names have a way of getting around, especially if someone says them very loudly."

Charlie clutches his fork and hisses, "Well, excuse me, boss. I told you I'm not good at this spy shit. I wanted a nice, easy job—the one I trained for—but you had to listen to new boy over here—"

"I didn't take this job just because of him, Charlie. No one influences me more than I influence myself. You know me better than that," Gregory says as he frowns, and Charlie glowers into his empty plate. "I took this job because it was a good opportunity for the both of you to learn a thing or two about what you really want out of this life. It's not a long-term job; your muscles and training are only going to carry you so far as you age. The rest of the guys know that, but you two are too young to get it."

"Boss—" Charlie starts, but Gregory holds up a hand, and he falls silent.

"This is where you're supposed to be, in school, setting up better futures for yourselves. If you wanna stay with me and Vortex after this is over, I understand. But if you wanna leave, I understand that, too."

He leans back in his chair, wipes his mouth with a napkin.

"So think of this job like a litmus test. Bodyguarding

isn't about just standing around and looking intimidating. You're still on a payroll; you're still getting hired to do what someone tells you, no matter how weird or off it might seem. Sometimes clients need different things to feel safe; information-gathering might be one of them. So you gotta do it. That's the basis of it; you gotta do what someone else tells you to do, even if you don't like that."

"I'm fine with it," Charlie protests.

"You're only fine with it if it's simple, straightforward," Gregory corrects. "One different thing slipped in and you throw a fit."

"I've been doing just fine with this shit," Charlie fires back. "Ask Batman over here!"

Charlie looks to me defiantly, but beneath the fire I see the barest glimmer of hope in his eyes, pleading and small. He might not know it, but he's all but begging me to confirm what he's saying, so he'll look good in front of Gregory. Who am I to deny that?

I nod. "He's been passable. He knows how to ingratiate himself with people if he has to."

Charlie's face relaxes, almost grateful, and Gregory grins.

"I knew he would. I told you—you got a natural charisma, kiddo."

Charlie goes red down to his spiky-haired roots and downs a glass of water quickly. He isn't used to being praised, I can see that much. Gregory looks to me.

"How have you been doing, Jack?"

"I'm also fine," I say.

"Yeah? This job isn't too similar to your old one, is it?"

I suppress my flinch. "No, sir."

"And yet you've been sleeping with that girl to get the dirt on our friends," Gregory says quietly. "Why you? Why not Charlie?"

"Because she took a liking to him, boss," Charlie says. Of course Gregory knows every detail of what we've been doing. Charlie and I have been telling him.

"Is that it?" Gregory asks.

Charlie shrugs. "And because he's handsome, or whatever, I guess."

"It's true," Gregory says, looking back to me. "You are. And I told you to use every tool at your disposal for your jobs. So you do. Almost too well."

I narrow my eyes. "What does that mean?"

Gregory is quiet, staring back at me without blinking. Charlie looks between us, confused. Finally, Gregory calls for the check from the waitress, and Charlie boxes my leftovers into his container. Gregory and I watch him from outside the diner as he does it, methodically.

"His grandma is a lady of little means," Gregory says. "He learned to save food real quick in his life."

"He looks up to you," I say. I begin to pull out a cigarette and light it when a girl with purple hair passes by, laughing with her friend. My memory goes straight to Isis, to the scars on her wrists, and I slowly put the cigarette away.

Gregory is oblivious, chuckling instead. "I know he does. That's why I want him to think long and hard about being in this company. He's a good kid. Gruff, but good. Reminds me of myself when I was young. He deserves better than the long hours and the lonely life, that's all I know."

"And me?" I ask softly. "What do you know about me?"

Gregory squints at me, rubbing his jaw. "I know you remind me of myself when I was young, too, just in a different way. In the beast way."

I'm quiet. He scratches the back of his head absently.

"I know you've seen some shit growing up. I know you were sad, and I know you trained hard at the Ranch to get rid of that sadness. You tried to leave what you did behind there. They say the past repeats itself, and I believe it now."

"What do you mean?" I ask.

"Blanche. I told you, right? I knew her. I heard about you from her. I know what you did when she was your boss. The women, the money." Gregory shakes his head. "And then you joined up with my company, and you go right back to doing the same thing—sex in exchange for something."

"It's a tool," I say coldly. "Nothing more. You said that yourself."

"No, I know. I said it back then, because I didn't want to go easy on you. I wanted you to use your full potential to get what you wanted out of this. But is this—is this what you really want? It's not good money, Jack. It's not even decent money. And it's hard work, injuries, and long hours—"

"Will Cavanaugh will pay for what he's done," I interrupt. "At any cost."

"And then what?" Gregory grunts. "He pays for what he did, and then what? What happens to you, huh?"

I'm silent. I hadn't thought beyond that. I didn't want to. Making Will pay was my last wish, the only thing that kept me moving forward. If I lost that, if I accomplished that, there'd be nothing left for me.

"You're a good kid, Jack, and you're smart," he presses. "But that isn't why I recruited you. I saw you in that bar, saw that bloodlust I knew so well in my own eyes, and I felt damn guilty. I felt guilty someone else in this world had to feel as shitty and angry as I do. So I chased after you, after your secrets. And when that didn't work, I drove down to Las Vegas and bribed a dozen people and found you because I *was* you. Twenty-five years ago, I was you, and it tore me up inside. I had to teach you. I had to show you what I'd learned from tearing myself apart before you did the same."

I swallow hard. Gregory puts a hand on my shoulder.

"You're not Charlie. He's got a normal anger inside him, like everyone else. It doesn't command him like it commands us."

"You taught me," I say. "You taught me how to control it."

"I did my best," Gregory says. "But it's always gonna be hard. It's not as simple as turning a light switch on and off—you have to work at it for your whole life. But you only work at it if you want to keep living, keep going. If Will Cavanaugh is the only thing keeping you going, then you aren't gonna last long, Jack. No matter how strong you are or how well you took to my training. You need more than that. You need reasons. You need *people*."

I look down at my hands. The world seems to spin a little when I think about all the things I've done with them; I hurt people, I loved them. I chased a man until he died. I couldn't save Sophia. I abandoned my friends—what few I have left of them.

I abandoned Isis.

"I've made a lot of shitty choices." My voice cracks.

Gregory squeezes my shoulder. "We all do. Life isn't determined by the shitty choices you make—it's what you do after them that matters."

I'm quiet, Charlie's voice cutting between us.

"Boss! Are you heading out?"

I watch Gregory put on a smile and turn to Charlie, answering all his exuberant questions. We part ways, Gregory heading north to Columbus to meet with some new clients. During the car ride home, Charlie seems mildly happier, his usual scowl gone, replaced by a faint smile.

"He's a good man, isn't he?" I ask. Charlie snaps out of it, frowning.

"Y-Yeah. I guess."

"You like him a lot."

Charlie's frown deepens. "Whatever."

His reluctance to talk about his feelings clearly reminds me of a certain someone, though he uses fewer jokes than said someone. I watch the trees speed by outside the window. He and I have lived together and worked together for nearly two months now.

You need people; Gregory's words resound in my head.

"Gregory found me in a motel," I say finally. "Bleeding and beaten. My shoulder was dislocated. I'd broken three knuckles and my nose."

"Doing what?" Charlie grunts.

"Fighting," I say. "Drinking and fighting and waiting for someone to kill me."

Charlie shoots me a look, narrows his eyes. He watches the road for a moment, and then: "Gregory was the police officer who busted me."

I quirk a brow. "Really?"

"Yeah." He nods, then scoffs softly. "I had ten grams of coke on me from my old boss, and I was selling it to rich high school kids. There's a ton of them in San Francisco; it's easy money. My gang knew that and hustled it hard."

"So Gregory was a cop in San Francisco?"

"For a while." He nods. "Then he quit the force and started Vortex, and I went with him."

"You've been with him for a long time."

"Long enough. He's an old coot. But he isn't all that bad."

His half insult is transparent—he says it with a little smile. I lean back in my seat.

"So what's our next move?"

Charlie shrugs. "Brittany told you about Kyle and Will's drug buyer, right? We got him. She told you about what sort of computer setup Will runs, too, right? And you tried to hack that."

"Didn't get very far," I agree.

"Doesn't matter—at least you tried. So what else did she tell you?"

"Will Cavanaugh is afraid of the dark," I say.

"Brittany told you that?"

"No." I shake my head. "Isis did."

"She knows him?"

"Once upon a time." My stomach dances uneasily.

"That's great. Get Loudmouth to talk to Will, then. Maybe we can learn more."

"No."

"Why not? She's—"

"He hurt her." My voice sounds stony even to my own ears. "She doesn't talk to him if she can help it."

"Bastard," Charlie mutters under his breath. "Guys who hit girls are the fuckin' bottom of the scum barrel."

I don't correct him, but I feel a tendril of affection for him. He takes a right turn, then flashes me a look.

"We gotta get some hard evidence. On either one of them."

"We went to the pool party at Kyle's apartment complex," I say. "And I asked Brittany which one he lived in, but she didn't know. Apparently he's moved since they were together. But Will lives on campus, so he could be easier."

"And now we know he's afraid of the dark. Just stick his computer in a dark room, and we got 'im."

"It's not that easy." I frown. Charlie gives a rare laugh.

"It's never easy. But that ain't never stopped me before." When I don't say anything, he sighs. "You shoulda told me earlier Isis knows Will."

"Why?"

"Because then I wouldn'ta scared her off so quick. Any info we can get is useful. Shit, she seems like she's got a better brain in her head than Brittany, anyway. She could be way more useful."

"This is her abuser we're talking about," I snap. "I'm not going to put her in that position."

"You ever ask her if she wants to get back at him?" he asks lightly. I'm quiet again, and he scoffs. "Can't just jump right to protecting people, dumbass. You gotta let them make their own decisions, too."

"But if she does, she'll—"

"Get hurt?" he asks. "More hurt than what he's already done? I don't think so. She's got you this time around. You tell me you like this girl, and then you don't ask her if she wants to get even with him? Talk about being a hypocrite."

"You don't know anything," I snarl.

"Yeah, I don't," he agrees. "And neither does she. Because of you."

I glower at the distant trees. Charlie Moriyama is a lot of things—crude, brash, hot-tempered—but he's not an idiot.

And for once, he may be right. My heart whispers with hope; I could invite Isis to help us. She could agree. We could work together, and for a brief moment, I could be beside her. It's a tiny seed, but it blossoms over the night into a full tree, a copse, and finally a sprawling forest. We could be together again, and even if it were nothing more than being in each other's presence, silently, it would be enough. It would be enough to see her face, the lines around her eyes, the furrow of her brow, the smile I still see in my dreams sometimes. It would be enough to hear her voice, her jokes, her laughter. It would be enough.

I stare up at the ceiling from my bed and swear to myself that it will be enough.

But it isn't enough.

I throw on a jacket and grab my keys. The drive is short, and the autumn cold threatens to chill my fervor. But I won't let it. Isis deserves better. She has always deserved better.

I ring the doorbell and wait. Brittany opens it, wearing pajamas and a bewildered expression.

"Jack? What are you— "

"It's over," I say. Her face dims.

"What?"

"You and me," I insist. "We're over."

I turn before she can argue, but she grabs my arm and pulls me back with a vise grip. I expect her to be tearing up or angry, but her face is only sad.

"At least tell me why."

A piece of my heart tears again, the one that promised never to hurt other people wittingly again.

"I made a mistake," I say. "And I'm sorry."

She thinks on it, then releases my arm and nods.

"Yeah. Okay."

"I'm sorry."

"It's fine." She half laughs. "At least you came in person. No one else has come in person to tell me that before. It's been texts or emails. So thanks."

She shuts the door in my face, and she has every right to. Something on my shoulders lifts, and my head feels lighter, clearer.

There's pain, in me and because of me, but I can do better. I have more to give than just pain.

chapter fourteen

4 YEARS, 0 WEEKS, 1 DAY

IN THE ENTIRE HISTORY OF PLANET EARTH, no one has been more of an idiot than I have. Except God, or the big bang, or whatever you wanna call it, because it made this place, and us. Because that was, objectively, a very bad move.

Anyway, God and I are tied for universe's biggest morons because I did something equally stupid, which was to hurt myself. For years. By keeping a nasty secret inside me.

I thought I was stronger than the traumatic event, which is entirely true except for the part where I forgot to admit it was a traumatic event to begin with, because, as Jemma tells me after I pass out on one of the cots in her office and wake up to birdsong and a Styrofoam cup of coffee she hands me, no matter what happened, or for how long, it still happened. Just because it wasn't prolonged or penetrative doesn't mean it wasn't rape.

He still held me down and masturbated on me.

It was still rape.

Jemma invites me to come in next week to talk some more when she changes my bandage again, and I agree. She's not a therapist, and she's not getting paid to do it, but she's taking a chunk out of her free time to listen to me talk, and I'm grateful. Also, sore and worn out and mentally exhausted from reliving the entire event in one night, but mostly grateful and ready for nine pizzas.

But I walk differently now, like all the space in my body was replaced with helium overnight. My shoulders feel lighter; my head feels lighter. I flip my hair dramatically as a couple walks past and realize I don't actually harbor the urge to barf on them anymore.

Nameless, though, is a different story.

I duck into the front office and grab a cup of water, the office ladies' chattering following me out the door.

"Summers? That's impossible. He's such a nice-looking man." One lady sighs.

"Well, one of the students did it," another lady says. "And we had that harassment complaint against Summers a year ago that the dean refused to listen to, remember? The poor girl dropped out."

"Do you think it's true, then?"

"College students do a lot of silly things," the first lady says. "But they don't typically write 'pervert' in fake blood on doors unless they have a good reason to."

"If he's been inappropriate to the female students, so help me, I'll—"

"Campus security is interviewing his students now, you know..."

The door shuts and their voices cut off, but word of my exploits doesn't stop. It filters around a few people eating cream puffs on the steps of the culinary science building.

"Ew, blood?" A girl wrinkles her nose.

"It deserved to be written in shit," a guy scoffs.

"I've always thought he was *too* nice," another guy says, shaking his head.

"Why does a guy with his looks need to perv on girls? That's sleazy as hell." The scoffing guy scoffs again.

I keep walking. A group of frat boys sees Summers crossing the lawn and hoots at him, and he drops his notebooks and scrabbles to pick them up. The snide glances and doubting whispers are proof I've turned the school against him. It's proof I've still got the magic, sweet-ass Isis touch that strikes fear into the hearts of evildoing men everywhere—

"Isis!" Kieran runs up to me, a scowl on his face. "I told you not to do anything!"

"Yes, well, orders and I don't exactly jibe. I mean, we jibe, but it isn't smooth and it isn't pretty to look at."

"They're going to bust you! They have cameras everywhere on campus!"

My stomach twists unpleasantly, but I shake it off.

"Never fear, they spontaneously combusted because of my hotness."

"Nothing is spontaneously combusting, and you're going to get kicked out!"

"Then we must make do with what little time we have."

"Isis—" I feel his hand on my wrist, jerking me back. I whirl around and plant my feet and clear my throat.

"I know that kiss was nice," I say. "And we kissed a lot for two people who met each other next to a shirtless guy throwing up on some petunias, and you're a really nice guy and you look sort of Scottish, which is always a good thing, ladies love kilts, not me specifically but most 'ladies' in air quotes, denoting roughly seventy percent of women aged eighteen to thirty-eight, and I know you think you like me as a person, and that you want to date me and that we'd get along well, but here's me, overturning your hopes and dreams. I don't wanna date anyone. Or that's not true, actually, the butthead I want to date just doesn't want to date me. So. So

I was just trying to get over him. And I was using your lips to get over him like a terrible person in a movie would, a villain, but I've always been the villain or the dragon and I'm sorry. I'm really sorry. I'm a dragon and I burn stuff down and I'm sorry."

Kieran's green eyes well with shock, and his grip goes limp. I tear away and leave behind another person I hurt, and I'm sorry for it, but I'm not going to beat myself up for it. I hate walking around with black eyes on my heart all the time.

I march away so hard I don't even notice when Diana passes me. She squeals, backtracks, and catches up with me.

"Isis! There you are! We've been looking everywhere for y—"

"Not now, moon goddess, I have boys to confront."

Diana laughs and slows. "What about the county fair tonight? You said you wanted to go."

"I'll be there!" I shout, and push through the door to the boys' dorm. I take the stairs two at a time and knock hard on his door. There're three seconds of silence, and then it opens. Jack looks like he's taken a casual jog through a meat grinder, if said meat grinder ground only the souls of good-looking boys.

"Hello," I say crisply. "I want you to help me kill Will Cavanaugh."

Jack's ice-cold eyes crack a little with surprise as I say Nameless's full name out loud for the first time in four years. I suddenly remember my priorities.

"Oh, but actually we can put that off for a while. First, I want you to come with me to the county fair tonight, and if Brittany doesn't want you to, I don't care. You're still coming."

I expect him to refuse or get angry, but his eyes crinkle on the outside—the Jack version of a smile.

"All right."

"I'm driving."

"All right."

"Meet me by the Psychology Building at nine."

He nods and opens his mouth to say more, but I quickly pivot and walk away. I can't have any more words with him—not until I've practiced what I want to say. Six hours and a flurry of closet-raiding is all that stands between me and figuring that out. Yvette watches with the casual interest of a hurricane observer as I chuck socks and pants and shirts over my shoulder.

"Where were you, though, seriously?" she asks finally. "Diana and I thought—"

"I was talking to a nice lady," I say. "And she helped me figure some stuff out. Contrary to popular belief, strangers work nicely when divulging your desperately nasty secrets."

I hold up the pink blouse, and Yvette makes a cooing noise.

"Oooh, that one."

The Isis of a day ago would have wrinkled her nose and thrown it aside. I should do that even now. But for some reason I pick it up and pull off my shirt, replacing it with the blouse. I test the waters, pivoting in front of the mirror. I wait for the voices, for Nameless's voice whispering how ugly I am. For once, nothing happens. I can't hear him when I look at my own reflection. No insults, no sneers, no nothing.

He's gone.

He's not gone, because he's on campus and in my scars and my nightmares, but right now, in this mirror, he's gone.

The blouse is cool and airy on my skin, the ruffles flickering with my every move. Yvette helps me pick out jean shorts and lends me an old, ratty army surplus jacket that looks balls rad and is perfect for the cool fall weather. Yvette pulls my hair back from my neck and puts it in a ponytail for me.

"You look way hotter like this," she says.

"I just want people to look at me and think *I want to give her a million cash dollars*."

"Why are you so obsessed with money?"

"Because with it you can buy stuff and also things."

Yvette laughs and shakes her head. "I want to give you maybe a ten. And a dime. A single dime."

I hold out my hand expectantly and she riffles through her wallet for a single dime. I tuck it into my bra for good luck.

I practice in my head what I want to say, over and over and over and under; through all the possible loopholes of conversation I create counterarguments, quips, and the finest of snarks, but they all drain out of my ears when I see Jack waiting for me near the parking lot. He leans against a peach tree, hair combed but still somehow messy, with dark jeans and a red flannel shirt on. His legs are so long, his shoulders so broad, his face proud and fine like a lion's. It hits me just then—he's getting older. I'm getting older. Time isn't waiting. I spent four years of my time mourning over someone who was never worth it to begin with.

But this boy. This stupid, wonderful boy just might be worth it.

"It's not a lumberjack carnival," I say as I approach. He looks at his shirt beneath his leather jacket, then speaks without turning around.

"I just like flannel."

"You and the entire hipster populace of Seattle," I say. Jack smirks and follows me to the car. We drive in utter silence, but a not-weird silence, until the carnival tents and the tip of a neon-highlighted roller coaster come into view.

"I've got the tickets," I say as I pull into the parking lot and we get out. "So you have the honorable privilege of buying me all the food I want."

"All the food you want? Woman, you want the rough equivalent of a third-world country's monthly intake."

"Does that make me gluttonous or evil?"

"Both," he offers, and takes the ticket book I hand him. He pauses under the archway into the carnival, the moonlight making every tree black and every cloud silver. The lights on the Ferris wheel and roller coaster and pharaoh boat beckon, the smell of greasy popcorn and hot dogs mixing with the dry, crisp smell of autumn leaves.

"The last time I came to one of these was with Sophia," he finally says. My heart turns into a ton of lead and lands like a weight on a cartoon character's head, except the character's head is my solar plexus.

"Shit. L-Let's go," I say quickly. "We don't have to do this. I didn't mean to—"

Jack's warm fingers encircle my wrist, and he holds me there. It isn't a rough grip, like Kieran's. It's loose. I could rip away if I wanted to, but I don't want to.

"I *want* to," Jack says, voice soft but steely as he meets my eyes. "I want to go to this, with *you*."

I melt a little around the edges, but I remember who I am and stick my tongue out and skip under the arch, leading the way.

"Don't say I didn't warn you."

I make him buy me a sundae and a corn dog and a slushy.

"Milady," he drawls. "Your appetite is like a horse's."

"Your face is like one, so it's all balanced in the end."

"We're in college now. You're officially banned from doing 'your face' jokes."

"But that's like, ninety-five percent of my comedy routine!"

"Alas, Horatio." Jack sighs. "However shall you make a living now?"

"I can't make a living as a college student!" I protest. "I'm supposed to be broke, and drinking all the time, and doing the nasty like…everywhere. It's a complicated list of demands."

"You don't have to do it like Hollywood says you do. You can just be you." His eyes soften.

"Sometimes it just…feels like I'm in the wrong place. It feels like I should be doing more with my life by now, you know?"

His hand ruffles my hair, and I look up at him, half shocked. He grins a little, in that barely-an-actual-smile Jack way.

"I know."

My tongue is blue and it hurts with all the pure sugary goodness of an exploding Peeps factory, and Jack says I'll die and I tell him my willpower is stronger than diabetes, and he laughs at me but then I laugh at him when we go on the pharaoh and he looks like he's going to shit himself the higher we get.

"Are you okay?" I shout at his white face. His lips are thin, his fists clenched, but he manages to yell back.

"Oh, I'm just fine."

"You look less 'fine' and more vampire-y! If you're a vampire you have to tell me before I eat the garlic breadsticks down there!" I point at the breadstick stand.

"I'm fine!" he snaps.

I put my arms up and whoop when we reach the apex, our stomachs lifting out from our abdomens, and he swears brilliantly and throws his arm over my chest as a mock-seat belt even though I don't need it because I already have the big black one over my lap.

"You're scared of heights!" I breathlessly exclaim as we get off. Jack wobbles a little and grips the edge of a nearby trash can.

"I am not *scared*!" he insists, green around the cheeks. "I have a perfectly valid wariness of being suspended fifty feet above the ground in a wildly swinging pendulum."

"Physics protects us." I pat his back, rubbing it sympathetically. "The only way we would've died is if the center axle went loose. Or if we all weighed eight hundred pounds."

I pick up a cotton candy from a stand and look at him expectantly to pay. He grumbles, fishing a five from his wallet.

"The way you're going, you'll be at eight hundred in no time."

"And I'll be equally sexy as I am now." I sniff haughtily and bite off a chunk of floss. Jack's smirk returns, and he leans in so close to my face for a second I think he'll kiss me and everything slows around us, the lights blinking in half time and people's voices low and distorted, but he takes a bite of the floss and pulls away with it and time catches up. I decide to punish him and start toward the roller coaster. Jack gives a massive groan but follows dutifully.

After he's stopped almost-hurling into yet another trash can, I take pity on him and wander toward the games alley. Goldfishing, water balloon tossing, shooting ranges, this place has it all. Jack strides after me.

"Hey, slow down," he says.

"Your request has been carefully considered by the Board of Me, and denied."

"You really should've brought Kieran here," he presses.

"Why? Don't like carnivals?"

"No, he's just—" Jack furrows his brow. "Aren't you and him…?"

"No. He's fine, as a friend. But no. Too straightforward. Cute, but too normal. And in the long run, being normal is a huge no-no. Along with, you know, being a serial killer, but normal is like, number two—number one point five-ish."

I can feel Jack staring at my face, and it makes some deep

part of me squirm uncomfortably, so I pick up a shooting gallery rifle and aim it at his forehead. He looks appropriately terrified.

"Wrong way," he deadpans.

"No, no, this is the right way," I insist.

"Miss, please, the targets are behind you," the high school guy running the booth says nervously. I turn and eye him, then the sign, then the huge stuffed panda that's a prize for all five targets. It's perfect. It's Ms. Muffin but huge. Mr. Muffin. I want him.

"Give me some of the bullets you're sweating," I say to the booth guy. The guy chokes and airs out his dark armpits.

"Excuse me, miss?"

"Six shots isn't enough," I clarify. "Gimme more."

"Six shots is plenty," Jack steps in, handing the guy some tickets and taking the rifle from me. "Watch and learn."

"Oh, this'll be good, and by good I mean hilarious." I lean against the booth and watch him position, narrowing one eye. He pulls the trigger, the shot sailing cleanly into the bull's-eye of the first target and exploding in pink paint. Jack turns to me, quirks a brow in an "I told you so" way, and I scoff.

"So what? You've practiced a little with some squirt guns. Big whoop."

Jack moves on to the next, and lands that, and the third and fourth, each taking just one shot and each perfectly in the center. The booth guy whistles and squints a lot, like he thinks it's a hallucination, and Jack looks at me before the fifth target.

"Bodyguard school's been good to you," I admit. "Or you're actually a serial killer."

"I have a talent for hurting things." Jack perches the rifle on his cocked hip, and it's so insufferably arrogant I want to shove him into the ball pit next to us and/or furiously make out with him. "But we always knew that, didn't we?"

He laughs, and it's despairing and his eyes are a little cold, and I regret ever bringing up the killer comment, but before I can apologize, he positions and aces the fifth target. The booth guy offers him the prizes, and he debates for a half second before settling on the giant panda. Jack turns and hands it to me, and I swallow my gasp.

"What are you—"

"I saw you drooling over it. It's yours."

"Nay." I shove it back in his hands. "Give it to Hemorrhoid. She's your girlfriend."

"We were never really dating," He puts it on my head, the legs flopping into my eyes. "And I told her yesterday I didn't want to see her anymore."

I quash the thrill that runs through my veins and assume an appropriately lofty expression.

"*Tsk*, *tsk*. It's almost like you use these women and throw them away like tissues."

"Historically, most women have used *me*," he says darkly. I hug the panda to my chest and try not to dwell on the pain in his voice. He always hid it so well, but now I can hear it clearly. We really are getting old.

"You ever think about that?" I ask, trotting along the games alley in an attempt to keep us moving, keep us light. "That escorting maybe affected you more than you want to admit?"

"I've told you before and I'll tell you again, it meant nothing to me, I felt nothing—"

"You felt used," I interrupt. "You were reluctant, no matter how much you insist it was a mutual business arrangement. And reluctance is not consent. It's reluctance."

He's quiet. I point at the Ferris wheel and smile back at him.

"C'mon. It's slow, and if you don't look down it's almost

like you aren't suspended a million miles in the air."

The Ferris compartment sways and Jack looks a little queasy, but the lights of the carnival below are too beautiful for even him to ignore. We watch the arcs of pink and green and spots of blue and white flicker on and off as we ascend, the music getting fainter. Our knees are almost touching.

"How is your arm?" Jack asks. I look down at the Band-Aid and shrug.

"I won't turn into a zombie, so. That's one good thing."

"I was worried," he says tentatively. "Not that I have the right to be worried about you any longer. But I was very concerned and I couldn't help it. I'm glad to see it's doing well—that you're doing well."

"Am I doing well?" I laugh. "I can't tell anymore."

"You look better," he says. "Something in your face isn't so sad anymore."

I look out the window. I burn to tell him what I told Jemma, but it's not the right time. Telling him what happened would bring Nameless into the Ferris wheel with us, and right now I just want it to be me and him, and no one else.

"If you squint, the carnival kind of looks like a galaxy from up here," I say. "Minus the cryogeysers."

Jack smirks. "Oh, I don't know, the ice cream carts get pretty cold."

If this were a movie, the Ferris wheel would get stuck or something, or fireworks would go off, but it just pauses at the apex, a short pause, and Jack's looking at my face again and my stomach feels like it's shriveling and growing all at once and I should say something, this is the moment I should say something, every movie ever has told me so, but the moment passes, and the Ferris wheel starts going down but I can't let anything get in my way anymore, especially not a giant LED hamster wheel—

"Isis, you're talking out—"

"I love you," I blurt. "I'm sorry. I'm sorry for saying it, but I love you. And you don't have to…you don't have to do anything, or say anything, I mean, I could just drive you home right after this if you never want to talk to me again, I'd understand, because girls saying 'I love you' is something you get a lot and you hate it, I bet, but I realized a lot of things lately and the biggest thing is that I probably love you, I'm not sure, but I think so, and it's not very romantic or confident to not be sure, but I barely even know what love is, I *just* sort of learned the definition, but I know that what I feel for you fits that, and I want to learn more, and I think you would help me learn, but also I just love you, no weird creepy learning involved, I just love *you*, you stupid idiot, so if you could just—if you could just love me back, that would be really great, but if you can't, I mean, I understand, it's hard, and also I'm hard and not your type and it would be too much work for a broken person, so maybe instead you could just pretend to love me, and not work so hard, and I could be a nice distraction for you, or you could use me for…I don't know, sex, or keeping your mind off things or getting less broken maybe, and I wouldn't mind, as long as you pretended—"

Jack leans in and this time, it's a kiss, and it doesn't sear my soul or make me woozy like the books say, but I can taste him and smell him and he's kissing *me*, me of all girls, and when he pulls away he's smiling the sort of kind smile I only ever saw him give Sophia, except now it's on me, all golden and sweet and genuine as he rests his forehead on mine, and that smile is better than fireworks. And maybe I do feel a tiny bit woozy.

"Moron. There would be no pretending," he says. "Because I love you, too."

I freeze, trembling, not daring to believe it.

"D-Do...do you mean that?" I whisper. "Do you really, *really* mean that? Because...because I don't want to get my hopes up again—I just—I couldn't take it if they were smashed again, you know? It hurt."

I laugh, on the verge of tears, and Jack cups my face in his hands, ice eyes locked on mine, clear and bright.

"I love you," he says. "Ever since that night in the sea room, I've wanted to love you. I've wanted to take all the hurt away, to hold you and protect you and make you laugh, and smile, and show you what love is. I've wanted to show you for so long that you are worthy of being loved for exactly who you are. And I tried to deny that, I tried to convince myself...that I wasn't good enough, that I would do nothing but hurt you. And I have. And I'm sorry. I was afraid. I was afraid of loving someone as delicate and beautiful and unique as you. I knew I only had one chance, and I was terrified I would make a mess of it, and you'd only become sadder and more convinced you were unlovable. I was afraid of my own shortcomings, and because of that I hurt you."

I sniff, and Jack thumbs away an escaping tear.

"I'm so sorry," he whispers. "I love you, and I'm so sorry."

I grip the flannel of his collar and kiss him again and again, and he runs his hands up and down my spine and cups my cheek gently, and I've never wanted anything more than for this moment to never stop, but I do want it to stop, because I want more, more than this, I am hungry and empty and I want to be full and the Ferris wheel attendant opens our door when we hit the ground and I pull Jack out and away, laughing, letting the wind dry the happy tears in my eyes as we half run, half stumble back to the car, stopping to kiss against a darts booth and a doughnut stand, the smell of sugar and sweat in our hair, and in the darkness of the parking lot I try to unlock the door as he kisses my neck and

I elbow him to stop and he laughs and gets in the passenger side, and the entire ride back to the dorms he tickles the inside of my palm with his fingers.

"This might ruin everything! We might not be able to be friends after this in the conceivable history of forever. There's still time," Isis says as we get out of her car and she locks it. I double around and reach for her hand. She squeezes it, blushing brightly. "We can just be friends, still. Or enemies. We can go back to the way things were."

My chest swells, and before I can stop myself I tangle my fingers in her hair and pull her toward me, kissing her hard. Her shock melts to eagerness, breath sweet and shallow and distinctly *her* against my mouth, and I pull back.

"I want you, Isis. Not as a friend. Not as an enemy. But as the most beautiful girl I've ever known."

There's a pause, a suspended thread twisting in the wind. And then she smiles.

She half pulls, half drags me, the both of us laughing when I nearly run into a glass door of her dorm. She fiddles with her keys and the door swings open; her roommate, she says, is sleeping over at someone else's dorm. The thought of having her all to myself, in a closed room with a soft bed, sends ripples of hot anticipation down my spine. She kisses me again, kicking off her shoes as I kick off mine, pulling me toward the messy paisley-spread bed. She is a fire that burns brighter, scorching every thought from my brain. Her fingers run over my chest, and I shrug off my jacket to give her better access, to feel her more keenly. I bite at her lip, and she bites back, a spark of almost-pain nudging me that much closer to the sweet edge. Her hands are insistent, roaming over my shoulders, my back, sliding lower to my navel—

"Isis—" I grab her hands and look her in the eyes. "Listen to me. I can't…I can't give you all of what you want. I'm just starting to rebuild myself. So. This is your last chance. You should find someone who isn't so broken."

She frowns and leans into my chest, murmuring.

"That sounds so boring."

"I'm serious, Isis, you deserve better—"

"And so am I!" She looks up, eyes flaring and bottom lip set stubbornly. "I don't care about what you can or can't give me. I just want you. Even if you're broken. Nobody else. Just Jack."

The sudden surge of excitement to my heart at her words is nigh painful. I crumble like a dry sand castle against her wave, edging her down onto the bed with hasty force. I freeze and sit up, afraid she'll be angry, or frightened and shaking, but she laughs and holds her arms out instead.

"C'mon, butthead."

Her hair's splayed out against the pillows and her blouse is hiked up, showing a bare wisp of her creamy hip bone. With soft slowness, I lean down and kiss her exposed hip, nudging the blouse higher with my nose and kissing upward. She giggles, but it quickly turns to pleased mewls as I reach the edge of her bra. I pull up and look her in the eyes, tugging at it.

"This comes off."

She quirks a brow and sits up, grabbing the hem of my shirt. "So does this. Only fair."

I pull it off in one swift movement and watch her eyes light up as she takes me in. She rests her lips against my skin, kissing each contour and indent of muscle, and when she reaches the lowest part of me I can't suppress my audible breath hitch.

"Isis—"

She buries her nose in my skin and sniffs. "You smell good, like honey."

I growl and push her gently back on the pillows. "And you"—I inhale her wrist, her hair, between her breasts, which earns me a squeal and a bop on the head—"you smell like summer and cinnamon. I could eat you. I *will* eat you," I add. Isis flushes.

"I-If I had known you were into cannibalism, I would n-not have agreed to this in the first place."

"Too late." I smirk, licking her neck. "You're mine now. Bon appétit."

Isis gives a little sigh, tensing her shoulder when she gets too ticklish. We laugh, and I pull her blouse off, slowly, tentatively. She can't look at me, eyes darting this way and that to avoid my gaze as I take her in.

"May I?" I ask. She nods, lip set stubbornly again. I run my fingers over her stomach, milk-smooth and soft, with paler lines running vertically around her belly button.

"They're gross," she says. "Stretch marks. Sorry."

I lean in and kiss them, each one, kiss up to her wrist burn scars, kiss every scar I can see, and she gives a soft cry, arms suddenly darting out to pull me up and kiss me fiercely, needy and hot and more eager than ever before, and then she's on top of me, kissing my collarbone and my neck, my arms, my chest, and down to my navel again in a whirlwind of soft lips and warm breath.

"Isis, you—"

"Shhhush up," she says quickly, unbuttoning my jeans with alarming ferocity and yanking them down to my ankles. She smirks at my black boxers, then looks up at me.

"That is entirely your doing," I offer. She just hums happily and rubs her hand down me in response. And I dissolve. I've imagined this, over and over, but nothing can compare to the real thing, to the real Isis, smirking and flushed and half naked. It's all my dirty fantasies come to life, all the aching need for her touch culminating in one moment.

But no. This is not how our first time should go. I flip us over, and she squeals, a pout on her lips. I kiss it away between murmurs.

"There will be…plenty of time…for you to tease me," I say, one long kiss for each pause. "But tonight…this is about you…and what I can do for you."

"You can lie down and let me figure out what this dick fuss is all about," she huffs.

"Like I said, there'll be time for that. But right now I want to make you comfortable. And then make you scream. In that order."

She squeaks and hides her face behind her hands. "Don't say stupid shit like that, idiot."

I smirk and unclasp her bra, inching it aside.

"H-Hey!" she protests, crossing her arms over her chest. "Don't look!"

"You got to see mine," I lament.

"That's because yours are small and pathetic."

"It's true." I glance my lips across the thin skin above her chest, tracing her veins. "Compared to what you're hiding under your arms, mine are very underwhelming."

"And floppy," she adds, more out of spite than anything. I'm very toned.

"And floppy," I agree. She relaxes slowly, so slowly, and finally her hard edge evaporates, a blush replacing it as she hastily puts her forearms over her eyes.

"Fine. Look."

The ordinary person would overlook her considerable assets, because that's exactly what she wanted them to do. Her clothes were always a little loose, one size too big on purpose.

But I'd caught enough glimpses to guess at the truth, and now I confirm it. Soft-looking, round, and perfectly teardrop-shaped, with the right breast barely noticeably larger than the left. They quiver, and it's then I realize she's shaking.

"Hey," I say. "Isis, what's wrong?"

She shakes her head. "They're weird."

"Look at me, Isis."

She peeks over her arms.

"Can we agree that I've seen many breasts in my life?" I ask. She frowns and sighs.

"I know, I get it. They're really weird compared to the hundreds of other perfect ones you've seen—"

"They are beautiful."

"You're just saying that."

"No, I'm not." I lean down and kiss the swell of one. "They are the most adorable I've ever seen. And they're turning me on. Your whole body has me on point. But I'm sure you know that."

I smirk, and she squirms pointedly, her fingers scrabbling for her jean shorts. I undo the top button for her, and then she stops me.

"Um. Wrap your willy. Um. Before you get silly."

I chuckle before turning and rummaging through my discarded jacket. I pull a condom from my pocket.

"I always carry one with me," I say. "Habit."

She frowns, no doubt displeased at the thought of the others who helped form that habit. I lean in and kiss her neck, moving to her ear and murmuring.

"Oh, don't give me that face. For months now you're the only one I've thought about using it with. You're the only one. God, Isis, you're the only one I've wanted for so long—"

She cuts me off and kisses me, her tongue darting out and mine eager to meet it. I pull back, fingers dancing down her tensing and relaxing stomach. She helps me pull off her jean shorts, and when she throws them they land on her computer, and we both laugh. I pause at the hem of her underwear—white with a green ribbon—and look up. She isn't shaking, which is a positive. She isn't rigid or tense.

"If you ever feel uncomfortable, let me know."

"Okay." She swallows.

"I mean it. If you don't want to do this anymore, at any time, tell me. And I'll stop."

She nods, and I sigh and lean in, putting my forehead against hers.

"Please, Isis. Promise me. Promise me you'll communicate with me. I can see the visual clues, but I'm not a psychic."

"I know." She sighs. "Sorry. Okay. *Okay*." She takes a deep breath, hard determination in her eyes. "I promise. Now shut up and kiss me and take off those dumb boxers."

And he does, but he ignores what comes out of it, preferring to pay attention to me.

"Are you okay?" He looks up, panicked.

"Do that again," I demand.

And he does, over and over until my arms are coiled around him and my thighs are practically crushing him, and his fingers are different, they're longer and more slender and can reach all the places I never could, all the places that make me pant and twist and finally, *finally,* explode soundlessly.

"H-Hey, dumbo."

He sits up. "What is it?"

"What about you?"

"That's a very dangerous game you're playing."

His hiss spikes. The ice of his eyes is all but spring water now, soft and pleasure-hazed. He throws his head back, and I kiss his exposed throat, and suddenly I'm down on the pillows again, his hands on my shoulders and his bangs shading his eyes. He licks down my neck to my breasts, and I arch. Faintly, I hear the crinkle of plastic and a sudden pressure, and I should be afraid or hurting more, my brain and my past tell me this should hurt and be terrifying, but I feel safe as he slides in easily with slow, careful movements.

I'm full, and a little uncomfortable, but it's fading and I don't want to tell him just yet. Not when his expression is as achingly satisfied as that. His groan is hoarse, and he dusts my neck in kisses.

"I-I'm sorry. Are you all right? I should've asked, I should have warned you—"

"It's okay," I insist. "Really. Didn't hurt at all."

He looks doubtful, and I smile.

"I'm telling the truth."

"Promise?" he asks.

"Promise," I say. "Just…maybe don't move all that much. For a while. It's kind of new territory."

"'Virgin territory' is the term I believe you're looking for." He smirks. I punch him with my pinkie. We stay like that, him breathing and me breathing and me getting used to the feeling of someone else. Finally, the pressure lessens.

I feel him, for the first real time, and moan.

"Jack, ah—"

"Say it again."

"Jack." I curl around him, my legs moving higher of their own accord, linking around his back.

"Oh hell." He groans into my shoulder. "I missed you. I missed you, Isis. It feels so fucking good to hear you say my name."

I say it many, many more times. Loudly and involuntarily.

chapter fifteen

0 YEARS, 0 WEEKS, 1 DAY

JACK DOES NOT ESPECIALLY APPRECIATE me taking all the blankets in the universe.

Or staring at him while he sleeps.

I know this because A) I know Jack, and he doesn't like being ogled unless he's being paid for it, and B) every time I pull on the sheets tangled around his legs, he grimaces a little more in his sleep. So I do what any decent human being who respects another person would do and keep pulling.

Jack groans and shields his eyes, the early-morning sun painting his tousled hair gold. It slants down his chest, making shadows on his bare belly, his neck, his throat. I want to nuzzle into the hollow of his shoulder and live there forever. It feels so surreal—like any second an annoying teen-movie alarm clock will start chirping in my ears and I'll rouse awake into the real world, in my real bed, alone and cold and sad and convinced no one will ever love me.

But he kissed me.

He kissed my stretch marks and my scars.

He treated me like a person to be respected, like a thing to be worshipped and handled as gently as precious glass.

He kissed the most frightened part of me, and it isn't so scared anymore.

He's here. And I can hardly believe it.

I can hardly believe a boy so handsome, so regal and smart and kind and interesting wanted to—burned to—sleep with me.

~~*No one else is going to want you.*~~

Jack wants *me*, for who I am.

And it's even more amazing he stayed after, that he's still here, that he didn't change his mind and leave. He's not a figment of my imagination. He's here and he's real, and he smells the same as his room smells, and I wallow in it, try to drag out every second of the luxurious golden haze that is this warm disheveled bed with this warm disheveled boy in it whom I happen to like an annoyingly huge amount.

Finally, Jack cracks one sleepy blue eye open, sees me staring, and laughs hoarsely.

"Good morning, you creepy, beautiful thing."

"I was plotting," I say. "How best to murder you in your sleep."

Jack leans in, planting a soft kiss on my palm. "Make it long and drawn out. I love suffering."

"Exactly why I'm making it short and snappy. Neck-snappy, to be precise."

He pokes at my forearm. "You couldn't snap my neck if you tried."

I scramble up and sit on him, trying to wrap my arms around his neck. He fights me off weakly and finally pulls me down into him, laughing.

"You are *vicious*."

"I believe the term you used was 'hellion,'" I correct in his ear.

He runs his hand lazily up and down my spine. "How are you doing? Pain-wise?"

"I'm broken in two and will never walk again," I deadpan.

"Yes," he hisses, tightening his hug. "Now you can never escape."

I roll my eyes and roll off. "Let's go. The day awaits, glorious and full of future disappointment. And food."

He doesn't get up, watching me pull on shorts and a T-shirt instead. He groans and shoves his face in the pillow.

"I don't want to go. I hate it out there. I want to stay here forever."

"I don't have enough Doritos in this room for 'forever,'" I insist, and wince when an ache shoots through my pelvis. Jack jumps out of bed, balancing me on his arm.

"Are you all right?"

"Everything is sore and I'm dying."

"I warned you."

"No, you didn't! There was no warning involved! Just a lot of gross dirty talk!"

"And laughing. A lot of good laughing."

I blush, and he wraps his arms around me and pulls me back down onto the bed. He sighs into my hair.

"It's been years since I've laughed like that. Thank you."

"*Tsk*, *tsk*, what kind of escort are you? I'm supposed to thank *you* for sex. Or pay you." I lean over the side of the bed and fumble around for anything other than dust. My hand finds the bra dime Yvette gave me, and I press it into his palm. "Here. For your services."

Jack growls and bites my neck. "I think I'm worth a little more than that."

"I don't know," I singsong. "You gotta prove it first."

He flips me on my back, and I squeal. He leans his forehead against mine.

"Prove it? Then what was last night?"

"A warm-up," I decide. "Appetizer. Except ew, let's not

bring weird food analogies into this please. I don't want to be compared to a restaurant."

"You're the best restaurant ever. Three Michelin stars," Jack asserts. I push him off and he laughs, pulling his boxers on. Yvette chooses that exact moment to walk in the door and get a face full of Jack-dick. She stares at it, then at me, then at Jack's face, and nods like a candid art appreciator as she proclaims, "Nine out of ten."

I, Isis Blake, have decided sex is okay.

I have a ~~little~~ large mental library of what is okay and what is not okay, and sex gets lifted from the not-okay book and slapped into the okay book over the course of two weeks. Jack and I shuttle back and forth from my dorm to his, alternating when our roommates are out and stealing quiet moments and making them not so quiet. I learn his every mole, every tiny scar from his childhood, every weak spot. There are so many huge, dumb problems looming, like the tape Nameless has, but I shove them and Nameless aside and bask in my newfound Jack obsession. The former Ice Prince is ticklish behind his ears and his knees and his hips (his sharp, delicious hips), and also he is still very much the Ice Prince—cool and collected and logical. Nailing each other hasn't changed that. In fact, nothing about us has really changed. I thought sex would break us apart or change us into a formless sappy mush. But that's not the case at all. I retort something, he snaps something back. I force gummy bears into his begrudging mouth, he holds me back from tackling the idiot who ran over my shoe with a skateboard. We fight. We fence. We argue the finer points of the most complex debates in human history.

"Santa is real," I say as I pick up my burrito from the food counter.

"He's not," Jack corrects, sidestepping a cafeteria worker with a full stack of dishes.

"Two words have never convinced anyone ever of anything."

"Yes, they have. *It's shit*," Jack says.

"What's shit?"

"The prequel Star Wars films."

"Oh, see, now you're *right*, and I have to take back what I said because I was *wrong* and you've convinced me utterly with only two words. Ugh. I hate being wrong."

"I love being right." He sighs, and I kick him under the table, except he is too fast, so all I kick is wood. With my shinbone.

"Ow."

He kisses my head. "You brought this on yourself."

I throw my face on the table and fake-sob. "I have bruises everywhere. I'm a bruise farm. Magnet. Bragnet. One day the future people of the world—who won't know what bruises are because technology will be so advanced no one ever gets one—will come to me, and I will show them my skin, and it will be the greatest contribution to human civilization."

This impresses Jack so much he takes a sip of soda.

Sometimes I catch him smiling at me when I'm jabbering on about stupid shit. But that's the only thing that's really changed.

Sex used to be this weird, scary blob of lace panties and ladies who scream like they're being hurt in porn all the time and *what if I smell funny; what if my chin looks fat from any angle ever during it*. It used to be me thinking I'd have to shave everything smooth like a dolphin every single day of my life for a guy to not be grossed out by me. It used to be me, angry at sex and hating it, and bitter because the only person I thought I loved used it to hurt me. Sex was a sword

I didn't want to be cut by again, a tiger that mauled me once before, and I'd gladly walk into a pit of corrosive tar before I'd go in that tiger's pen again.

So I suppose Jack Hunter is a pit of corrosive tar. But we already knew that.

"Objection, your honor," Jack contributes. "I am not a pool of base acid."

I kiss him on the cheek and stand. "I'm going to the library to taunt an animal dumber than me. Boys count."

"Don't encourage them." He rolls his eyes. "They might develop a crush on you and then I'd have to end them."

I stare pointedly. He sighs.

"Gently. And in accordance with UN humane procedure."

Jack leans up for a kiss, and I lean down. He nibbles playfully at my bottom lip before he pulls away.

"I'll see you later, then."

"Your room or mine?" I ask. He smirks knowingly.

"I was thinking something a little different tonight."

"Oh yeah?"

"I have to report to my superior," he says. "But we're trying to make it look as casual as possible. So she's put me on a dinner reservation with her. If you came, I'm thinking it would look even more natural."

"See, hell no, I've watched enough movies to know this is where you bring me to the CIA and they kidnap me for experimentation."

"There'll be no kidnapping. But there will be crème brûlée."

I consider this proposal for an astonishingly lengthy two point five seconds.

"Yes."

"Meet me in my room at eight, and wear a dress."

"You just want to see me in a dress, perv."

He smirks. "I want to see you in everything. And nothing."

The library is much quieter and contains less sexiness than wherever Jack is currently, but I'll live with it. For now, I have someone decidedly less sexy to bother.

Nameless has been on my list for so long, but only now do I have the strength to start plotting his ultimate demise. Only now do I have the courage to point all my dire expertise and rage at his throat. Now that I know for sure Nameless is wrong—that I've always been perfect and worth loving—I can fight him instead of run from him. Jack must be rubbing off on me in more ways than one; the fact that I haven't busted down Nameless's door and shanked him yet is a clear sign I've learned to control my anger like a true Ice Prince. Gasp. The horror!

People say you're supposed to love yourself on your own. And I tried. God knows I freakin' tried for four years.

But now that I know someone else loves me, it's so much easier to grow the courage to start loving myself.

It's not fast, and it isn't all happening right away.

But it's a start.

The only dress I brought with me to Ohio State is a green pleated dress I bought for prom but never wore. Jack's in a white button-down shirt and slacks, which suddenly makes me paranoid I'm underdressed.

"You look lovely." He smiles and I curtsy.

"Does this place happen to be enormously fancy?" I ask. We walk to his sedan, and I bunch my skirts up and settle in the passenger seat with the grace of a drunk hen with huge buttocks.

"Not especially." He pulls out of the parking lot.

"Will I get kicked out for spilling soup on myself? Because I really enjoy spilling soup on myself. It enhances my overall life experience of being a slob."

"As long as you don't scream about aliens, you'll be fine."

"What! Aliens are included in my traditional prayer to the dessert gods!"

He gives me a long look that basically translates to "please don't scream about aliens."

"Ugh, fine," I huff. "I'll pretend to be normal. Just don't act surprised when I keel over and die of a pulmonary embolism. Cause: sheer boredom."

He pulls my hand up with his free one and kisses it wordlessly.

The restaurant is a small black-glass building wedged in at the end of Main Street. Jack opens the door for me and I slip in, the hostess flashing me a brilliant smile and Jack an even more brilliant one. Jack asks for Vanessa's table, and the hostess leads us through rows of dark-wood booths lit with candles. A woman with severe, long black hair and wearing a fancy blue silk dress sits there, stirring an iced tea. She gets up and makes a weird forced smile as she leans in to hug me.

"It's been so long!" She laughs and hugs Jack in turn. We all sit, except my butt is slightly more bewildered than theirs.

"Um. Hello," I say. "I'm Isis, and also confused."

"Jack's told me much about you." Vanessa smiles. The waiter comes along, and she looks up. "Do you two want something to drink?"

"Water will be fine, thank you," Jack says, and looks to me. I squirm.

"Um, just a Coke would be good."

The waiter nods, and Vanessa and Jack watch him retreat with eyes so sharp I'm surprised his back doesn't start bleeding.

"Is he a threat?" Jack asks in a low voice, perusing the menu without looking at Vanessa.

"No." Vanessa shakes her head. "But he followed me from

the hotel earlier today, so we should stay alert."

"Whoa, wait, *that* guy?" I whisper. "He looks way normal."

Vanessa smiles at me. "The best ones always do. Let's throw him off with a little boisterous conversation, shall we? How are you doing in school, Isis?"

She raises her voice, and I play along and mimic her, even if I have no idea what's going on.

"I'm failing chem." I sigh. "I hate it so much—it's worse than calc by a thousand times. Also, I farted during the exam, and I'm pretty sure Professor Brown knew it was me because he wrinkled his nose and sniffed a lot and gave me a C-minus for 'incorrect exposition,' which is chem teacher speak for fart, I'm pretty sure."

Vanessa laughs. "Well, at least you know what you're *not* going to be majoring in, hmm?" Her eyes stay on me, but she lowers her voice and aims it at Jack all in the same breath. "Have you got the recording?"

"I, on the other hand, enjoy chemistry," Jack says, his voice louder as well. "But I'd never pursue it as a degree. It gets far more complicated by third year, so I'm thinking of something simpler in the sciences." His voice lowers again. "It's on a USB in the napkin."

Vanessa nods sympathetically. "When I was your age, I switched my major from biology to physics. Less icky cells, more clear numbers. Much easier."

"Yeah, except biology gets all the cool stuff like wombats," I say. "Have you seen how cute their ears are? A number could never compete with a wombat. Well, maybe the number eighty-three could."

Jack and Vanessa give me blank looks.

"Because if you tilt it, it looks like someone making a kitty face!"

The dead silence in the face of my utter hilarity makes

me squirm. All of a sudden Vanessa lurches, dropping her napkin on the floor and wrinkling her nose.

"Oh, damn."

"Here." Jack slides his across to her. "Use mine."

Vanessa smiles and takes it in her lap. "Thank you. Are you ready for midterms, Isis?" she continues smoothly.

"Honestly I'm more ready for shrimp scampi." I point at the menu.

"Of course! You two must be starving. Not that your college doesn't serve good food! On the contrary; I've heard they have a wonderful selection."

"It's mostly burritos, but I'm not complaining. My intestines do sometimes, though. Speaking of which, I gotta pee. Where's the—"

Vanessa points toward the back and smiles. "On your left."

I slide past Jack, who grips my hand and squeezes it.

"You all right?" he asks.

"Uh, I'm about to eat *food*. I'm all sorts of fine."

He smiles and lets go, and I start toward the bathroom. I catch a glimpse of our waiter watching me, but when our eyes meet he quickly looks away. Way to be subtle, suspicious guy.

Even the bathrooms are fancy—marble countertops and soap that doesn't smell like a movie theater's. I stare at myself in the mirror, my makeup less like a raccoon and more like a cat, and realize I've grown up. Not much. But a little.

It's a start.

When Isis is gone, I turn to Vanessa.

"She's very pretty." Vanessa smiles. "Much prettier than I assumed."

"What?"

"Oh, nothing. The girl you described on the phone…they normally don't look like that. Humor comes to the plainer girls easier."

Her backhanded compliment doesn't faze me. I clear my throat.

"Terrance's admission is on that USB I gave you. He says both their names very clearly."

Vanessa smiles, looking over her menu intently, too, but our focus is everywhere except there.

"An admission from a drug dealer isn't enough," she says. "But it helps. This and direct key logs should be enough for our team to work with."

"How are you going to get a key log on them?" I frown. "Will is wary of me—I've tried to approach him multiple times, but he always slips away. Kyle is less smart, but Will's warned him. They both avoid me."

Vanessa stares at me, hard, and I know enough about her body language now to understand it's an order to change the subject.

"She and I've been going out," I say quickly. "For several weeks now. She's my first actual girlfriend in a long time."

"Ah, that's right." Vanessa smiles. "You were always the playboy type."

"May I take your order?" The waiter comes up behind us, and I grin.

"Yes, thank you. I'll have an order of the shrimp scampi for the missing lady, and the salmon fillet for myself."

The waiter nods, eyes scanning our table with a too-focused intensity. Looking for us passing evidence, no doubt. Is he a friend of Will's?

Vanessa taps her finger on the menu. "And I'll have the lobster rolls. With the salad. Thank you."

The waiter nods, taking our menus and briskly walking off.

"He's definitely not subtle, is he?" Vanessa asks, stirring her tea. I nod.

"Will is nothing if not outwardly friendly. He must've told his friends in this town to keep a lookout for me."

"Now how are we going to go about this?" She purses her lips thoughtfully. "He'll obviously tell Will you've met with me, a suspicious not-college student. Will may bolster his defenses, and you'll never get anywhere near his computer."

"Then what do I do?" I ask.

Vanessa muses over this. "Isis. You said she knows Will, right? He hurt her once and is tormenting her at school now. If she could act as bait—"

"I'm not going to put her in that position," I say quickly. "Ever."

"You'll be there to protect her, of course."

"That isn't enough," I say. "I'm not going to ask her to do anything she isn't comfortable with, period."

"Very well. It's just that there are few other options, since Will and Kyle are so careful. There may be hope yet if we let her contribute."

"Let me do what?" Isis is back, sliding past me into her seat. "Were you two gossiping about me while I was gone? Ten million years' dungeon for the both of you!"

I'm quiet, as is Vanessa. Isis, ever allergic to silence, squirms.

"I'm serious! What were you two talking about with me in it?"

"It's nothi—"

"We need someone to plant a device on Will Cavanaugh's computer in order to gather enough data to arrest him," Vanessa leans in and whispers. "And I heard from Jack that you know Will."

I expect Isis's expression to flicker with discomfort and pain, but instead she lifts her chin.

"I do. I hate him."

Vanessa smiles. "Fabulous. Then I'm sure you want to see him arrested even more than we do."

"Or killed," she says lightly. Too lightly. So lightly it's frightening. "I'm not picky."

Vanessa smiles wider. Isis cocks her head as if thinking.

"You're with the government, right?" she asks.

"Yes."

"Isis, you aren't doing this," I say firmly. She smiles at me.

"The only thing I'm doing is eating my shrimp scampi and then maybe possibly dessert."

The waiter drops our food off and leaves. We eat, carrying on a false conversation that leaves me uneasy for some reason. Vanessa is being far too kind to Isis, the two of them looking through pictures of cats on her phone. I won't allow her to drag Isis into something that might get her hurt, or worse. I realized my mistake by bringing her here, in the direct line of fire.

Now that I have her, I'm never going to lose her again.

Dinner ends, and Isis orders apple pie. Vanessa pays our bill and smiles at me.

"I really need to get going. You two stay and have fun a little longer."

"Where arsh yew goin'?" Isis looks up with a mouthful of pie.

"I have some business I need to take care of," Vanessa says, and nods to the both of us. "Have a good night."

"Bye!" Isis waves frantically, then looks at me. "I like her."

I wipe pie filling off her cheek. "She's an operative. She doesn't like you. She's just pretending."

Isis frowns grumpily. "I could do it, you know."

"Do what?"

"Plant that device. Will likes messing with me. I'm sure he'd let me in his room if I knocked."

"Isis, no. You're not going to confront him. He's already put you through enough."

"Which is why I need to confront him." She sucks her finger free of whipped cream thoughtfully.

"You're not," I say firmly, "going to plant the device. You'll leave it to me. This is my job, not yours."

She stares at me, dark eyes so innocent and wide. Finally she shrugs.

"All right."

"I'm serious, Isis."

"As a heart attack," she agrees. "I promise I won't. It's all you, baby. Ugh. Did I just call you baby? You are a baby. A whiny baby. With a nice butt."

I can't be mad at her for long, my smile strained but still there.

In the car, I clear my throat.

"If Will ever tries something, if he threatens you, you can always come to me. You know that, right? I'll take care of it."

"I know," she says idly, staring out the window.

"I'll protect you," I say. "I swear it."

"Hush up." She leans in. "And kiss me."

Her lips are fire and apple and cinnamon spice, driving all worries from my mind. We never quite make it home. I pull over at a nearby park, and Isis straddles my lap, and we kiss until the sun disappears behind the trees. My hand slides up her dress and her smell and pants cloud the car in a deliriously succulent haze. When she's on the verge of losing control, she buries her head in my neck and bites it.

"I love you," she whispers. "I love you, you stupid idiot."

I stop my ministrations, and she whines. I lock eyes with her, watching her pleasure-fogged expression contort with want. Sweat mists her forehead, her chin, and I kiss it.

"Sorry," she tries. "I'm sorry I called you an idiot. Please—"

I laugh and resume my work, and she gasps.

"We're both idiots," I murmur into her ear.

Later, much later, days later, when we've drunk ourselves silly of each other's bodies and brought each other to the brink and back again so many times I've lost count, I return to that restaurant and ask after the waiter. The hostess informs me he quit, and to give a letter to anyone asking after him.

Jack,

I hope you're enjoying her. God knows I did.

Have you checked in with Belina Hernandez recently?

Yours sincerely,

Will

My stomach goes cold. How does he know about that? Did Isis tell him? No—she never would, and I shouldn't underestimate his sleuthing skills. Of course he knows about that. I've been sending the last of the money to Belina, but I've never visited her personally. It was always too painful. I'd sit outside her house in my car sometimes, trying to force myself to go in, but it never worked.

If Will knows about Belina, he knows about that night, and Joseph. If he told her what I did—

My feet fly over the cement. He told her first. He ruined what I'd been working up the courage to do for years. She hates me. She's called the police, and they're coming to investigate me. I'll be thrown in jail. I won't be able to see Isis, or hold her, or protect her from Will. That's what he wants. He wants me out of the picture, gone, and he knows a grieving widow would throw her rage at the person who killed her husband, indirectly or not.

He's using that night to get rid of me.

I break more than a few speed limits driving back to Northplains, the setting sun like blood over the horizon. Belina's house looks the same as ever, yet this time I can't let my fears keep me from knocking on the door. But those fears are compounded twice now—she knows what I did. I'm walking up to the woman whose husband I had a hand in killing. I feel like puking, but I tamp it down with long, deep breaths.

I have to do this. If I don't, I may never see Isis again.

That thought is fire in my brain, the pain forcing my legs into motion, my arms into opening the car door. Every stair feels like I'm fighting against the pressure of a thousand blocks of iron on my back.

My hand knocks on the front door in slow motion. The wait is torture, but eventually a round-faced woman answers the door, her hair in a bun and tired lines around her eyes. She wears a dirt-stained apron, as if she's been cleaning all day. Her dark gaze travels up me, down me with no expression, and then she speaks.

"Jack, right? Come in."

I blurt the first thing I can. "Mrs. Hernandez, I—"

"Come in," she repeats softly, holding the door open wider. There's a thick silence between us, the fire in my head reaching flames into my heart, burning it alive. Is she planning revenge? Is she luring me in just to have me arrested?

No—I'm in no position to suspect her of anything. I took her husband from her. I inhale a breath and walk in, and she closes the door behind me. The house is simple, clean, with yellowing walls and many crosses over the doorframes. It smells delicious, like long-cooked meats, but my nerves are so bad I notice it only faintly. She leads me into the living room with several paisley couches and an ancient TV.

"Please"—she motions to a sofa—"sit. Would you like some water? Juice? I can make coffee, too."

"I'm fine," I say quickly. "Mrs. Hernandez, I came because—"

"I know why you came. I saw the video."

The fire in my body consumes me now, down to cinders. My hands start to shake. Will showed her the video? How does he have it in the first place? It's over. She's seen everything, and I'm a monster, solidly and fully. No amount of money can hide that fact. I will never be able to make it up to her, no matter how hard I try.

I feel something in me puncture, deflate. Something I've held for so long, so carefully. I bow my head and clench my fists on my knees.

"I'm sorry. I'm so sorry. Whatever you want to do, I'll accept it," I manage hoarsely. "I won't run."

"I know you won't," she says, faintly smiling. "You didn't run when faced with five grown men with dark intentions against that girl you loved. Why would you run now?"

I flinch, but the feeling of her hand on mine makes me look up. Her eyes are soft.

"Joseph fathered my children. He built this house for me, so many years ago. We loved, for some years, and we hated for others. Then the hating years became more and more frequent. And then one day, he took a bottle to my littlest one."

I suck in a breath, but her smile grows.

"It was the last straw," she says. "I began filing for divorce. It drove him further into his darkness, and he began to drink."

Belina puts her other hand on mine, eyes sincere and pressing.

"When I saw him in that video, harassing that young girl, I knew he wasn't the man I'd married. And I knew, too, that perhaps it was for the best he disappeared. Before he could hurt my children, or anyone else."

"Belina, I swear to you—"

"Ah-ah." She holds a hand up. "I saw it, Jack. I know only two things—you were young, barely a child, and he was wrong. You were scared, and he was still wrong. I don't want any more apologies from you. I don't want police or lawyers. I only want the truth."

So I tell her. Everything. Every bat swing, every dollar sent, every cover-up by Avery's parents, every ounce of Sophia's life. Of my life. And when it's over, she puts her arms around me and holds me close.

"You have been very brave, Jack, for a very long time."

We sit there, watching the moon outside the window, and I feel a single trail of wetness slide down my face.

chapter sixteen

0 YEARS, 1 WEEK, 5 DAYS

"YOU ARE FIRED from being my best friend!" Kayla screams. Even her two-in-the-morning Skype face is Beyoncé-flawless. I want to be her except I don't, because the idea of dating Wren is almost basically like incest, because he is so little-brothery to me, and also breasts that enormous would make me trip at an inopportune moment, like, say, over the lion's cage railing at the zoo, and I'd die.

"Stop talking about my boobs! You're fired!"

"Kayla," I whine attractively. "Kayla, listen, I am not fired, you are *fired up*."

"Hell yes, I am fired up!" She slams her water glass down and it splooshes all over everything. "Why didn't you tell me sooner?"

"Because!" I blush. "Because. Because I was *busy*."

Kayla smirks knowingly, and I yell.

"Shut up!"

"I didn't say anything!"

"Shut up anyway!"

"Finally!" She ignores my request. "God, it took you two *forever*."

"A year and some is not forever."

"You could have a baby in that time!"

"Ugh, no, please. No grubs. Promise me you won't have a grub."

"I will have nine hundred grubs just to spite you. Speaking of grubs, you're using condoms, right?"

"*Yes.*"

She just giggles. "Aren't they weird? Like weird little plastic socks."

"I will put one on your head and suffocate you."

"I'm sorry!" She throws her hands up. "I'm just happy you finally got what you wanted in life!"

"Jack is not all I wanted in life." I roll my eyes. "What I want in life is a stable yet satisfying career in the field of my choosing and a giant house made of a single doughnut."

"And Jack."

"And Jack can come sleep in my doughnut house sometimes. Yes."

Kayla stares at me, smiling with increasing amounts of dorkishness.

"What?" I snap.

"You really are in love."

"Ugh."

"I'm serious! What other boy would you let sleep in your doughnut house?"

"Heath Ledger."

"Yes, but he's dead."

"Ughhhh. People who are dead can totally sleep in my doughnut house."

"Wait." Kayla looks like she's been struck by lightning and/or has come up with the most brilliant hypothesis this side of teenage girl science. "Is doughnut house a euphemism?"

I groan and roll myself up in a blanket and then roll on

the ground like a particularly floral sausage. Skype beeps with another call, and I bolt up.

"Oh, hang on. I've got another call coming in."

I flip over to it, and Vanessa's face greets me.

"Oh, hi! It's you!"

"It's me," she agrees. She looks different without all her makeup on, and she's in some kind of fancy hotel room. The bedsheets are too perfectly made. "I assume you found the note I wrote you in your phone?"

"Yeah! I'm kind of amazed you managed to type all that out while just pretending to look at my pictures."

If you're still interested, I'll contact you via Skype from twelve to three a.m. My username is kv2009dia@msn.com. I found it in my notes app the next morning.

"I didn't want Jack to see it," she says. "What I'm proposing would make him angry, and I want him focused."

"So…" I glance at my phone. "You want me to plant the key log thingy on Will's computer, or whatever?"

"Precisely."

"Okay, I'd love to do that for you and all, but I'm gonna need some incentive."

Vanessa nods. "Of course. I'd be happy to pay you—"

"Uh, no. I don't want money. I mean, I do want money, always, but not from you."

"Then what do you want?"

I knit my lips and debate the validity of telling a possibly-government agent a very dirty secret. Her face is so set and determined, and it's then I realize she doesn't care about anyone else's business. It'll all get shoved aside as information, a means to an end. It's Will she's after.

"So, Jack did something. A long time ago."

"The Hernandez disappearance?"

I squirm. "Uh, yeah. How did you—"

"I know all I need to know."

"So then you know the Feds gave the tape of that, um, incident, to Will's friends. So they could clear up the tape for them."

"Regrettably, yes."

"Aren't you guys hunting Will and his friends? So why—"

"There is little cooperative communication between us and the federal government," she says quickly. "Call it rivalry, call it human pride, but mix-ups like this happen very often. We don't tell the Feds what we are doing and to whom, so we sometimes end up arresting people they've…*enlisted* for help."

"Right. Well. I'll do the whole key log thing for you. But. But I want you to make that footage go away. I want you to make it stop going to the Feds. Or anyone. Forever."

Vanessa purses her lips. "That's an awfully big request. You're asking me to tamper with evidence in a federal cold case."

"I know. But. If you do it, I'll do the key logging thing. Tonight. Right away. Just make it disappear."

A tiny voice in my head begs to ask her to make the footage Will has of me defacing Summers's office go away, too. But Jack's dilemma is more important. Jack's means jail. Mine just means getting kicked out of college, and one is definitively worse than the other. So I stand firm.

Vanessa ponders it, then sighs.

"All right. You put the key log on tonight, and I'll make some calls."

"Thank you," I breathe. "Thank you so much."

"I'll have my associate drop the key log off in a brown paper bag, in the right-side garbage can outside Ciao Bella. That's the café on your campus."

"Duh. I've been there a thousand times."

She fixes me with a stern look, and I fall quiet.

"You'll attach the key log to one of the USB ports on his computer. Any one will do, just make sure it's all the way inside. All I need is for the key log to stay in the computer for four hours. After that, I'll be able to access his hard drive anytime I choose."

"USB port, all the way inside. Got it."

"I'll know when it's done. Expect a call from my associate in the next few weeks. He'll tell you when your 'reward' goes through."

"Right."

"And Isis," Vanessa says. "Be careful. Will is not a good person."

"I sort of already know that."

Vanessa logs off, and I switch back to Kayla.

"Everything okay?" she asks. "You look kind of sick."

"Sick nasty rad," I correct.

"No, like, throw-up sick."

I'm quiet, staring at the darkness of her bedroom as she stares at the darkness of mine, seven hundred miles away.

"Hey, Kayla?"

"Yeah?"

"Would you still be my friend if…if I dropped out?"

Kayla furrows her brow. "Of course, dumbass. Do you not, like, like it there?"

"I thought I would! I thought I really wanted to be here. I thought it would be great, and it's been okay, but. It's just boring," I say. "School is boring. I wanna go places, and see new things. Things that aren't textbooks. I want to travel! I wanna get out of this state, this country. I just wanna…*go*. Except—"

"Your mom," Kayla finishes for me. "You've looked after her for so long! You deserve some vacation time away from family!"

"But she'll be— She and Dad will be disappointed in me, and the money they spent to send me here—"

"They won't have to pay anymore if you drop out!" Kayla laughs. "And I dunno about your dad, but I know your mom. She's so sweet. She'd want you to be happy, not miserable."

"You don't think it's stupid? You don't think I'll be ruining my future forever or something?"

"Uh, no? You're Isis Blake! You're not me, or Wren, or even Jack. You're not like other people. You're hilarious and quick and good, and most importantly you're *you*. You'll be just fine, no matter what you do with your life. Nothing is ever ruined forever. And I'll always be your friend."

My eyes well up with tears, and so do hers. She laughs, wiping her cheeks.

"As long as you go for what makes you happy, everything will turn out okay. I promise."

Eight hours later, I try my very hardest to look like I'm not doing possible spy things. I wear a bright yellow skirt and a shirt with flowers on it, and I smile and say hi to everyone, even Heather. Spies are not friendly. No one will ever know I am doing spy things.

"Are you doing spy things?"

"Jesus H. Christo!" I yelp, and whirl around to see Charlie glaring at me. "How—how did you—" I lean in and whisper. "*Can you read minds?*"

"You were thinking out loud," he deadpans. "Ugh, and that yellow is hideous. Word of advice, if you wanna be a spy, wear black."

"I'm not a spy!" People stare. I immediately lower my voice. "I am not a *spy*. I simply…threw an important paper away. On accident. Yeah."

Charlie looks at my hand buried in the trash can and then stares pointedly at me.

"Many papers," I correct. "An entire notebook. Full of papers."

"Here." He grunts, putting his hand in and pulling out the paper bag, wiping the banana peel off it. "Weirdo. If you want drugs, you can get them like normal people do and go pick them up from the dealer. That way, you don't have to dig around in garbage. Everybody wins."

"Right. Um. Thankyoubye."

I fast-walk away as quickly as I can. I run into the glass door of my dorm and denounce the devil loudly, rubbing my sore forehead.

"Boy, you really suck at this being-subtle stuff," Charlie says. I hide behind a pillar.

"Go away," I whisper. "Shoo!"

"You're usually a lot chattier than this."

"I just get a headache when people say too many dumb things to me all at once."

"You know, for what it's worth, I like you better than that Brittany chick. But now that she's gone, Jack and I gotta do it all the hard way."

"What's the hard way?"

"Sneak in. Ugh. I hate sneaking."

"You were pretty shitty at it in the forest," I agree.

"I was chasing you because we thought you knew Jack."

"Well, it didn't feel like a chase, that's how sucky you were."

"You screamed."

"We all make mistakes sometimes."

He rolls his eyes, and I stamp my foot.

"Look, it's great you are here and doing things like breathing, but I really must go."

"Oi!"

I feel a hand on my wrist and whirl to see Charlie holding me back.

"What is it?"

"I just—" He goes red from the roots of his spiky hair all the way down to his chin. He can't meet my gaze. "I wanted to say sorry."

"For what?"

"Chasing you. Calling you rude stuff. Just— I'm sorry, okay?"

I can tell it's paining him to apologize. He definitely doesn't do it often. I smile and ruffle his hair.

"You're forgiven."

"Hands off the merchandise!" he squawks, and I laugh and walk away.

I take the stairs two at a time, leaving him behind to ponder his life mistake of ever speaking to me. I open the paper bag in my room; the key logger is a flat black plastic bit no bigger than my thumbnail.

"Is that a piece of poop?"

I whirl around and hide the key logger in between my fingers. Yvette is sitting on her bed, painting her nails their usual cheery death-vampire black.

"It's a bargaining chip for my soul," I say. "I'm playing a high-stakes game against Satan! It's actually kind of invigorating. Do you wanna help?"

Yvette shoots me a doubting look. "Like, horns and red skin and big scary fork Satan?"

"Sort of. Think more hair and fewer pointy bits, but exactly the same level of evil."

"So, a guy."

"Yup. I gotta get in his room and plant something in it, but I don't wanna get trapped. Because he will trap me in there if he can help it, since he enjoys watching me squirm."

"Fucking sadist," Yvette spits. "Okay, so you go in there, and I bust you out. Right?"

"Subtly."

"What does that mean?" She wrinkles her nose.

"It means instead of busting down his door and alerting him to the fact that I've planned this and am messing with his shit, you gotta make a distraction."

"Who's making a distraction?" Diana asks as she walks in. "And can I help?"

"You're hired." I point at her. Yvette fills her in as I dig in my closet for an appropriate battle outfit. Something cute but not too cute. I want to remind him of what he ruined, distract him with his own "triumphs" long enough to blind him to what I'm doing. I pick dark skinny jeans and a tight shirt, even though it makes me sick to my stomach to think of baring any of my curves in front of him. This is for Jack. This is so he doesn't end up in jail because of that stupid video that ruined his life, Sophia's life, Wren's and Avery's.

"We could pull the fire alarm," Diana says. "The boy's dorm will empty fairly quickly, and I doubt even someone like this guy will want to stick around with that siren in his ear."

"Perfect. God, you're a genius. My girlfriend is a genius." Yvette kisses her on the cheek. Diana blushes.

"Oh, stop."

Yvette goes over to the window and opens it, yelling.

"*My girlfriend is a genius!*"

My mouth is a happy open *O* as I look at Diana, whose blush is now frozen on her shocked face. It's a bold move full of courage and love, and it's so different from the Yvette I know, who whispered her secret to me from over a pillow a month ago. Diana gets up and they start kissing, and I clear my throat only when I see bits of tongue.

"Ahem! Payback brigade, attention!"

They both laugh, trying to separate and turn toward me in a salute all at once, but they bump noses and legs and then we're all laughing on the floor, and I know without a shred of doubt I'll be all right.

No matter what happens after tonight, I'll be okay.

Yvette and Diana agree to pull the fire alarm if I don't come out in ten minutes. That gives me two minutes to get up the stairs, and eight minutes to chat Will up enough to distract him and plant the key log. But if I fuck up—

I shake my head. No fucking up! Not on the menu. Not now, not ever. Never was. Fucking up is the fish sticks of the Life Options restaurant menu—nobody orders it, and nobody likes it. And if you do order it, it was an accident and you regret ever living.

I rush up the stairs and forcefully catch my breath outside Will's room. I smooth my hair and try to look like I didn't just run straight up three flights. My hands are shaking. I feel like I'm going to puke.

And then my cell phone goes off.

I scrabble to answer it before it alerts Will.

"Hello?" I whisper, moving away from the door.

"What the hell do you think you're doing?" Jack snarls, sounding as though he's walking very quickly. "Get out of there, right now."

"Don't come here," I demand. "I'm serious, Jack. Stay away. How did you even—"

"Charlie told me you were acting strange. Isis, you can't go in there with him. You need to stay the hell out of this. It's my job, not yours! You could get *hurt*."

"It's worth it," I say. "If I do this, you'll be okay. So. Just let me do it. Please."

"No! No, I'm coming to get you—"

"Jack," I say with all the force I can muster. "You ran away after Sophia's funeral because you needed to. I need to go in there now. Alone. It's the same."

Jack's silent, then lets out a feral snarl of frustration. "No."

"Yes."

"No, Isis, *please* no."

"He won't hurt me this time."

"You don't know that!"

"I don't. You're right. I don't know anything. I don't know if the sun will rise tomorrow, or if I'll contract some horrible disease or get hit by a car, or if Will might hurt me. I don't know where I'll be in three years, and I sure as hell dunno where I'll be in ten. I don't know if *Game of Thrones* will ever be finished! I don't know if anyone I love will die soon, and I don't know if a meteor is gonna come down and smite us all into ash. I don't know if I'll have eggs tomorrow for breakfast or not." I laugh. "But I do know I love you. That's... that's really the only thing I *do* know."

"Isis—"

"Please, Jack. Let me do this. I'll come back in one piece. I promise."

"You *promise*," he says, his voice hopeless and small and steely.

"I promise, idiot."

"I love you," he says. "God, I fucking love you, you moron."

Jack hangs up first. I hang up and face the door at the very last. Except there's no door. There's only the chest of Will Cavanaugh in front of my face. I back up quickly, and he chuckles.

"Isis! So good of you to come. I heard your voice and was concerned, so I came out to check, and lo and behold, here you are! What a pleasant surprise."

I set my expression, trying to make it unreadable.

"I want to talk to you. In private."

"Of course you do." He smirks. "Let's go. My roommate's out getting dinner. I guess mostly everyone is, at this time of night."

He leads me to his room and shuts the door behind me.

"Don't lock it," I say, feigning a hint of terror in my voice. But he does anyway, double checks the lock, and smiles.

"Can't have you running off now, can we? We have important things to discuss!"

Will claps his hands and sits on the bed, then motions for me to sit on his chair near his desk. And his computer. Bingo.

"So!" he says. "Should you start, or should I? Or will you just sit there struck dumb like you always do and let me walk all over you?"

"That would be nice for you, wouldn't it?" I snarl. He makes an "oooh" noise.

"So you've got some spark back in you, huh? And here I thought it was all gone. Is it because Jack fucked you? How predictable."

"You're not worth the breath it would take to speak to you," I say. "But I'm going to do it anyway, because this was something I should've said to you a long time ago."

"Oh, let me guess! Is it one of your resounding 'fuck you's? I love those so much. I miss those, you know. But ever since you and Jack got back together, you haven't so much as looked at me."

"And you don't like that, do you?"

He taps his chin thoughtfully, then nods. "Of course. I told you, Isis—you're mine. Jack's an idiot, thinking a few pity fucks will make you his."

Will gets up, circles me, then grabs my hand. I pull away, panic making my muscles strong, but he rips my fingers open and grabs the key log from it.

"Well now, what's this?" He laughs.

"It's n-nothing," I scramble. "Just a piece of dirt—"

"It's a key log. Did you really think I didn't know? I saw you and Jack walking around, kissing and making stupid faces at each other, and I knew he was getting you in on this. He's after me, and his fucking partner's after me, and now you're after me. But it won't work, because—" He snaps the key log in two, grin wide. "I'm just that much smarter than you."

I stare at the fractured remnants. *He* doesn't know it isn't my only key log, and I can't let him see that in my face. Will flops on the bed again and sighs.

"Good try, though. Entertaining, at the very least."

"Is that all…? Is that all I was to you?" I choke. "Entertaining? Nothing about us—not one single time—was because you liked me?"

"Oh, don't get me wrong. I liked you very much." He smiles. "I thought you knew that."

"But you—you can't like someone and call them names. You can't like someone and—"

"Yesss?" he leads. "Go on. Say it."

I take a breath, the deepest breath. I fill my lungs with strength, with Jack's smell and memories of his laughter and his hands, of Diana's and Yvette's laughs, of Kayla's teary smile. I look Will in the dark eyes and hold my gaze there.

"You can't like someone and rape them."

His eyes go wide, and he whispers. "Rape. Is that…is that what you thought it was? Oh God, no. I was trying to have sex with you! That's how much I liked you!"

My instinct is to squeeze my eyes shut, to block out the memories, but I force myself to unblinkingly stare at him, through him.

"I told you to stop. I said it clearly many times."

"It's true. You did. Except girls are weird—they never say what they really want. And I know you did. You hung around me like a starving dog begging for scraps. You were a stupid little girl who kept changing her mind and didn't know what she wanted, so I helped you along."

His words turn to a hiss, his anger refreshing. This is the real him, the one he hides behind fake grins.

"I wasn't stupid," I say slowly. "I just didn't want you."

He stands all at once, tall and exploding from the bed.

"You did."

"No, I didn't."

Will has no control over himself. He just puts a silk screen over his ugly face and hopes people won't look or pry too hard. But I've pried the hardest. I've stabbed him where it hurts, deep in his ego, and his handsome faces twists into an ugly mockery—a gargoyle, a vampire of old.

"You fucking bitch!" He slams his hands on his desk. The computer rattles. "You were a fat, fucking ugly bitch! You were lucky I even let you hang around! You were so fucking lucky I even *wanted* to touch your fat, stinking carcass! No one else did. *No one else does*. Not even that fucking pretty boy. He's just fucking you because he pities you. He sees how pathetic and ugly you are, and he's taking pity on you! You're an idiot for thinking he wants you—you of all people!"

I sit still, transfixing my eyes on his face, not away from it. I always used to look away, too afraid that his eyes would bring up memories. Will puts his furious red face in mine, and it's all I can do to not bolt up and dive through the open window away from him.

"I had you first!" he seethes. "He's got my trash, my discarded meal, my fucking *garbage*! You're nothing. You're nothing without me. I got you friends, I got you popularity, I fucking taught you how to smoke and drink and steal and not be a pathetic fucking loser. You're mine! You're mine, and to anyone else you're an empty, useless bitch. *Fucking. Useless. Garbage.*"

With his every word, something deep inside me starts to come loose. It's hardened and dark, like old amber on the skin of a tree, and it wiggles free bit by bit. Will laughs, an insane sound.

"You liked it. I know you fucking liked it."

And with that the dark thing pops free, off the bark of my insides, and floats up and away, out of me, out of the top of my head, and I suddenly feel so light and exhausted.

Whatever Will used to be in my memories, whatever he'd done to me in the past, suddenly lets go of its grip on me and disappears into the air. Just like that. All at once, after years and years of pain.

"You never loved me," I say hoarsely. "And I hated it."

"You hate me." He grins, maniacal. "You'll always hate me. You'll always think about me, no matter where you are."

"No, I feel sorry for you." I stand and sigh. "I'm going to leave through that door and never think about you again."

It happens so fast I lose my footing and fall—Will lunges for me and pins me to the ground with his knees. Fear streams down my back, my spine, my face, like the ice-cold claws of a dread monster made of razors.

"Get off!" I scream. "*Get the fuck off me!*"

"You think you're better than me?" He sneers, spittle landing in my eyes. He grabs my flailing wrists and pins them to the floor, too. "You think you've got the fucking right to feel sorry for me? I'll show you sorry. I'll make you more sorry than you ever wanted—"

I spit in his face. It hits him on the eyebrow and drips down, and he looks horrified for a split second before he knees me hard in the ribs. I cry out and try to squirm away, try to kick him and punch him, but there's nothing to kick and punch with, everything is pinned down by his heavy, furious weight.

It's going to happen again.

It's going to happen again.

It's going to happen again and I can't stop it.

No.

NO.

I can stop this. I have to stop this once and for fucking all!

I twist my body around and kick hard, my foot meeting a soft bit of disgusting flesh between his legs, and Will wails and curls off me. It's not a lot, his stubbornness clinging to my body, but it's enough to give me the leverage I need to kick him off like the leech he is and race for the light switch.

"No!" he shrieks, the room flooding with total darkness. The only light is the faint streetlight from the window, and he scrabbles to sit on his bed and directly in that little square.

"You bitch!" Will snaps, shivering. "You fucking cunt! I'll kill you when I find you. I-If you get near me I'll fucking *kill* you!"

I stay low, like a panther. The tables have turned. I'm the predator, the wild thing in the darkness to haunt his nightmares. I unlock the door, just in case I need to run. Yet I get the feeling I won't need to. He's terrified, that much is clear in his voice. I have the power, and I'm drunk on it, seething with a smile that can barely contain my laugh.

"You're pathetic," I say. Will immediately lunges for my voice, but I sidestep him, and when his fingers touch emptiness he recoils back into the light.

"You're a disgusting human being."

I sidestep again, farther back, and he swipes wildly at nothingness.

"Fuck you!" he screams.

"I pity you, because you'll never know what it's like to be loved." I laugh, dark and hoarse. "Your daddy never taught you. He taught you the opposite. And with that nasty attitude, no one in the world is going to try to teach you otherwise."

"Shut up! Shut your fucking mouth!"

"You're going to rot forever inside yourself," I whisper. "You're going to be afraid of the darkness forever, the real darkness, the dark inside you. It's there forever. And no one will ever care about you enough to try to pull it out. You will never care about yourself enough to try to pull it out. But I have cared about myself. I've tried for years, and I've finally done it, and I'm leaving you behind in it."

Will's face crumples in the dimness, and I smile.

"So yes, I pity you, Will Cavanaugh."

The door behind me slams open, light flooding in from the hallway. Jack, breathless and furious, tumbles into the room, takes one look at the situation, and strides over to me, holding me in his arms.

"You took too long. Did he touch you?" He cups my face, looking it over with all the gentle intent of a doctor.

"No." I smile up at him. "Not much, anyway."

Jack tenses, eyes solidifying to the most subzero temperatures I've seen yet. The room itself seems to go cold as he fixes his twin icebergs on Will. Will's eyes dart around, focusing on the exit behind us, and he musters up a mad dash but never quite makes it, because Jack trips him and in two seconds he has Will pinned to the ground, his arm twisted behind him and his cries echoing.

"Fuck! Screw you, asshole! Let me go!"

Jack looks up and stands on Will's arm, using him as a footstool to reach the light on the ceiling. He pulls the bulb out, throwing it against the wall. It splinters in fragments of glass.

"Isis," Jack says calmly. "The lamp."

I oblige, stepping over Will and maybe dragging my foot a little so it hits his face. He swears, but he swears harder when I yank the lamp out by the cord. I'm about to throw it at the wall when Jack stops me.

"No. The bed. I'll hold him. Use the cord and tie him to it."

"No! Shit, shit, fuck, no! You can't do this! You can't fucking do this to me! Isis, don't let him do this!"

I ignore his pleas as Jack fixes his arms around the iron bedpost sunk into the floor. I tie the cord twice, and Jack ties it a third time, yanking it to check the tightness.

"It should be about seven hours until sunrise," Jack says. "And I'm sure we can persuade your roommate to spend the night somewhere else. Somewhere…quieter."

"The window," I say casually. "It should be covered."

"*No!*"

"You know, it really should," Jack agrees, smiling as he pulls the comforter from the bed and throws it over the window's curtain rod, blocking out all the light from outside.

"Isis! I-Isis please!" Will pants, tears and snot dripping down his nose. "You can't do this! I liked you! I cared about you—"

Jack punches him so hard I hear the crack of bone. He leans in, grabbing Will's collar and sneering in his face.

"You will *never* speak to Isis again."

"Isis! Plea—"

I turn away just in time to avoid seeing the second punch. But then I look back, because I deserve that much. Blood from his nose drips down his chin and mouth, and he pants, a thin sheen of sweat over his terrified face as Jack and I retreat.

"The joke's on you, Will." I laugh. "The key log you crushed was a fake I made from a soda bottle. I can't believe you thought I was stupid enough to only have one. I planted the real one when you locked the door, when we first walked in. How many hours do you think it'll take for them to find all the nasty shit you've been doing on that computer of yours? Probably more than it'll take for you to see sunrise."

"*No! No!*"

"Ah, the noise," Jack says. He rummages through a nearby

dresser and pulls out a shirt, handing it to me. "Should I do the honors?"

"I will," I say. I rip the flimsy cotton down the middle and walk up to the pathetic boy I used to love. Will whimpers, the threat of another punch keeping him from speaking.

"Tell me why," I say, squatting at his level. "Why did you hurt me?"

Will looks to Jack, who remains emotionless. Will tries a smile.

"I didn't, Isis! I liked you! I thought you knew that!"

He struggles weakly as I force the cloth in his mouth. Not his throat, because I don't want to kill him. I thought I did, but I really don't. I want him to live. To suffer in the darkness like I did, except for the rest of his life.

I walk back to Jack, Will's muffled screaming the last thing I hear before I shut the door and total darkness consumes him.

I manage to find Diana and Yvette before they get anywhere near the fire alarm. I'm too exhausted to track anybody down, so they offer to find Will's roommate for me, a mousy boy with big glasses, and tell him what's happened. He sighs in relief, saying he hates Will, and God bless us for fucking him over. He stays in Diana's dorm, and they, curiously, stay with him. But I'm too exhausted to be very curious for very long about it.

Jack helps me into my room and collapses on the bed with me.

And I cry, and he strokes my face and my arms and waits.

chapter seventeen

TWO YEARS LATER

I'VE DECIDED THE SUN is out to end me.

A lot of things are out to end me—cancer, animatronic dinosaurs, general death. But out of all the dire and dangerous things in this world, the sun has to be the worst of them. It grows our food and keeps us warm in the vast infinite cradle of space-time, so it forces us into the illusion we should be grateful for it, when in fact it's very hard to be grateful to anything blinding your eyes with a cheerful saw blade of ultraviolet rays.

"Ugh." I roll over on my beach towel. "Can you cool it for, like, five seconds?"

The sun brightly declines. I sip my Barbie-colored fruity drink from a fancy glass and try to pretend it doesn't exist.

"Where the heckle—" My hands scrabble for my sunglasses, and I shove them on my face. "Ahh, temporary relief. So sweet, so transient, so Gucci."

"Mademoiselle!" a voice rings out. I groan and sit up, watching Gregory stride his way through the sand toward me. Even the southern French villagers, used to bright and colorful Mediterranean clothing, stare at his atrocious green-

and-orange Hawaiian shirt. When we said "come visit us and have a vacation," he apparently didn't get the memo that he wasn't visiting a tropical island.

"Gregory, you're an eyesore," I complain. Gregory laughs and offers me a hand up, his eyes taking in my white swimsuit with the low-cut back.

"And you, madam, are quite the opposite."

"No!" I protest as I stand up. "No, no, no, look at these thighs! I'm far too young to be a madam. Try again in like, seven thousand years."

He chuckles. "Very well. Come on, he sent me to fetch you and for some reason he's antsy as fuck-all."

"Antsy? *Jack?*" I quirk a brow, picking up my towel and drink and slipping on my sandals, trudging through the sand with Gregory. "Are we talking about the same human being I'm in regular personal contact with?"

"The one and only."

"Are you hiring him again? Please say yes, *please*! I want those amazing little chocolates from Paris again—I want them with all my crappy idiot heart."

"God knows you deserve them, putting up with him all the time," Gregory huffs. "He's been so off-kilter lately. Not that I'd know, but we do keep up in emails."

"Oh, I know." I nod. "I've seen those emails. It's always you, begging him to come back to Vortex."

Gregory laughs. "Can you blame me? He's Jack."

"He *is* Jack!" I agree. "Which is why he left in the first place. Teaching is a viable career, too, you know."

Gregory's eyes crinkle like a father's around the edges. "He'll be a good teacher. And that glare of his? He'll have the most well-behaved students, I bet."

Gregory walks with me up the beach to the tiny dirt road that splits the village in two. It's been two years since Jack and I first visited, and eventually stayed, but still the villagers are a little wary of us, the American couple. But I'll win them over. Or wear them down. Whichever comes first. I wave at the villagers as cheerfully as I can.

"*Bonjour! François! La bouche un petite chienne!* Oh dear, they don't look happy about that last one."

"That last one didn't even make *sense*," Gregory emphasizes, and makes little *pardon* noises at the offended nearby villagers. I walk briskly past him and up the cobblestoned road. The village is tiny; children carrying boogie boards and floats bob and weave between bikes and too-slow couples. Two old men in stodgy caps take turns playing chess and drinking wine under the eaves of a flower shop.

Toward the edge of the village the cobblestone fades, replaced with a well-worn dirt road. Tall summer grasses sway on either side. I scoop up yellow and purple and white wildflowers, a honeybee fighting me for a particularly beautiful orange blossom.

"Go on!" I shoo her. "There are a thousand more; you can afford to donate one to the poor humans!"

Gregory chuckles, looking out at the ocean and the small farmhouses we pass.

"I'll miss this town. You two've picked the best place in the world to settle down, I reckon."

"Hey! No one's settled! We're going to Cambodia next year!"

"What's the difference?"

"Settlement means like, minivans and baby barf. Home base implies we are *explorers* of the *highest caliber*. And after Greece—after that it's back to Ohio."

"That's the plan, huh?"

"Yeah." I kick a pebble down the path.

"Do you miss your family?" he asks softly. I nod.

"We stayed with my mom for two weeks after, planning stuff. We've Skyped, but…it'll be good to see her in the flesh. And bones. And all the other parts of her."

Gregory laughs. I watch the village crowd, mesmerizing in its fluid dance. I got kicked out of college the day after I confronted Will. He didn't leak the video of me defacing the office or anything. I told them myself. I wanted them to kick me out, maybe. Or maybe I just wanted to come clean about everything.

I hugged Diana and Yvette good-bye, promising to keep in touch, and then I packed my things and left with Jack for Northplains and Mom's house. Those two weeks after dropping out were some of the best in my life. Mom, Jack, and I hung out, playing board games and going to the zoo and making delicious meals together. I was so happy that when we got the news about Will's arrest I barely batted an eyelash. Barely. But it was still batted. He got seven years in an Ohio jail for aiding and abetting a criminal organization, and that's the last I heard of him.

After the night I confronted Will, I never heard from Vanessa again. I did, however, get an email four days later from someone claiming to be a "friend" of hers, who told me all recorded instances of the tape of Jack and Sophia and the others had been destroyed. It'd be easy to distrust Vanessa's promise, but when Will's arrest popped up in the news so quickly and he was sentenced so thoroughly, I knew she'd never leave something unfinished. I scratched her back, and she scratched mine, and that was the end of that.

When I told Jack, he'd held me close, wordlessly and tightly.

He quit Vortex shortly after that. Charlie came to my house, banging on the door and demanding Jack come back, but not because he liked him as a partner or anything. Jack went out and they talked, and eventually Charlie left, the spikes of his hair wilting a little in disappointment. Then Gregory visited, gave Jack his pay for Vanessa's job, and it was enough for us to travel. Jack wanted to leave, and I wanted to visit somewhere. Anywhere but Ohio.

But first, good-byes were due.

Kayla and Wren couldn't make it to see us off, so we planned to visit them instead when our airplane to Europe stopped at Boston. There were a lot of happy tears and ruffling of hair and promises to keep in touch. Promises that were kept, daily, with my internet connection and a lot of time zone planning.

Even before the airplane, there were other good-byes.

I said good-bye to Mom the only way I knew how, with tears and a hug and a cheek kiss and swearing I'd be back. Mom laughed and hugged me back, insisting she would be all right on her own. We call every day, and sometimes Skype, and it was through Skype she introduced me to Harold, a round, pudgy man with a warm smile who always wore sweater vests and treated my mom like a precious vase, a queen made of diamonds. She's seemed happier than I ever could've thought possible after Leo, but when I get back to Ohio, I'll be sure to check up on Harold's sincerity. It's not that I don't trust him; I just don't trust anyone. But for now, she seems all right.

After my mom, we visited Jack's mom. Mrs. Hunter answered the door covered in paint stains and with her customary messy bun. When she saw Jack, she dropped the glass jar full of murky paint-water she'd been holding and flung her arms around him and sobbed. He'd called her before that, of course, but it was the first time she'd seen him since he left after Sophia's funeral. I cleaned up the glass bits while Jack held her and soothed her and Mrs. Hunter wailed. Finally, when she'd calmed down enough, she invited us in for tea, and Jack explained where we were going. She tried to get us to stay—we could live at her house, she insisted—but we managed to convince her we needed some time away. She pulled me aside just before we left and thanked me for finding him, for being with him, and my heart melted on the edges as she hugged me. She made me swear to make Jack call her at least twice a week, and I Scout's-honored it.

Eventually, Jack and I visited Avery's house. The massive town house was chilly inside, all marble and white walls with no paintings or tapestries or even stains. Avery's parents weren't there, too busy with a case in Columbus, but Avery was. She came down the stairs, then froze when she saw it was us. Jack and I talked that way, her on the stairs and us in the hall. She didn't look as bad as she did at graduation—she wasn't as thin, and some color was back in her cheeks. Her hair was as vibrant red as ever, if not more so. Her eyes were skittish, though, and she was still too small. And she kept her mouth silent, no matter what we said.

"Isis!"

Halfway out the door, Avery called out to me. I turned, and she was at the bottom of the stairs, face earnest and honest in a way I'd never seen it before.

"Have fun," she said, green eyes boring into mine. She wasn't smiling, wasn't frowning. But her expression was saying more than her words ever could. "Have fun" was also "be safe" and "thank you," but silent and hidden in that reluctant, subtle-as-a-hidden-knife Avery way. I knew it, and she knew it, and finally I smiled.

"You got it, Avery Bobavery."

Jack drove us to Belina's house. We had to all but fight off her invitation to stay for a delicious-smelling dinner. She hugged Jack in farewell and cupped his face with her hands like he was her own child, saying something in Spanish I couldn't understand.

Later, in the car, Jack told me she'd told him to live well and happily.

And then came the harder good-byes.

We visited Tallie's grave one last time with a picnic. We had sandwiches and wine, and I poured a little cup of lemonade for Tallie and put it on her grave, and we talked about how cute she was, imagining all the different ways she could've grown up. It should've been sad, something like that, but Jack and I couldn't stop smiling. When the sun set behind the lake, we packed up, and Jack's hand went to the white bleached-wood cross that served as her marker.

"What are you doing?" I asked. Jack stared at the cross, then looked up at me with a soft gaze.

"They should be together," he said simply.

"We can't just deposit a baby skeleton on her grave," I say. "The police will be all over that."

"No, you're right. But we can take the rest."

So we took the cross. Sophia's grave was serenely quiet, the graveyard empty and painted metallic by the golden sunset. Jack put Tallie's white cross on the grave.

Jack let me talk to her first, alone. It didn't feel right, visiting together, so we took turns. I told Sophia everything about what happened at college—from the bad food to the classes to Yvette and Diana to Will. I told her everything, just like I used to tell her in the hospital. She'd want to know. She couldn't do college, so she deserved to know.

Jack took much longer than I did, and I sat beneath a tree a ways away and let him have space. He knelt at the grave for two hours, and sometimes his lips would move. I don't know what he was saying, but it was personal, and important. That much I could tell from the way he clenched his fists.

And then, all at once, his fingers went slack, and he

approached me, and together we got in the car and drove to the airport.

I'm so lost in my memories I don't realize Gregory's led me out of the village and up the dirt path that leads to our cottage.

Gregory breathes the fresh air in deep. "How're you doing here, anyway? Picking up the language at all?"

"Well, there's honey and bread and lots of fruit in the fall, and I can't speak a word of French, but at least my boyfriend can." I smack my lips. "Boyfriend. Ugh, that word *still* tastes funny. There should be another word. Prince, maybe? No, that's too regal. Significant other? Ugh, too suburban. Buttbear?"

I pause, then turn to Gregory.

"I think I've struck *gold*."

"Buttbear sounds like a disease." He sighs.

"Exactly! Haven't you heard? Love is a disease, and the only cure is death. And sad breakup songs."

Gregory shakes his head. We walk in silence, me skipping and him sticking to the shade of the oak trees. We pass another farmhouse, all white stone and logs and dogs chasing goats around.

"I've heard," Gregory starts, "that a funny, beautiful girl has an internet advice show that's gotten very popular lately on a certain you of the tubes. Something about…a network approaching her? And a contract?"

I wave him off. "It's nothing big, really. People just like to watch me flail around and say weird things. That's pretty much been my entire life. So really, they just like to watch my life. Not bad for a girl who got kicked out of college for defacing a professor's office, huh?"

"But you make enough to live here," he presses.

"Yeah. I mean, Jack helps, too. A little."

We share another smirk. Gregory and I both know Jack helps a lot. The pay Gregory gave him was more than enough to last us for two years. But now that Jack's getting his teaching degree at the nearest French college, things will be a little different. He'll want to start work again—his plan is to teach high school science. Which I find hard to believe, since I know he's a dunce. A smart dunce. But a dunce nonetheless.

"He's *your* dunce," Gregory corrects my out-loud ramblings, and I roll my eyes and run up to the gate that is the entrance to our house.

It can't really be called a house—more like a run-down shack planted next to a peach tree. The walls are white stone reinforced with wood. The windows are a little crooked and don't keep much heat in the winter, but our woodstove takes care of that, and the roof never leaks, so it's the small things that count, really, and also the big things, because we have the biggest claw-foot tub and the fattest gray cat named Oolong sitting in the windowsill sunning himself. I dash up to the door and Oolong raises his head, giving me a thorough and vastly intimidating once-over before purring himself back to sleep.

"The party has arrived!" I herald my own return and throw my towel on the back of the chair and survey the kitchen—sea glass and shells decorate the windowsill by the rusty sink; mugs of morning coffee still sit on the counter next to stringy remnants of the waffle-maker's mess. I fish around in the fridge and look up as Gregory seats his weary butt at the kitchen table. The chair protests loudly.

"Do you want milk? Fresh from the cows next door. Or—ooh! We still have some wine left from last night."

"Water will do fine," Gregory insists. I pour him a glass and pop my head into the living room. My laptop and the camera equipment I use to record videos are still in a pile on the ugly yet hella charming paisley couch. The woodstove is cold, only used for the chilliest of nights, and the pile of wood next to it is high. Jack must've refilled it.

I tiptoe through the living room and into the bedroom. The door's open, the queen-size brass bed just as unmade as we left it this morning. Jack sits at the desk in front of the windows overlooking the sea, talking to someone on Skype on his laptop. His disheveled tawny hair catches the sun, his lazy flannel and jeans only making his back look broader. But I hardly have time to appreciate it, because at that exact moment I see who he's talking to.

"...but what if I ask her and—"

"Wren!" I scream, launching myself across the room and hanging over Jack's shoulder. "Look at you! I can't believe you're graduating early, you dumbass! Or, shit, I can't call you that anymore, can I? You have a college degree!"

Wren, his glasses perched on his nose and his stubble dark, laughs.

"No, you can't."

"I think you should still call him that!" Kayla chimes from behind him. "And hi, you. Love the tan you're working on."

"Hi, sweet stuff," I coo back at her. "It's been too long."

"Isis, we talked last night."

"Too long! You should come back. I miss you and the house misses you and the shitbaby cat misses you," I lament. Jack reaches up and strokes my back with one hand, the other clicking around on Skype.

"All right you two, I should go," he says.

"Right! Talk to you later." Wren smirks.

"Good luck!" Kayla beams. Jack growls and shuts the laptop quickly.

"Hey grump-ass! What's the frown for? Wait, don't tell me, Oolong took a crap on the bed."

Jack sighs and entwines his arms around my waist, pulling

me into him. "No."

"Diiiiddd he eat your hair gel again?"

"No," Jack murmurs, resting his head in the crook of my neck and sniffing my hair. "You smell like ocean."

"I smell like *questions*!" I correct, and turn to face him. "What's got you so worked up, huh? You've been out of it for days. And every time I catch you on Skype with Wren you always exit out so quick! Are you two sharing porn? Is this a porn thing? Am I a widow now?"

"He's going through puberty!" Gregory shouts from the kitchen.

"Shut up!" Jack shouts back, then quickly adds, "Sir!"

Gregory's chuckles can be heard from here, and I laugh with him, but Jack hugs me close and it's then I know something's really wrong.

"Hey, hey you." I pull away, cupping his face. "If you don't tell me what's wrong right now, I'm going to die. And then fly away. Or, wait, reverse those two, I don't think dead things can fly unless they are zombies-slash-angels and I am most certainly not an ange—"

Jack's mouth is so close to my ear. "Marry me."

I freeze, a horde of icy tingles cascading down my body. "W-What?"

He groans and nuzzles into my neck. I can feel the blush on his cheeks with my own skin.

"Don't make me say it twice."

"Jack, what the fuck—"

"Marry me," he repeats. "Marry me. I want you to be my wife, Isis. I want you to—I want you to be mine."

"I am yours, idiot." I kiss his neck.

"I know. But I want everyone to know. I want your mom and dad to come out, and my mom, and I want Wren and Kayla here, and Diana and Yvette, and Charlie—"

"You think he'd come?"

Jack laughs. "Of course. He might be prickly, but he likes me. I think. He'll bring his grandmother. You'll love her; she's much nicer than he is. I just want them all here, with us, I want them to see how happy we are, and I want them to celebrate with us, and I want to see you in a white gown smiling and cutting a cake and being happier than you've ever been."

I mull it over. Marriage is huge. Marriage is the fairy-tale endgame for every movie heroine in Hollywood's narrow view of happiness. It's clichéd. The me of two years ago would've rolled my eyes at the idea of it. But if you put Jack in the marriage picture, it suddenly doesn't seem so bad. It seems fun and interesting. Spending the rest of my life with him sounds sort of perfect.

"You haven't seen your parents in years," Jack presses. "And I haven't seen mine. Just imagine this house filled up with people—"

"They'd sleep…on the table?"

"Imagine the village motel filled with people," he corrects. "All the people you love. You could show them around, we could go to the beach and do fireworks, you'd make the best cake known to mankind—"

"Every cake I make is the best known to mankind," I say haughtily. He pokes my belly, and I giggle and twist away, but he leans in and captures me again.

"And you'd be…you'd be Isis Hunter. If, *shit*, if that's all right with you. You obviously don't have to, I'm perfectly content being with you like this, but I just thought, I don't know, I just thought—"

I turn and kiss him, shoving him onto the bed and sitting on his stomach playfully.

"Okay. So I marry you. What's in it for me?"

"I devote myself to you," he answers, face serious.

"You are already quite devoted." I smirk, kissing down his jawline and into his collarbone.

"I protect you. As much as a hellion like you needs outside protection."

I laugh against his chest and trail my mouth down it.

"I become yours," he adds. "In every way."

I kiss the hem of his jeans. "You already are."

He pulls me up and kisses me hard and fierce, flipping us over and pushing me into the pillows, gently nipping at my ear.

"Then it's easy, isn't it? All that's left is one silly white dress, and a cake, and our families."

"You just want to see me in a wedding dress." I snicker. He looks me up and down and gives me a cocky smirk as he gently snaps the thigh of my swimsuit against my skin.

"Can you blame me?"

"I blame you for everything. World hunger, Ronald Reagan, Lady Gaga"—I inhale as he presses his knee between my legs—"my current about-to-be-ravished state."

He laughs, and the sound rings so clear and true in the house I want to kiss him again, and again. Forever. But he knits his lips instead.

"So, is that a no?"

I lace my arms around his neck and bring him closer to my face.

"Who do you think I am? I'm Isis Blake. I try everything once. Or four times. If it's cheap enough and tasty enough—"

Jack's ice eyes are serious and hard, and I lose my joking edge.

"—and I'd be honored to try marriage with you—"

Jack smiles.

"—you big stupid idiot."

bonus content

Read on for a
never-before-seen
scene from a brand-new POV!

knife kid

EVEN AFTER TWO YEARS, Isis still calls me Knife Kid.

Everyone who hears it sort of flinches and looks at her with one question in their eyes: *Don't you know his real name?* I always wanna correct them—of course she does. She sent me her wedding invitation, after all. How else do you think I got here, dressed up in a too-big-for-me tux, in this big pasture in the French countryside?

Everyone's gathered on rickety plastic lawn chairs, in their nicest clothes, a light rain coming. No one seems to mind, though. Isis's mom has a huge smile on, her dad absent. He's supposed to be sitting next to her, but apparently Isis told him he couldn't bring his new wife and family, so he refused to come. Sounds like her dad might be a bit more of an asshole than mine, which is saying something. Instead of Isis's dad, Jack's mom sits next to Isis's mom, and they clutch each other's hands, misty-eyed at what's to come. Kayla and Wren, looking the same as they did in high school except a little taller, sit in the next seats, whispering to each other excitedly.

Go figure—the hottest girl in school and the nerdiest

guy in school actually *do* get together outside of Hollywood movies.

And somehow, beyond all belief, Avery is here. Avery, the nasty social butterfly, the bully hidden in Balenciaga, is here. I remember back in senior year, she dropped out for a few months, and we only ever saw her again at graduation. Something about her mental health? I don't know. I never knew her and never cared to get to know her. But it's weird, seeing her sitting here without an ounce of makeup on, her red hair let loose and natural and her dress nowhere near designer. She used to smirk at everyone, like it was her default face to sneer at those lower than her, but now her expression is just…mild. She looks around at the pasture and the other people here like she's seeing them for the first time. We lock eyes once, and I give her a nod. My jaw nearly drops when she smiles back at me, so small but so honest I barely believe it's the same girl who bullied the shit out of everyone I knew. Never in a million years did I think someone as spoiled and mean-spirited as Avery could change for the better. I thought she'd always be a heinous asshole. But maybe I was wrong.

Maybe some people really do change.

Two girls I don't recognize at all are next to Avery, one of them Goth-looking and the other short and cherubic. They kiss every so often and play with each other's hair. Isis said they were from her college or something. Can't remember their names. But Isis introduced me to the lady on the end: her aunt Beth. That was who raised her, apparently. I eye the colorful scarves Beth draped around her every angle and suddenly realize why Isis is so flashy in everything she does.

The "priest" isn't really a priest at all but a big guy with white hair and a tweed suit. Apparently he was Jack's boss or something, but he's also licensed to get two people married.

His eyes twinkle as he looks over my head, and that's how I know they've finally arrived.

We all turn at once to see Jack and Isis walking up the thin row between our chairs. Jack looks dapper as hell in a black tux. Life's unfair—guys like him just get more and more handsome as they get older. But unlike the scowling dude I knew in high school, this Jack looks happy. I mean, I used to see him get a little happy when he and Isis would fight, but now? Now it's like comparing a bud to a full-blooming rose. He's practically giddy. It's hard to tell, since he's always quiet and tame with his emotions, but his smile says it all—Jack Hunter is, for once in his life, genuinely happy. I never thought I'd see the day.

Isis, on the other hand, is and always will be the complete opposite—she can barely stop jumping up and down. I can't help but smile when I see her. She's always had that effect on me, though—on everyone. No matter how she's feeling, she's so obvious about it we all sort of end up feeling it, too. She shimmies in her dress like she can't contain all the energy pent up in her body. It isn't a fancy dress—no ruffles, no lace, just a plain white sundress. It suits her. What you see has always been exactly what you get with her. Her hair's in a long, loose ponytail, and she clutches a tiny bouquet of wildflowers, the same as the ones dotting the field around us.

As the two of them walk down the aisle, they can't look away from each other. Well, Isis can, of course, waving madly to her friends and family before smiling back at Jack. But Jack? Jack can't bring himself to look away from her face, not once.

They stop in front of the tweed-suit man, and he smiles at both of them and blathers the usual speech about "in sickness and in health." Isis asks him to hurry it up because the cake back at their cottage looks so good, and he laughs.

Jack insists the cake will still be there when they get back. She's using the cake excuse, but even I can tell she's trying to get us all out of the rain. She pretends to be irreverent, but she cares the most about us out of everyone.

The tweed man finishes with a "you may kiss the bride." The two of them lean in, Isis's face so red you'd think this was her first time kissing him or something. Finally, their lips meet, and the little crowd explodes with whistling and clapping. Even Avery puts her hands together.

When the chaos settles, Isis ushers us across the pasture and back into the cottage where it's warm. She fishes towels out of nowhere and insists everybody dries off. We mill around in the living room until Isis and Jack wheel out the cake—a massive tower of sponge topped with the most horrific icing job I've ever seen. Chunks of cake are ripped out from the force of whoever iced the damn thing, two tiny stick-figure people, one with blue eyes and one with brown, prodded deep into the top of the cake. Isis declares it doesn't look like much, but she made it and she "promises it tastes good or your money back guaranteed." Everyone laughs, and Jack just shakes his head with a smile.

Isis's warm eyes find mine in the crowd, and she dashes over and takes me by the arm, leading me to the cake. She presses something cold and metallic into my hand. I look down—it's a knife.

"Would you do me the honors, Knife Kid?" she asks. I nod and poise the knife over the cake.

"Sure."

"Wait, wait, *wait*!" Kayla screeches. "You can't just cut it! You have to say something first!"

"Like what?" I grunt. "I'm not good with speeches. That's Isis's thing, not mine."

"I'd settle for just one word," Jack insists.

"Maybe two, if you're feeling generous," Isis teases. I sigh and think, the silence in the room deafening. I look at Isis's face, then Jack's, and then I look around. It's *crazy*. It's crazy that I'm here, with them, at their wedding. Life moves so fast and so strangely. And yet I know without a shadow of a doubt, Isis and Jack will do just fine.

I glance back at them and grin.

"You'll be okay."

It's not much. I've never been good with words or saying the right thing at the right time. It's not a grand speech, worthy of applause. For a second, I almost feel stupid for saying it. But then I see Jack's chest swell with something like pride or gratitude. Isis's eyes get a little watery, in that special way people's get when they're on the verge of happy tears.

I raise the knife and cut into the cake, the people behind me cheering.

Don't miss Sara Wolf's exciting new fantasy series, BRING ME THEIR HEARTS, coming in 2018!

Zera is a Heartless—the immortal, unaging soldier of a witch. Bound to the witch Nightsinger ever since she saved her from the bandits who murdered her family, Zera longs for freedom from the woods they hide in. With her heart in a jar under Nightsinger's control, she serves the witch unquestioningly.

Until Nightsinger asks Zera for a prince's heart in exchange for her own, with one addendum: if she's discovered infiltrating the court, Nightsinger will destroy her heart rather than see her tortured by the witch-hating nobles.

Crown Prince Lucien d'Malvane hates the royal court as much as it loves him—every tutor too afraid to correct him and every girl jockeying for a place at his darkly handsome side. No one can challenge him—until the arrival of Lady Zera. She's inelegant, smart-mouthed, carefree, and out for his blood. The prince's honor has him quickly aiming for her throat.

So begins a game of cat and mouse between a girl with nothing to lose and a boy who has it all.

Winner takes the loser's heart.

Literally.

Read on for a sneak peek!

Chapter One

King Sref of Cavanos watches me with eyes of a raven circling a corpse—patient, waiting to devour me the second I let my guard down. I briefly debate telling him humans don't taste all that good, until I remember normal girls don't eat raw flesh. Or fake their way into royal courts.

Normal, I think to myself. *Completely and utterly normal. Bat your eyelashes. Laugh like you've got nothing in your head. Old God's teeth, what in the flaming afterlife do normal girls do again?*

I look to my sides. There are three of us; three girls in cake-pink dresses, kneeling before King Sref's throne. The other girls would know. I'd ask them, but we're currently busy drowning in expensive lace and the silent stares of every gilded noble in the room. Well, the other two girls are. I'm doing more of a "laughing internally at the way they carefully tilt their gorgeous heads and purse their pouts" thing. Look More Attractive than the Girl Next to You is the name of the game their mothers have been teaching them from birth.

Mine taught me how to die and not much else.

"You are all as lovely as rose blooms," the king says finally. His face is weathered with a handsome age. Dignity carves lines around his steel-colored eyes. The smile in his eyes doesn't reach his lips, though, a sure sign it's only half sincere. He is old, he is powerful, and he is bored—the most dangerous combination I can think of.

"Thank you, Your Majesty," the two girls echo, and I quickly mimic them. I've nicknamed them in my head—Charm and Grace. Charm and Grace don't dare look at anything but the marble floor, while my eyes dart about, thirsty for the rich silks of the nobles' clothes and the gold falcons carved into the majestic stone columns. Three years stuck in the woods serving a witch makes your eyes hungry for anything that isn't a tree or deer droppings. I can't raise my head for fear I'll be singled out, but I can look just high enough to see the feet of Queen Kolissa and her son. Crown Prince Lucien d'Malvane, archduke of Tollmount-Kilstead, Fireborn, the Black Eagle—he has a dozen names, all of them eye-roll-worthy. If there's one thing I've learned from my single day at the royal court, it's that the more names someone has, the less they actually do.

I haven't seen more than his booted toes, and I already know he's useless.

And soon, if I have my way, he'll be heartless.

"As the newest additions to our illustrious court, I welcome you," King Sref says. His voice booms, but out of decorum, not of passion.

"Thank you, Your Majesty," Charm and Grace say, and I echo. I'm starting to get the hang of this—thank everyone a lot and look pretty. Infiltrating the palace might not be so hard after all. Queen Kolissa's saccharine voice rings out after the king's.

"I hope you will bring honor to your families and uphold the ideals of this great nation," she says.

"Thank you, Your Majesty," we respond.

I hear the queen murmur something. A deep voice softly says something back, and then the queen's voice gets an inch louder—so quiet only the three of us, kneeling at the foot of the throne, can hear it.

"—say something, please, Lucien."

"That would be pointless, Mother, and I tend to avoid doing pointless things."

"Lucien—"

"They're only looking for rich husbands or status. They don't care about anything worth a damn. And they certainly aren't worth my breath." The prince's voice is laced with dark venom, and I flinch. It's nothing like his father's carefully emotionless tone or his mother's sickly sweet one. Unlike the rest of these restrained nobles, his emotions burn hot just beneath the surface. He hasn't learned how to hide them completely, yet.

"It's a tradition," the queen insists. "Now say something to them, or so help me—"

The screech of a chair resounds, and the prince's voice demands of us, "Rise."

The two girls, graceful as swans, lift their skirts and stand. I bite back a swear as I do the same and nearly trip over my ornate shoes. Note to past self: two weeks of training isn't nearly enough time to teach someone to walk in a pair of ribboned death traps. How Charm and Grace do it so effortlessly is beyond me, but the blushes on their faces aren't.

I look up to the prince, now standing on the top step before us. Even without the elevation advantage, I can see he's tall—a warrior's height, his silver-vested torso lean and his velvet-caped shoulders broad. A year? No, he's two years older than my teenage form of sixteen; the corded muscles tell me that much. I can see why they call him the Black Eagle now; his hair is blacker than a raven's, windswept about his face and long in the back, kept in a single braid that traces his spine. His face is his father's in its prime: a proud, hawkish nose and broad lips, cheekbones so high and dignified they border arrogance. His eyes are his mother's—a piercing gray-black, midnight on dark iron, yet sharpened to a fine, angry blade point while the queen's are subdued. He is all pride and sable darkness. The girls beside me all but salivate, and I do my best to look bored. On my way here I saw much better-looking boys. Dozens. Hundreds.

All right, fine—there was only the one, and he was a painter's model in the streets of the artist's district, but none of that matters, because the way Prince Lucien sneers his next question wipes every ounce of attractiveness from my mind.

"A lady isn't merely a decoration," he says, words rumbling like thunder. "She is the mother of our future, the teacher of our progeny. A lady must have a brain between her ears, as must we all. For what is beauty without purpose? Nothing more than a vase of flowers, to wither and be thrown away."

Books written by the smartest polymaths have told me the planet is round, that it rotates about the sun, and that there are magnetic poles to our east and west at the coldest parts, and I believe them, yet in no way can I believe there's someone who exists that's *this* arrogant! The nobles titter among themselves, but it quickly dies down when King Sref holds up a hand.

"These are the spring brides, my prince," the king says patiently. "They're of noble lineage. They've studied and practiced much to be here. They deserve more respect than this."

Someone's getting scolded, I think with a singsong tone. I tamp down my smirk too late—Prince Lucien sees it, curls his lip at me, and throws his sharp, dark gaze to the king.

"Of course, Your Majesty." His disdain at calling his father "Your Majesty" is obvious. *Consider yourself lucky, Prince,* I think, *that you have a father at all in this cruel world.*

"But"—the Prince turns to the noble audience—"all too often do we equate nobleness of blood for soundness of mind and goodness of judgment."

His eyes sweep around the room, and this time, the nobles

are dead silent. The shuffling of feet and cough-clearing of throats is deafeningly uncomfortable. I haven't been here long, but I recognize his stance. It's the same one young forest wolves take with their elders; he's challenging the nobles, and by the looks of the king's white knuckles and the queen's terrified face, I'd guess it's a dangerous game he's playing.

"Let us welcome the spring brides as the kings of the Old God did—" The prince sweeps his hands out. "With a question of character."

The nobles start murmuring again. The silver half circles with three spokes through them dripping from every building in the city weren't exactly subtle; the New God Kavar rules here in Vetris. The Sunless War was fought for Kavar thirty years ago, and the Old God's followers were slaughtered and driven out of Vetris. His statues were torn down, his temples demolished. Now, saying the Old God's true name in the country of Cavanos means jail, and carrying on an Old God tradition is a death sentence. The king knows this—and covers for his son quickly.

"The kings of the Old God were misguided, but they built the foundation upon which this country thrives. The roads, the walls, the dams—all of them were built by the old kings. To erase them from existence would be a crime to history, to truth. Let us have one last old tradition here, today, and shed such outdated formalities with grace."

It's a good save. You don't have to be a noble to see that. Prince Lucien looks displeased at his father's attempts to assuage the nobles, but he hides it and turns back to the three of us.

"Answer this question to the best of your abilities, in front of the court, here and today: What is the king's worth?"

There's a long moment of quiet. I can practically hear the brain cogs of Grace and Charm churning madly beside me.

The nobles murmur to one another, laughing and giggling and raising eyebrows in our direction. A swamp-thick layer of scorn and amusement makes the air reek and my skin crawl.

Finally, Charm clears her throat to speak.

"The king is worth…a million—no! A trillion gold coins. No—seven trillion!" The nobles' laughter gets louder. Charm blushes beet red. "I'm sorry, Your Majesty. My father never taught me numbers. Just sewing and things."

King Sref smiles good-naturedly. "It's quite all right. That was a lovely answer."

The prince says nothing, face unimpressed, and points to Grace. She curtsies.

"The king's worth cannot be measured," she says clearly. "It is as high as the highest peak of the Kilstead Mountains, as wide as the Endless Bog in the south. His worth is deeper than the darkest depths of the Twisted Ocean."

This time, the nobles don't laugh. Someone starts a quiet applause, and it spreads.

"A very eloquent answer," the king says. The girl looks pleased with herself, curtsying again and glancing hopefully at Prince Lucien. His grimace only deepens, and she falters.

"You, the plain one." The prince finally points to me. "What say you?"

His insult stings, but only for a moment. Of course I'm plain compared to him. Anyone would be. I'm sure the only one he doesn't think plain is the mirror in his room. I hold his gaze, though it burns like sunfire on my skin. His distaste for me, for the girls beside me, for every noble in this room, is palpable. He expects nothing from me, from anyone—I can see that in the way his eyes prematurely cloud with disdain the moment I open my mouth.

"The king's worth is exactly one potato."

There's silence, and then a shock wave ripples through

the room, carrying gasps and frenzied whispers with it. The massive Celeon guards in silver plate mail flanking the thrones grip their broadswords on their backs and narrow their catlike eyes, their tails swishing madly. Any one of them could rip me in half as easily as paper, though it wouldn't kill me. It'd just betray me as a Heartless—a witch's servant—to the entire noble court, which is considerably worse than having your insides spilled on the marble. Witches are Old God worshippers and fought against humans in the Sunless War. We are the enemy.

I'm the enemy, wearing the mask of a noble girl who's just said a very insulting thing about her king.

The queen clutches her handkerchief to her chest, clearly offended at my words. The king raises one eyebrow. The prince, on the other hand, smiles. It's so slow and luxurious I barely see it form, and then all at once his face is practically gleeful. He's handsome, I think to myself—handsome enough when he isn't being a hateful dog turd. He tames his expression and clears his throat.

"Care to elaborate, or should I have you thrown in the dungeons for slandering the king right here and now?"

He's enjoying the idea of throwing me in the dungeon a little too much for my taste. I raise my chin, carefully keeping my shoulders wide and my face passive. Strong. I will make an impression here, or I will die for my loose tongue. It's that simple.

Except it isn't that simple.

Because I can't die.

Because unlike the girls next to me, I'm not here to impress the king and win a nobleman's hand in marriage or a court position for my father.

I'm here for Prince Lucien's heart.

Literally, not figuratively. Although figuratively would

be easier, wouldn't it? Making boys fall in love is easy—all it takes are sickly sweet compliments and batting eyelashes and a low-cut dress or five and they're clay in your hands. Not that I'd know. I haven't spoken to a boy my age since my family's death, and my own, three years ago.

No, I'm not here for the easy way. I'm here for the organ beating in his chest, and it will be mine, by gambit or force. In order to get that close, I must earn his trust. I must prove I'm different, that I'm worth noticing. I'd do anything to get close—even wear that low-cut dress. But for now, all I have are words.

The prince expects idiots and sycophants. I must give him the opposite. I must be brilliance itself, a diamond dagger in the flesh of his stagnant noble life.

"The king is worth exactly one potato," I repeat. "A king is the steward of his people—they trust him to lead them, to take care of them. To a commoner, one potato can mean the difference between starving for the winter or making it through to spring. To the king's people, nothing is more precious than one potato."

The murmur that goes around the room is quiet, confusion written on the nobles' faces. They have no idea, I'm sure, of what it's like to starve. My memories of many winters going hungry as a child resurface, but I push them aside. Father is dead. Mother is dead. They are gone. I no longer eat human food. I have a new family now, and they need me. If I get lost in the past here, I forfeit my future.

I lock eyes with the prince once more. His face, too, is confused, but in a different way from the crowd's. He looks at me like he's never seen a person before, as if I'm some odd specimen kept in a cool cellar for later study by a polymath. All trace of the venom in his gaze is gone, replaced with a strange, stiff sort of shock. I should look away, but I don't. I can't. I make my eyes sing the determined words my mouth can't say.

I am no flower to be ravaged at your whim, angry wolf—I am your hunter, bow cocked and ready. I am a Heartless, one of the creatures your people fled in terror from thirty years ago.

I let the smallest, hungriest smirk of mine loose on him.

If you were smart, you'd start running, too.

The girls at my side are staring. I don't look at them. The queen's hands are away from her chest, her smile faint as she squeezes King Sref's arm. Finally, the king laughs. Nothing about it is bland or subdued; it leaks with the hoarse edges of unbridled amusement. For the briefest moment as he smiles at me, he looks ten years younger.

"What is your name, clever little bride?"

My mind says, *Zera, no last name, daughter of a merchant couple whose faces I'm starting to forget; orphan, thief, lover of bad novels and good cake, and indebted servant of the witch Nightsinger, who sent me here to rip your son's heart from his chest.*

I dip into a wobbly curtsy instead and spill my lie with a smile. "Zera Y'shennria, Your Majesty; niece of Quin Y'shennria, lady of the House of Y'shennria and the Dead Wastes. Thank you for having me here today."

Thank you, and I'm sorry.

As sorry as a monster can be, anyway.

acknowledgments

Lovely Vicious is a series straight from my heart to you, the reader. It's a series I wrote for the high school me—a girl who was sick and tired of the world and the people in it, a girl who slowly but surely learned the beauty of life again. Isis is a past me, and I love her and Jack to bits. Thank you for following their story. If you liked it, then you and I are the kind of people who'd hang out together forever. Let's chill, drinks on me.

People say one of the hardest things to do is write a book. And it is. But it really doesn't feel like it when you have such excellent help. To Stacy Abrams and Lydia Sharp, thank you so much for your tireless effort and amazing insight. You've made this book a hundred times better. To the entire Entangled crew—thank you, from the bottom of my heart. You've done so much for me and this story.

To the community, reviewers, book bloggers, and librarians—rock on so hard. Keep rocking until all the rocks in the world turn to sand, and then throw a huge beach party. You've earned it. You work so tirelessly for so little, read so many books for so little thanks, and keep your ears and minds and hearts open to each story. I can never thank you enough for your reviews and support. God bless the heckie out of you.

And last but not least, thank you, Jack and Isis. It's been a wonderful ride, and I'll be there for eternity—or at least until I lose my mind with age—smiling down on you like a creepy yet well-meaning godparent. I love you two. Live well. Live happily.

Collect all the books in the Lovely Vicious series

Love Me Never

Discover where Jack and Isis's relationship first heated up in *Love Me Never*, available now.

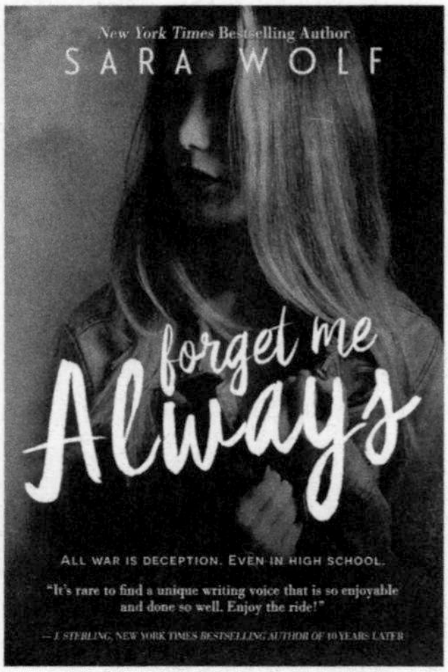

Forget Me Always

Don't miss the continuation of Jack and Isis's story in *Forget Me Always*, available now.

Grab the Entangled Teen releases readers are talking about!

Violet Grenade
by Victoria Scott

DOMINO (def.): A girl with blue hair and a demon in her mind.
CAIN (def.): A stone giant on the brink of exploding.
MADAM KARINA (def.): A woman who demands obedience.
WILSON (def.): The one who will destroy them all.

When Madam Karina discovers Domino in an alleyway, she offers her a position inside her home for entertainers in secluded West Texas. Left with few alternatives and an agenda of her own, Domino accepts. It isn't long before she is fighting her way up the ranks to gain the madam's approval. But after suffering weeks of bullying and unearthing the madam's secrets, Domino decides to leave. It'll be harder than she thinks, though, because the madam doesn't like to lose inventory. But then, Madam Karina doesn't know about the person living inside Domino's mind. Madam Karina doesn't know about Wilson.

Lost Girls
by Merrie Destefano

Yesterday, Rachel went to sleep curled up in her grammy's quilt, worrying about geometry. Today, she woke up in a ditch, bloodied, bruised, and missing a year of her life. She's not the only girl to go missing within the last year...but she's the only girl to come back. And as much as her dark, dangerous new life scares her, it calls to her. Seductively. But wherever she's been—whomever she's been with—isn't done with her yet...

Other Breakable Things
By Kelley York and Rowan Altwood

Luc Argent has always been intimately acquainted with death. After a car crash got him a second chance at life—via someone else's transplanted heart—he tried to embrace it. He truly did. But he always knew death could be right around the corner again. And now it is. Luc is ready to let his failing heart give out, ready to give up. A road trip to Oregon—where death with dignity is legal—is his answer. But along for the ride is his best friend, Evelyn. And she's not giving up so easily.

Proof of Lies
by Diana Rodriguez Wallach

Some secrets are best kept hidden...

Anastasia Phoenix has always been the odd girl out, whether moving from city to international city with her scientist parents or being the black belt who speaks four languages.

And most definitely as the orphan whose sister is missing, presumed dead.

She's the only one who believes Keira is still alive, and when new evidence surfaces, Anastasia sets out to follow the trail—and lands in the middle of a massive conspiracy. Now she isn't sure who she can trust. At her side is Marcus, the bad boy with a sexy accent who's as secretive as she is. He may have followed her to Rome to help, but something about him seems too good to be true.

Nothing is as it appears, and when everything she's ever known is revealed to be a lie, Anastasia has to believe in one impossibility.

She will find her sister.